RUNEBREAKER

Also by Alex R. Kahler

ALEX R. KAHLER

THE RUNEBINDER CHRONICLES BOOK TWO

RUNEBREAKER

HARLEQUIN® TEEN

ISBN-13: 978-1-335-01732-1

Runebreaker

Copyright © 2018 by Alex R. Kahler

Printed in U.S.A.

For those who burn

"Repent
and pray our Lord will forgive.
Repent
and bathe thy darkest sins
in the fires of His mercy."

—Sermon of Brother Jeremiah,
2 P.R. (Post Resurrection)

PART 1

TO BE A MONSTER

CHAPTER ONE

FEAR PULSED THROUGH AIDAN AS HE KNELT BY THE grave.

Fear, and something darker. Something stronger.

Power.

"I'm sorry," he whispered. "I'm so sorry. I'll save you."

He pressed his hands into the soil while lightning strobed above and rain lashed against his skin. Reached deep into the Sphere of Fire burning within his chest, that magical center of energy that guided him forward like a second conscience. Power blossomed within him, flooded him with heat as flames wrapped through his veins and twined down his fingertips, traced crimson lines across the rumbling earth.

Not just rumbling. Someone screaming.

Distant screaming. A boy, begging for him to stop.

He couldn't stop. He had to save her.

He had to bring her back.

Aidan reached deeper into that damnable light within.

Power reached back. Fire burned through him, cast away all doubt, all fear.

"Stop!" the boy called.

Aidan ignored him. Barely heard him through Fire's siren song. Why should he stop, when he was so close to getting everything he'd ever dreamed of? Why should he stop, when he was so close to making things *right*?

"Please!" the boy called. Closer, but not close enough to douse Aidan's flame. Only enough to be a nuisance. Fire raged that this boy—this *nothing*—should try to stop him. Nothing could stop him. No more.

Not even death.

Aidan looked up.

The boy ran toward him, and in that moment Aidan knew the boy was a Hunter like him. From the accent, American— like him. The boy wore the same blacks, albeit a different cut. Water pulsed in his gut, sending thick raindrops whirling around him. And he carried a bladed quarterstaff.

Aidan knew something else in that glance.

The boy wanted to end him.

The boy was too late.

Lightning flashed and the ground rumbled, graves spilling forth bones as the soil before him churned. Power was every-thing. Fire was everything. And there, deep below the earth's surface, he felt the power connect. Felt the spark of life flare.

Felt her awaken.

A hand shot from the earth. Black nails. Soot skin.

Fire pulsed in his heart. Victory. *Victory.*

"No!" the boy screamed.

Aidan narrowed his eyes. "You are too late, Tenn," he said in a voice that was not his.

Aidan raised his earth-covered hands. Reached deep through the flame within while the buried woman pulled herself from her grave.

And when he sent his power forward, a billow of hell-fire and rage, he saw the boy try to defend himself. A shield of water, hissing and steaming against the fire that burned brighter than a star. His water was no match for Aidan's fury.

There was no match in the world for Aidan's hate.

Fire burned through him. So bright he was a sun. So bright he felt nothing but flame, but ecstasy. So hot, he was no longer himself. In Fire's embrace, he was omnipotent. He was a god.

He gave in to that glorious heat, that terrible strength, and poured every last piece of himself into the fire burning against the intruder's shield.

The barrier disintegrated. Flame engulfed flesh.

And then, like choir music to his ears, Tenn screamed as his veins boiled to ash and steam.

Ash and steam.

Ash and heat and steam.

And screams.

Aidan woke covered in sweat, his dream burning away as awareness broke through the haze.

Flames coiled through his room.

Fire licked up the walls, curled over his bed like crimson petals. Billowed from *him*.

He stared at his hands in distant fascination as fire twined around them, making his tattoos writhe like serpents on his skin. The tattoos on his knuckles: **BURN THEM**. A promise. A demand.

Another scream, and he looked up. Someone stood at the foot of his burning bed.

Someone covered in flame.

The figure before him screamed out again, clawed at the flames eating his skin alive. Fire billowed from Aidan, cocooned his room in heat, in ecstasy. Curled against the intruder like a lover.

Aidan wondered if this was another dream.

It had to be. There was no way his Sphere had opened up in his sleep. No way Fire had acted without his will guiding it. This was a dream, his subconscious acting out, because the alternative was beyond impossible. Yes, he felt the flame. Yes, his lungs choked with smoke. But he had had similar dreams before—dreams of flight or fire or sex, dreams that felt more real than waking life. He'd even been aware of them before. Just as he was aware now.

Aware, but completely detached. Completely unable or unwilling to stop it.

He watched. And he waited for the dream to end as some small part of him wondered, idly, who the burning figure was, and if it mattered when it was all just a metaphor.

It was only when the figure dropped to the floor and the screams stopped that Aidan realized it maybe wasn't a dream.

Realized he wasn't waking up.

And when Fire winked out from his chest and the flames disintegrated like an afterthought, Aidan realized he had killed someone in his sleep.

Maybe it was the trace of Fire still burning in his veins, but he also realized, deep down, that he didn't truly care.

CHAPTER TWO

"DO YOU HAVE ANY IDEA WHAT YOU'VE DONE?"

Trevor's voice sparked a note of frustration in Aidan's chest. The man standing before him didn't even have the nerve to sound angry. He just sounded defeated. No—worse—he sounded disappointed. Bloody Water mages and their bloody emotions.

"I had a bad dream," Aidan replied.

Even though Aidan was American, his voice had taken on the semblance of a Scottish brogue from three years of being stranded here. Too much time hanging out with Trevor. Too much time *shagging* Trevor.

As he stared stoically at his co-commander, however, he knew that there wasn't such a thing as *too much* when it came to that. Trevor towered above him—not that that was surprising, since most people towered above Aidan's 5'5" stature. Years of using Water might have paled Trevor's skin, but his eyes held no watery softness.

"This isn't a joke, Aidan," Trevor said.

"And that's why I'm not laughing."

Trevor's room was next to his. He had been there, at Aidan's door, moments after the fire—and Vincent's screaming—had stopped. One glance at the ash and destruction, at the body still smoldering on the floor. One glance, and Trevor's hand had gone to his mouth in horror. Aidan would never forget the way Trevor's eyes had flickered from the body back to him. He would never forget the low, shocked tone in Trevor's voice when he'd dragged Aidan back to his office.

Aidan wondered if someone had been sent to clean up the mess, or if this whole incident was just between the two of them.

Something in Trevor's face told Aidan that this wasn't going to be swept under the rug. *Although whoever was left in my room could easily be swept under a rug.* He bit down the thought and suppressed a giggle.

"You killed a fellow Hunter," Trevor growled.

"*I* didn't do anything," Aidan replied. Despite himself, his words shook. Not out of emotion, but out of dawning truth: the Sphere of Fire had opened unbidden in his sleep. One could only access the Spheres with concentration. Even after being attuned to Fire three years ago, he'd only been able to use the elemental power by reaching for it. He'd never heard of a Sphere opening on its own.

As if it had a will. A consciousness.

He could only imagine what sort of sentience a Sphere like Fire would have. The thought filled him with awe.

"You expect me to believe Fire opened on its own. *Killed* on its own." Trevor's voice rose and grumbled with anger, his fists trembling. "Vincent is dead because of you!"

Aidan took a step back.

He'd seen Trevor sad. He'd seen Trevor frustrated. They'd led armies together and suffered as many defeats as they had victories. But he had never seen Trevor struck so suddenly by rage.

"It wasn't my fault," Aidan said. He hated how his voice sounded small. Hated how he felt like he no longer had the upper hand. It didn't suit him.

Instinctively, he wanted to reach for Fire, wanted to coax the Sphere to life from the embers in his chest. If only for the strength. If only for the assurance that it was—and would always be—there.

That would definitely not be a wise idea.

"You're right," Trevor said. He stepped back. Leaned heavily against the desk. "It's my fault."

"Because you're the one who sent him in to wake me up?"

The moment he said it, he knew he'd pushed Trevor a centimeter too far. Those strong eyes widened, fists slammed back against the desk.

"Because I knew you were dangerous!" Trevor yelled. "And yet, I kept you around anyway."

Aidan had pushed him too far, but that didn't keep Aidan from pushing his co-commander further. He hated pity. He hated self-deprecation. Both were weaknesses and he refused to empathize with those who wouldn't fight.

"Then I guess his death is on your conscience," Aidan said.

The worst part was, that did the trick. Trevor practically deflated against the desk, and Aidan felt the tables turn.

"I should have you executed for this."

"Like hell," Aidan said. "Scotland's army follows *my* lead. Kill me, and you'll never overtake Calum."

Trevor didn't say anything, not at first. The guy stood there, staring at his feet, and Aidan knew he wasn't just thinking about the truth in Aidan's words. They were so, *so* close to overthrowing the Howl that ruled Scotland. Calum was one of the Kin, one of the six original Howls that had taken over the world and turned it to shite, and he lived in his castle in Edinburgh like a damned king, ruling over them all.

Aidan had spent the last year devising a way to overthrow the bastard. Trevor wouldn't toss that away, not when so much was at stake.

But as he stared at his co-commander, Aidan knew that the logic of victory and defeat wasn't the deciding factor. He could see the faint glow of the Sphere of Water churning in Trevor's stomach, and that told him everything he needed to know.

Every human carried the five Spheres within them. One for each element—Earth, Water, Fire, Air, and Maya—all lined up along the spine, all invisible to the layman unless attuned to a Sphere. To the majority of the population, the Spheres were simply energy centers, vortexes that kept the body and mind functioning.

Then, maybe four years ago, someone had learned how to tap into the Spheres. Had taught mankind how to use the Spheres residing within to manipulate the elements without. A few simple tattoos, a hell of a lot of concentration and will-power, and bam. Magical fucking powers.

The modern miracle, ads proclaimed. The ability to heal any ailment with a touch of Earth. To change weather patterns with Air. To coax crops to grow with Water. To win wars with Fire.

Magic should have been the end to world hunger and poverty.

Obviously, it didn't take long for mankind to weaponize it.

Cue the creation of monstrous Howls and the Resurrection and the end of civilization. Cue the need for Hunters like him. People trained in magic who could fight back against the evil mages who followed the Dark Lady, and the monsters those necromancers created.

Howls were human, once. But necromancers learned how to tap into the host's Spheres, how to drain them to the point of exhaustion, and further. To the point where the Sphere didn't create energy, but consumed it. The process twisted the human host into something otherworldly, a creature craving whatever Sphere had been drained. Howls were just the blanket term for these monsters. Kravens were born of Earth and needed flesh. Bloodlings, Water. Incubi, Fire. And Breathless, Air. So far, no Howl had been born of Maya. Yet.

But there were subtler drawbacks of magic. Case in point: Trevor, who—whenever he used Water—became a mopey pile of emotional rubbish. Aidan knew that his co-commander was drowning in a dozen emotions. Worrying what the others would think. Terrified he'd fail Glasgow's—and the rest of Scotland's—population. Wondering if maybe he *was* the reason Vincent was dead, and maybe it was he who should be executed, rather than Aidan. Trevor felt personally responsible for every bad thing that happened within the Guild.

It was a vicious cycle Aidan knew all too well.

And so, he used it to his full advantage.

"Without me, Glasgow will crumble in a week." Aidan took a step forward, letting the low cinder of his words fill the space between them. "The soldiers love me. They would *die* for me. If you kill me, they'll lose trust. They'll lose *fear*.

And an army that doesn't trust and fear its commander is an army destroyed. Would you really let the last hope this country has of survival die out because of one accident?"

Aidan felt his lip curl in victory, even before he let his final words hammer home: "Kill me, and you won't just have my blood on your hands. You'll have executed your entire country."

Trevor swallowed. Hard. And Aidan crossed his arms over his chest. He knew Trevor. He'd be angry and sad and confused, but he would never kill unless absolutely necessary. He would never kill someone he loved.

No. Trevor wasn't a threat. Aidan just had to let this blow over, so he could figure out what had actually happened in his bedroom that morning. He didn't want to think about it, didn't want to question why Fire had done what it had. He didn't want to mistrust the only thing he had faith in—himself.

But there, lingering in the corners of memory, were traces of a dream that made his breath catch and his heart hammer with fear and need. He knew, somehow, that the two were connected.

Not that he would place any weight in dreams.

"You're right," Trevor whispered, breaking Aidan from his thoughts. "I can't kill you."

Aidan smiled. He began to turn. He needed to go find a new bedroom, and clothes that didn't smell like smoke and burnt Vincent.

"But I can't let you stay."

Aidan stopped. Confidence flickered.

"You're dangerous, Aidan," Trevor said, looking up. "It's safer for…for everyone if you left."

"What?"

"I'm exiling you. Leave Glasgow. Leave Scotland." He made eye contact, and even though Water boiled in Trevor's gut, his next words were hard as steel and harsh as flame. "If I see you again, I'll kill you with my bare hands."

"You can't—"

"I am."

High-pitched ringing filled Aidan's ears, and with it, a burn in his chest. Fire wanted to open. Fire wanted to burn this room—no, this whole damn Guild—to the ground. To prove that no one denied Aidan Belmont.

"I gave my life to this Guild, to this bloody country!" The words didn't feel like his. They were too weak. Too pathetic. "You can't just force me away."

"You should have thought of that before murdering a comrade," Trevor replied. Sadly.

The ringing increased. Fire opened in his chest then, and flames curled around his hands, burned against his knuckles. His mouth opened, but he didn't hear what he said. He couldn't hear anything against the ringing, against the char and the burn. He couldn't feel anything besides anger, the need to make someone pay.

And then, strong hands grabbed him by the shoulders. Jerked him around.

"Aidan," Kianna said. Or maybe mouthed. "Get a hold of yourself."

He wanted to kill. He wanted to burn Trevor to cinders. But he couldn't kill Kianna. Would never.

He shoved her aside and fled.

CHAPTER THREE

AIDAN WANTED BLOOD.

Howl or human, it didn't fucking matter at this point. He didn't just want blood, he *needed* it, needed to make someone or some*thing* hurt, needed someone else's pain to feed the rage burning inside of him, the venom that made his limbs shake and his chest burn as he ran down the darkened subway tunnel. He needed to make someone scream the words stuck in his own throat.

Thankfully, in this new, broken world, there was always a victim on whom he could enact his vengeance.

He heard her crying as she ran. Stumbling and sloshing, her gasps echoing down the earth-and-concrete tube. He didn't know if they were actual tears, or if she thought it would grant her mercy. If the latter, she was about to face a rude awakening. Flames danced around his clenched fists, burning jagged shadows on the walls. With the Sphere of Fire raging in his chest, he felt *alive*. He felt alive, and he felt her life, too. The warm, flickering spark of her half-humanness.

His spark reminding him that he was mortal. He would one day burn out. And he would burn as hot and as bright as he could, while he could, and burn the whole world with him, until that day came.

Aidan hunted, and Fire raged, and the monster before him fled. Just as everything should be.

He could end her right now. One big burst of flame filling the tunnel. Burn her alive in moments. Or he could raise the temperature, singe the air from her lungs, make her screams immolate her throat. He could already feel it, the imagined tendrils of flame smoking through the tunnel like serpents, hissing for flesh as he guided their hunger. A thousand potential ends for her, a thousand ways to appease Fire's hunger, to offer her life at its devouring altar.

But that was too fast. Too fast. He smiled at the sound of her stumbled splash. He ran faster.

You're dangerous, Trevor had said. *It's safer for everyone if you left.*

The words sent flames spiraling around Aidan and acid boiling in his chest. His veins were fire, fire and anger, and he lost track of whether the Sphere fueled his fury or the other way around.

"Fuck you!" he yelled.

Leave.

Leave!?

"Who the hell do you think I am?"

He lashed out, a curl of flame snapping from the whorl around him, turning the memory of his co-commander's charge to ash.

"I'll show you," he growled through gritted teeth. He

barely heard his words through the incendiary roar of Fire. "I'll show all of you!"

Another lance of fire, this one spearing straight through the tunnel, turning the walls orange and making the waters hiss with heat.

The woman screamed. A splash.

He reached her in moments, everything inside him burning— his breath, his throat, his chest, his veins. His vision hazed red or maybe it was the flames that swarmed him, their heat a comfort, a hymn. He looked at her and felt nothing.

She was pretty.

He registered that, in the far-off corner of his rational mind. Even though her clothes were charred from his wrath, even though her skin was pallid and thin as rice paper. He towered above her, flames flickering off the disgusting water pooled around her, magical in its way—her watery, glittering halo. Magical if not for the fear in her bloodshot eyes.

"What was your name?" His words trembled with anger. He didn't normally ask this of those he was about to kill. But he wanted to draw it out. Fire hissed its agreement in his ear. *Make her suffer. Make her pay.*

"Laura," she said. Her voice trembled. Hunger? Fear? Did it matter? Her accent was thick, rolling through her mouth like clotted blood. *L-ow-rah*. Glaswegian. Once.

"I'm Aidan," he replied. "And I am going to kill you."

Her eyes narrowed, as though this was anything but inevitable. As though she had a chance if she chose to fight.

"And do you know why I'm going to kill you?"

She pushed herself up to a crouch, but he pointed at her. No dagger in hand. Just the flames wreathing his arm in a sheath.

"No. Stay down. I asked you a bloody question."

Laura didn't answer. Her lip pulled back in a sneer, revealing teeth filed to points and black gums. Even her nails were sharpened, clenched in clawed fists at her sides. Bloodlings—Howls pulled from Water—delighted in torturing their victims while drawing blood. Not that it would do her any good.

He could feel it, that tremor in her heart, that pulse of frantic life. The Sphere of Fire was life and heat and vitality. And it knew when it was about to be extinguished.

"I'm not going to kill you because you're a bloodling." He practically spat the word. "Not because you're in *my* city, hunting *my* people." He leaned in, poured more heat and anger into his voice, made the flames around him blue with rage to burn out the lie: this city wasn't his, not anymore. "I'm going to kill you because I'm pissed. Because you are in the wrong place at the wrong damn time. Which means your death is meaningless."

"I'm not meaningless," she hissed. "Not as meaningless as you."

"Everything about you is meaningless!" he yelled, and Fire raged in his chest.

Flames snapped out from his hand as he reached for her, and grabbed her by the throat. She couldn't scream, not from the heat burning the breath from her lungs, not from the pressure on her larynx. He squeezed, and he looked into her eyes as they widened, as more capillaries burst. She clawed at him, tried to relieve the pressure on her throat. Even she knew it was hopeless.

"I'm going to make you suffer," he hissed. "Not because

you've made your prey suffer. But because I want to make this hurt."

She *did* scream then, as he loosened his grip and sent a wave of flame billowing from his skin to hers, searing the pale white flesh, burning through her sodden clothing. The tunnel filled with the stench of hair as follicle after follicle curled and crisped and disintegrated. He grimaced against the smell, but he didn't let go of the power, didn't let up on the heat.

Didn't look away from her eyes.

Yes, a voice inside him whispered, feminine and cool as the deepest ocean, and just as unforgiving. *Make her suffer. Bring her to me. Bring her...*

Laura jerked.

Her eyes widened. Rolled back in her head.

Laura went limp as her inner flame flickered out.

No! No no no no what the—

"Howls are not free therapy."

He jerked up and nearly lashed out, fire billowing around him in rage.

Kianna stood beside him, a katana pointed straight at his chest. "Drop it," she commanded. Like he was a bloody dog.

He dropped the bloodling, let her corpse splash unceremoniously to the filth. That's when he noticed the tip of the dagger sticking through the bloodling's sternum.

"No," Kianna growled. Her voice lowered in warning. *"Drop it."*

Fire raged in his chest, screamed a thousand curses in his ears. His breath was hot and there was no way in hell he would release this. He was a god. A *god*! Who was she to make him bow?

"Don't make me kill you, love," she said, almost soothing. "Not like this."

Some small, straining voice in the back of his mind knew she would follow through. Told him that this was ridiculous. Kianna was a friend. Potentially the only one he had left. And she would kill him if she thought he was a threat.

He *was* a threat.

He should let her kill him. It would be better than—

No, Fire raged. Fire wouldn't be extinguished. Not yet. Not until he'd made the whole world burn. He couldn't do that if Kianna killed him first.

He took a deep breath. Tried to calm the anger, the hatred, the *shame*. It felt like smothering an inferno with a teacup in his chest, but he pressed harder, willed the Sphere of Fire into submission. It fought against him. *Burn her. Burn them all!* But he couldn't. He wouldn't. Anyone else, but never her. He forced the frenzy down.

His Sphere winked out.

Cold snapped through his body the moment Fire subsided, cold and darkness and a disgust so deep all life left his limbs in a heartbeat. He dropped to the floor and his head swam, the darkness spinning, spinning, as he cried out in pain and cold. His body convulsed with shivers and he squeezed tight into himself, trying to curl around that tiny pinprick of warmth in his chest. He couldn't find it.

Instead, the darkness closed in around him, pressed to his skin.

And in that darkness, he heard the voice, the woman, oceanic and terrible, beguiling him to come, come, *succumb*.

"Aidan, come *on*." Kianna's voice floated through the darkness.

Dimly, he noticed the black get lighter. But he couldn't open his eyes. Couldn't force down the shaking that kept him from moving a voluntary muscle. Couldn't hold back the tears.

What had he done?

"Jesus," Kianna muttered. "Pull yourself together."

A hand on his shoulder, strong and heavy. Kianna shook him. Roughly.

He took a deep, shuddering breath as the despair and fear washed off him in a wave. Opened his eyes.

Found himself staring straight into the open, bloodshot gaze of the Howl he'd murdered. Despite himself, Aidan cried out, sloshed backward as he tried to get as far away from the creature as he could. But his limbs still weren't his own—he didn't get very far.

Kianna stepped between him and the Howl, knelt down, and looked him in the eyes. He shuddered. He could still smell the Howl's blood. That was the curse of Fire—under its influence, you were a god. The moment it left you, you were nothing more than a husk of rapidly decaying meat. Against that warmth of immortality, regular life was a cold, terrible shell.

"Aidan," she said, softer this time. Calming. "Are your tits calm now?"

Well, *her* brand of calming.

He stared up at her, shivering, taking in the way the lamp at her waist played off her dark features—the sharp lines of her jaw, the folds of her leather jacket, the long pink-and-black locs. The pink that matched the pink skull T-shirt beneath her bomber, the black that matched her torn denim jeans. She was tall and imposing, Amazonian in those bloody platform boots he always told her she'd nicked from a goth teenager. Tall and imposing and a bitch to the core.

In other words, the only person in this damnable country he got along with.

The question was, why was she here after what he had done?

"Aye," he muttered. He forced down the last bit of weakness. At least the aftershock of Fire didn't take long to wear off. The lows were just as sharp and short as the highs. "I think so."

He reached up and took her hand. She helped him to standing and didn't say a word when he collapsed against her. She held him there, not saying a word, as the feeling came back to his legs with a wash of needling pinpricks. He kept his eyes open, even though he wanted to close them, wanted to sleep.

He didn't want to see the stare waiting for him in the darkness.

"How did... How'd you find me?" he asked as she helped him limp down the tunnel. He kept his eyes up as they passed the Howl.

Laura. Her name was Laura.

Guilt attempted to curl through him once more. He fed it to the muted flames before it could germinate, the seed of doubt burnt to ash in a heartbeat.

"Glasgow's Underground's a circle, love. And you were literally on fire. Not that hard to find."

His next words came out as a choked whisper. "What did you hear?"

"Enough to scare me," she replied. "If I could get scared, that is."

He didn't mean what he said in the tunnels.

Neither of them did.

They walked in silence for a bit, sloshing through the puddles, light glinting off subway rails that hadn't been used in three years. Glasgow's singular tunnel had been abandoned in the early days of the Resurrection—it was a miracle it hadn't flooded in the aftermath. Hell, it was a miracle the whole country hadn't sunk. Though there was always the chance tomorrow.

She helped hoist him up to the platform. He tried pushing himself to his feet, but he still couldn't move, not really, not when all of his muscles were busy shivering. She leaped up beside him, landing silently. In spite of the ridiculous boots.

"Those are ridiculous boots," he muttered.

"What was that?" she asked as she picked him up, slinging his arm over her shoulder. Her sword was sheathed again. Clearly she no longer saw him as a threat. He shivered and stumbled. Yeah. Clearly not a threat. "You say you want to sleep down here? Or was that a, 'Thanks Kianna, love, you're the best mate a guy could ask for'?"

"Definitely the latter," he said. His teeth chattered violently, slamming against his lip ring.

Something cracked in his mouth.

No bloody way.

Kianna stopped and looked sideways at him. "Did you just chip a tooth?"

He spat out the shard in answer. Well, tried to. It drooled down his lips and dribbled to the ground.

"Disgusting," she replied. "You have a problem."

"Aye," Aidan said. "Scotland's dental system hasn't improved since the Resurrection."

Kianna howled with laughter. Her voice echoed in the tunnels behind them, too loud. But there was nothing else out here. No one else. At least her laughter kept her from laying into him again. If anything, though, she was good at reading the mood. She knew that now was clearly not the time to lecture him on his addiction to magic.

They walked slowly up the stairs that led to the exit, their feet slipping up the smooth stones that were slimed over with moss and mold. At least he didn't hear any rain.

His kingdom for a full day of sunshine.

They stepped out and paused for Kianna to turn off her lamp. Above them, the arched plexiglass entrance to the Underground loomed like bruised ribs, the structure beaten and shattered by magic and miscreants. Beaten and shattered. Pretty much Glasgow in a nutshell.

Fog lay heavy on the ground, the once-crowded boulevard of Buchanan Street sloping up before them. Sooty sandstone and glass buildings scratched up through the haze, their forms obscured in mist. What was left of their forms, at least. Once, this place had been filled with shops and restaurants, the wide avenue crowded with people jostling bags or buskers playing flaming bagpipes. Magical. Luminous. Now the place was empty. Buildings toppled to bare bones, stone facades nothing more than battered skin. He stared at the wrecked memories and inhaled the scent of the place, the soot and the dampness and a tang his American senses could never quite place, something like stone, like sharp earth.

His kingdom.

But not anymore.

CHAPTER FOUR

KIANNA LED HIM UP THE STREET, THEIR FEET KICKING
loose rubble, the fog swallowing sound hungrily. They might
as well have been ghosts in the gloom, one tall and bladed, one
hunched and broken. He hated that he was the shattered one.

He had no idea where she was leading him. He had no
idea what the hell he was supposed to do with himself, no
idea where there was to go in this city. Save for the West
End, where the Guild had set up its base on the University's
grounds, all of Glasgow was abandoned and rubble. After the
Resurrection, the necromancers had done what they could to
tear down the city. First, the Howls came through, snatching
up anyone they could for food. Then the necromancers, snaring the rest for converts and demolishing centuries of architecture in the process. Maybe so humanity would have nothing
left to return or hold on to. But probably just to be dicks.

He and Kianna had barely gone a block when she turned
down what was left of a side street. She guided him over bro-

ken concrete and steel girders, everything coated in fog like a bad horror movie set. Except the monsters here were real.

Most of Glasgow had been abandoned, civilians evacuated to safety behind the Guild's walls, which should have meant there was nothing here for the Howls to hunt. The last few years, the streets had been fairly safe in their emptiness. But now, with most of the country's resources depleted, the Howls were hungry. Desperate. Scavenging in places they hadn't been seen. Like Laura, seeking a human to drain of blood.

Humanity might be losing, but that meant the Howls were losing, too. And they were more reckless when it came to assuaging their eternal hunger.

Now, Glasgow's streets weren't necessarily as abandoned as they once were.

"Where are you taking me?" Aidan muttered.

A shiver tore through him when a droplet fell on the back of his neck. *Please, just let it be condensation.*

Another drip. Moments later, the sky broke into a full-on downpour.

He shuddered and Kianna pulled him closer.

"Not much further, love."

He glanced at her. She sounded concerned. Like, actually concerned. And that concerned him. How much had she heard? How much would he have to explain?

"I'm okay," he lied.

She just grunted and kept her eyes on the rubble at their feet, navigating expertly over glass and stone, the crunch of their boots muffled in the fog and rain. He wanted to reach for Fire, to wrap the warmth over and through him, but he knew he wasn't strong enough. He'd drawn too much. Any more, and he might burn himself out or lose control entirely. Again.

Kianna pushed open a steel gate in the side of a tall, mostly intact building, the interior hallway remarkably untouched by the apocalypse. It was still covered in trash, but at least it wasn't caving in. She flicked her lantern on in the half light, directing him down the hall and up a flight of stairs littered with scraps of clothing and furniture. He noticed she made sure to lock the gate behind them.

Two flights of steps, the darkness dancing with lantern light. Then a hallway, the hum of rain outside. Everything here was steel and concrete, modern and sparse.

"What is this?" he asked. Why were they still in Glasgow? Trevor had told him point-blank he wasn't welcome here. Not that he really cared what Trevor said.

"A place for the night." She pulled a key from her pocket and opened a door.

Inside, the flat was clearly awaiting their arrival. A cold but set fireplace, a teakettle beside it. Rugs and pillows, wooden crates and bottles of water, food stores and weapons. Everything was so modern and untouched that for a moment his head spun with anachronism. If not for the weapons, he could almost imagine it was three years ago, before the mess of the Resurrection, when he'd first stepped foot on this accursed island.

"You've been preparing," he mused. His eyes snared on the empty fireplace. A shudder wracked through him, and he nearly toppled them both to the floor.

Shite. He'd drawn even more power than he'd thought.

If he didn't warm up fast, he would catch his death of cold. Literally.

She led him straight toward the fireplace and set him down somewhat gently on a pillow beside the hearth. Without speaking, she lit a match and set the kindling alight while Aidan shivered uncontrollably at her side. She noticed his helplessness, but save for a grunt to herself, she didn't say anything. She just peeled off his sodden jacket and shirt and threw them both to the nearby kitchen tile, where they landed with wet thwaps. He stared at his dark arms and chest dumbly, his myriad black tattoos making constellations over his skin: alchemical symbols, star charts, Norse war runes, **BURN THEM** on his knuckles, and even a sexy merman on his pec. All of those tattoos had become like a second skin, symbols of his countless victories. But now, his vision snared on the concentric circles and arched lines on his forearm, the mark that had attuned him to the Sphere of Fire three years ago. The mark that had helped him secure Scotland's survival and brought him up the ranks until he was co-commander in a country he never wanted to call his own.

The mark that had also, somehow, cost him every single one of those conquests.

Then Kianna wrapped a wool blanket around Aidan's shoulders, obscuring the tattoos and leaving him to take off his drenched trousers and pants himself.

"I figured this day would come," she said, settling herself by the roaring fire.

"Did you?" His teeth chattered. He was seconds away from asking her to come under the blanket with him. He needed the warmth.

"Have you met yourself?" she asked. "Only a matter of time before you pissed someone off enough to be exiled. Frankly, I'm impressed it didn't happen sooner."

She moved the iron kettle onto a rack by the flames while he scooted closer to the hearth. He looked around the flat, at the weapons, at the boarded windows, his heart dropping with every observation.

This was it. This was his future.

Then he asked the question that had been smoldering in his chest ever since she appeared in the tunnel. "Why are you helping me? After…after what I did?"

She shrugged.

"I hate everyone," she replied. "You, I just hate less." She paused and looked at him. He expected an interrogation. That's the least of what he'd earned.

"Sugar?" she asked. Then began scooping sugar into an empty cup before he could answer.

"How are you asking about tea at a time like this?" he asked.

"Because times like this always call for tea," she said. She wrapped the handle in a handkerchief and pulled the kettle from the flame, then poured the warm brown nectar into both of their cups. She handed him one, then took up her own in two hands.

For a while, she just regarded him over her cup, her eyes intent through the steam.

He wanted to ask her what she'd heard. He wanted to ask her if Trevor had changed his mind. He wanted to know if Vincent was actually dead, or if it had truly been a nightmare.

Her next words silenced any further questions on his part.

"There are worse things than exile, love."

He looked at her—his only friend left in the world—at the tea, at the fire.

He stared into the flames, remembering the sound of Vincent's screams. Remembering how little he'd cared when realization dawned.

There were worse things than exile.

He knew.

He'd done them.

CHAPTER FIVE

IT TOOK AN HOUR AND THREE MUGS OF TEA BEFORE he felt warm again. Even then, "warm" was an overstatement. Shivers still racked his body, but at least he was dry. The chills weren't from magic alone. No, that had lessened long ago. This pain was something he would never truly burn away.

Though he would sure as hell try.

Not once did Kianna bring up his meeting with Trevor, the "private" discussion she'd "accidentally" walked in on. Aidan didn't offer up any morsels of information, either. He just sat there, another cup of tea in his hands while he watched the flames flicker. She filled the silence with busywork, unpacking boxes of weapons and food, arranging gear in duffel bags. Making lunch. Even though it was clear she'd had this place set up ages ago, it was also clear she hadn't been entirely certain when they would need it.

There was a part of him—a small part of him—that wanted to feel sad. Depression lingered like a puddle of water on a smoldering board. He could feel the edges of it hissing away at the heat always burning in his chest, threatening to drown the flame, to quench the anger. He could feel the fire fighting back, trying to evaporate the sadness before it gained the upper hand. He felt the sadness, but he refused to let it win, steeled himself with Fire's strength.

There was no room in this world for sadness and regret.

There was only the flash, the burn, the energy and excitement. Life was a flame, not a flood. You lived and you burned and you burned out. Drowning was not an option.

"This isn't right," he said finally, pouring himself another cup from the nearly empty kettle. The handle was hot against his palm, probably too hot for most to bear, but for him it felt like a kiss.

The kind with more bite than blush.

"Insightful," Kianna muttered. She glanced up from the array of daggers spread before her. "I swear to Mary, you say life isn't fair and I'm chucking you out the window."

Aidan managed a laugh.

The water of despair still sizzled away in the corner of his heart, but the more he focused on his indignation, the more the water evaporated.

"He's going to regret this," Aidan said. He turned his attention back to the smoldering peat fire in front of them—the scent of burnt earth was as familiar to him as his own, now.

"Are you going to make him? Sounds an awful lot like treason. Especially when it looked like you were about to burn him apart there."

"I'm not a member of the Guild anymore."

Something hard hit the side of his head and thudded to the

ground. He jolted, sloshing tea all over the lambskin rug he sat on, and looked to the dagger now sitting at his hip.

His heart flipped with anger.

"You could have killed me."

"And yet, you live." She didn't even look up from organizing her blades. One fewer than before. "So clearly that wasn't my intent."

"What was?"

"To stop you from saying something I *will* make you regret. You're not a part of the Guild, but you're still a Hunter. Same as me. Unless you're thinking of switching sides and joining the Dark Lady's forces. In which case, the next dagger I chuck won't be hilt-first."

Aidan opened his mouth to say of course that wasn't what he meant, but the words were stuck in his throat. If he didn't want to join the Dark Lady, and he wasn't part of the Guild, where was he? There were only two sides to the coin: you either served the Dark Lady, the near-mythical figure who had caused the Resurrection by turning the first human into a Howl, or you fought against her. Didn't matter that the Dark Lady wasn't real, or at least no longer alive—her forces were fighting on without her. The Guild was the only thing standing in her way. Well, the Guild and the Church, but those zealots were as crazy as the necromancers.

Pissed as he was, killing Trevor would be an act of treason. Would declare Aidan a tool of the Dark Lady and every creature he'd dedicated his life to erasing. Was revenge really that sweet? The fact that he even considered it startled him. Maybe Trevor was right...

Quickly, he focused on the flames in front of him, poured

himself into the fire like an offering of ash. Doubt burned away, leaving nothing but a skeleton of steel underneath.

"I'm not joining her," he said, a flash of rage at the thought. For everything the Dark Lady and her minions had done to him, he would never join her side. If nothing else, he would make her pay. Even this, in its way, was her fault. "I just refuse to let Trevor get away with this."

"Don't worry, love. In a few days he'll realize just how worse off he is without you and come crawling back for you. Oh, I meant the Guild. The Guild is worse off."

Aidan glared at her.

Her stare was just as cold in response.

"Look, Aidan, Trevor did what he had to do. Honestly, he was more lenient on you than I would have been and you know it. Hell, if *you* were in his shoes, you know you would have issued a death sentence. Though that's mostly because you're a heartless prick. So don't pull any of this *woe is me* shite. You did something bad. You were exiled because of it. Move on with it and be thankful you weren't killed."

"So what do we do?" Aidan asked.

"Find another Guild? I'd suggest London, but there's no way in hell I want to go home."

Again, the hiss of despair against his flame, this time over the word *home*. Because she could go home. She could search for her remaining family, could find the familiar walls of her flat. He was stuck here. A thousand miles away from the mountains and forests that had once been as much a part of his world as the smiles of his family. As far as he knew, his hometown didn't even exist anymore.

As far as he knew, he'd lost more than just his mother during the Resurrection.

"They'll have heard," he muttered. "I won't be welcome anywhere."

"Then we just go rogue. Head over to Europe and find a Guild that hasn't heard about you…"

"I refuse to leave the country. I was stuck here, and I fought to make it mine. To make it *free*. I'm not leaving until Calum is dead and Scotland is liberated. Preferably by my hand."

Kianna snorted. "You and what army?"

He shrugged uncomfortably and went back to looking at the fire. He wanted to find his future in the flames, a path to victory, to vengeance. So many people had wronged him. So many still needed to pay.

"Maybe we don't need any army," he mused. "We could try to take Edinburgh ourselves. If nothing else, we go out in a blaze of glory like we always wanted."

Kianna didn't respond, and for a moment he let himself see that potential future in the flames: Calum burning to the ground as he overtook the Kin's castle, as he became the first to destroy one of the six who had destroyed the world. As Aidan didn't just vindicate himself—he became immortalized.

That was a thought that made Fire purr. To be known throughout the world. To be revered. *Worshipped*. That was the treatment Fire demanded. From the very first days, mankind crowded around the flame, seeking warmth. Safety. Nourishment. Fire had provided all of those, just as Aidan had provided for his people. For that, Fire expected nothing less than devotion.

Just as Aidan deserved.

Calum had crowned himself the Howl King of Britain early on, and no one had usurped his reign.

Normally, the Spheres created energy that sustained the body. But a necromancer could tap into the Spheres. Draw the energy out. Until the Sphere collapsed, and the Sphere started draining the host of those energies and nutrients. Unlike most Howls, Calum wasn't just created by magic, he was able to use it. That was what set the Kin apart, what had let them destroy the world—they could wield the Spheres as well as any human, whilst enjoying the superhuman side-effects of their conversion. He, like the five other Kin out there, was a force to be reckoned with.

But none of them had reckoned with Aidan.

Yet.

"It might be a bit crowded," Kianna muttered, drawing him from his dreams of victory.

"Crowded?"

She sighed. She rarely sighed. And when she looked at him, he felt a flicker of doubt.

"I heard Trevor before I left to find you. He gave the command. They're attacking Edinburgh tomorrow."

The flicker turned to a roar as anger overtook fear. Fire opened in his chest and he leaped to his feet, flames dancing around his clenched fists as the blanket dropped to his feet.

"What?" he roared. "That was *my* mission!"

Kianna stared up at him, calm and collected in the face of his wrath. The day he saw her flinch would probably be the day he saw her die. "Not anymore. You *were* supposed to lead them to victory. But Trevor must have known you wouldn't just sit around after being exiled. It's like you'd slept with him or something. Many times. Even after your best and only mate had warned you against it for reasons like this. Also many times. He knows you better than you know yourself, and he knows you'll never let someone else steal your thunder. And Calum is the biggest thunder this country has to offer."

Her eyes flickered down. Squinted.

"Also, I can see your prick. I think."

"When?" he hissed, completely ignoring her jab. Something shattered in his hand, and he realized he'd crushed the teacup. He didn't even feel it.

His blood sizzled as it fell to the floor.

"In the morning."

"No. When were you going to tell me?" he asked, his teeth clenched tight as his fists.

"When you cooled down," she said. She began packing up her blades, slipping them into various belts and pockets of coats strewn about the floor. "So, knowing you, after you died."

"You bitch. You were going to let them go to war without me?"

"Of course not, Aidan," she replied. "I was just going to let you get a full night's sleep first. So I could sleep, as well."

"We leave tonight." He would get a jump start on them. He would be there when the attack began.

"So much for that," she said. "This is why I don't tell you things until you absolutely need to know. A girl needs her beauty rest."

"Sleep when you're dead." He reached for a dry pair of boxers.

"Not even then," she said, deadpan. "I'll be too busy haunting your arse for getting me killed."

CHAPTER SIX

THEY DIDN'T LEAVE IMMEDIATELY.

He blamed Kianna.

Not that she ever outright forced them to wait until morning—no, she knew him better than that, knew the moment she tried to reason he'd dig in his heels and force his way. Instead, she took her time assembling all of her weapons. Then she insisted they actually eat something warm, while they had a dry place. Which meant beans on toast, a meal he'd come to expect and despise. Howls weren't the only ones starving on this cursed island. Then she suggested he take a nap, which he refused with a yawn.

And then she pulled back the curtain to the torrential downpour that was Glasgow's evening weather, casually mentioning that it would suck to have to trudge out there without magic or light to guide their way, as use of either would get them caught by the scouts Trevor had surely already sent out toward Edinburgh.

He hated admitting that she had a point.

If they left now, they'd be in sheer darkness. Sheer, wet, freezing darkness. He couldn't use Fire to warm himself or light the way, not without risking his former comrades stumbling upon him. Nor could they use the few working torches they had, for fear of the same.

He stood by the window, fully clothed, his daggers restocked, and shivered, watching the rain pour down the glass. He couldn't even see past the window into the street beyond, the night was so dark and the rain so thick. No way in hell he wanted to be caught out in that.

Maybe it was from being attuned to Fire, but he hated the rain and he hated the cold above all else. Oh, and large bodies of water.

God must truly exist, to fuck him over so badly by trapping him here and granting all three at once.

"We're screwed," he said, turning from the window.

Kianna was in pajamas.

Like, pink-and-black-plaid pajama bottoms and a pink tank top. She was literally the only Hunter he knew who wore anything other than black. Then again, she broke the mold on a lot of things—her attire was pretty benign in comparison.

She was snuggled up on the sofa, wrapped in a few thick quilts, reading a book. Probably a romance novel, knowing her. The kinkier, the better. Preferably with lesbians. "Hmm?" she muttered, not looking up.

He didn't want to take off his gear. Not that it was comfortable, but it felt like giving in. Not just to the night, but to any hope of a different future. He needed to keep moving. Fire wasn't an element of complacency—it had to be fed, to burn, to spread. If he lost momentum now, a small part of him screamed he would snuff out.

"This," he said. He flopped down on the sofa next to her and kicked his feet up, resting them beside her hip.

She shoved them off the sofa without looking.

"No boots on the furniture." She looked over the book at him. "I know you're from the mountains, but were you raised in a bloody barn?"

"No, but my neighbors had one." He reached down and began unlacing his boots. As much as it hurt his pride to stay in, he knew she was right—if they left now, they'd be captured or killed or both.

He wasn't going to burn out. Not just yet.

Not until *someone* paid for all of this.

"So why are we screwed?" Kianna asked. She flipped a page. Judging from the cover, there were definitely lesbians in this one. Which definitely meant they weren't leaving any time soon. "Despite the obvious."

He didn't know how to say it. No, he didn't *want* to say it. The words burning in the back of his throat.

We can't do this alone.

We need the Guild to survive.

If Calum falls and I'm not there, everything will have been for nothing.

Silence and the hiss and pop of the fire filled the room while he sat there, fingers twined through his laces, unable to move or speak. Any of those admissions felt like defeat. Fire cursed inside of him, telling him he was worthless if he failed after all of this, telling him he needed to fight harder, burn brighter, otherwise he was worth no more than the undead he hunted. If he didn't make his mark on the world, no one would remember him.

If no one remembered him, he might as well have never existed in the first place.

After a moment, Kianna put the book down and stared at him. "Why did you do it?"

"What?" Her words broke the spell and pulled him from his reverie—it wasn't depression. No, that was a heavy, sodden thing. When he turned inward, it was all knives and cauterization.

"Don't act stupid, twat. Why did you kill him?"

He'd been waiting for her to ask that question.

He'd been waiting since he ran off to the Underground, and he still didn't have an answer. None that made sense. None that would make her want to abandon him less.

"Because I wanted to," he said, tossing his boots toward the fire with a thud.

"Bullshit. I know you. You're an arsehole and you're reckless, but you aren't that stupid."

Aidan stared at his boots and the flames flickering off the polished black leather. He bit his lip as the memory came back—not the image, no, but the scent. The scent of Vincent's burning flesh, the char of his leather jacket, the singe of his hair. He could almost see Vincent's eyes in the fire's reflection, could almost see the fear.

Then Aidan shook his head and looked to Kianna, and the vision was gone.

"What do you want to hear?" he asked. "That I lost control? That magic is dangerous? That everything you ever warned me about finally happened?"

Rage was a slow build inside of him, but mostly, he was too tired to feel it. His words sounded as empty as the city he was exiled from.

"Those are my words, yes," Kianna replied. "I want yours."

He couldn't look at her. Instead, he stared at the tattoos on his knuckles: **BURN THEM**. The first of many. He'd gotten them the day after he'd received his Hunter's mark and attuned to Fire. As a reminder, a motive. A mandate. He'd spent his entire life after the Resurrection with only one goal: make the Howls pay. It had been the one thing guiding him forward, and the one thing keeping his rage in check. Burn them. Burn the ones who did this to him, to his world. Burn every last Howl and necromancer until he had the Dark Lady by the throat.

The charge wasn't meant to apply to his comrades, as well.

"I don't know," he finally said.

And there it was. The three words he wanted to hold back, because releasing them was the flood over his flames. He'd always known. He'd always been assured. Fire was his weapon and he would wield it against the undead until he died. Fire was *his*. To control and command. To carve a path straight to the Dark Lady's heart.

"That's not an answer, Aidan," Kianna said. "What do you mean, you don't know?"

Aidan shrugged, still staring at his tattoos. He could practically feel his mark burning against his right forearm.

"He pissed me off," he began, but that wasn't right, either. He closed his eyes.

"He woke me up."

"He woke you up," Kianna said. "Are you bloody well kidding me?"

Aidan shook his head.

The scent was still in his nostrils.

"He woke you up and you decided to kill him?"

"I didn't decide anything," Aidan said. His words were barely above a whisper.

"What?"

He couldn't explain it to her. She wouldn't understand. Couldn't.

She wasn't attuned. She didn't know how the Spheres sang and intoxicated. She didn't know. She never would.

"I didn't do it," he managed.

He hadn't meant to kill Vincent.

He hadn't done it.

Vincent woke him up. Woke him up from some dream he couldn't grasp. A dream with a boy calling his name, and a grave calling his soul. A dream that seemed to resonate deeper than anything ever had. A dream he didn't want to look at, because for some reason, it hurt like hell.

"It was Fire," Aidan muttered. "My Sphere. It…it killed him."

"I told you magic would bite you in the arse some day," she replied, but her voice was unsteady.

Kianna distrusted magic. No, that was too gentle—she *despised* it. Said that's what got them into this mess in the first place. Even though magic had allowed her to transition without surgery, even though it had saved her arse in battle more times than he would dare bring up, she would never be attuned. She would never wield the Spheres as a weapon or view magic as anything less than a curse humanity brought upon itself. He'd tried asking why, when they first met. When he was attuned and she stood by with disdain while watching him get tattooed.

He'd tried, but just like him, she didn't talk about her past. Or her feelings. Which was precisely why they hadn't killed each other yet.

Secretly, he'd always thought she was just scared of wielding so much power. Scared of what she would do with it. Or maybe she was just the ultimate hipster, denying herself magic when it had become mainstream. He'd never know. That wasn't the issue. The issue was that her aversion to magic was, in some small way, starting to feel justified.

Up until today, he'd believed that the Spheres were just weapons, no better or worse than the person who wielded them. He thought he'd been in control.

Yet, that very morning, Fire had proven that *it* was the master. *It* had taken control of *him*.

And Fire had only one desire: burn them all.

No matter who was offered at the stake.

CHAPTER SEVEN

KIANNA MADE HIM SLEEP ON THE SOFA.

He couldn't blame her, not after admitting to accidentally killing his comrade in his half sleep. It was another reason he didn't want to stay here, why he wanted to be on the road and as close to Edinburgh as possible: he couldn't trust himself. Not around anyone, but especially not around her.

He didn't think he could move forward if he accidentally killed his only friend.

So he lay on the leather couch, covered in quilts, while the fire smoldered in the hearth and Kianna snored from the nearby bedroom. He was tired. More than tired. But sleep was the furthest thing from his mind.

He wasn't worried. He wasn't thoughtful. He was just...*angry*.

After all Aidan had done for the troops—the battles won, the lives saved, the plans made—this one cock-up was all it had taken to get kicked out. One mistake, and everything he'd fought and bled for was thrown out the window. No one gave a shit that he was the only reason the highlands were

free. No one cared that, without him, they would have lost
the battle for Glasgow a year after the Resurrection. Without him, they'd all be dead or Howls by now, no question.
And now, he wouldn't even get to take part in the attack he'd
spent the last year devising.

He wouldn't be there when the castle fell and the first of
the Kin was destroyed.

He wouldn't be the one to liberate Scotland from the Howls
for good.

Someone else would get the credit.

Someone else would gain that immortality.

He lay there, fists clenched, and seethed at it. The injustice.
The stupidity. Fire smoldered in his chest, wanted nothing more
than to burn the whole flat down, to run back to the Guild
and make them all pay. It filled him with that want, that need.
To burn. To hurt. To feed. And as he stared at the embers in
the hearth, he realized how easy it would be. They wouldn't
be prepared for it. He knew the secret ins and outs of the place.
He could sneak in, murder Trevor in his sleep, and take the
Guild as his own. They would follow him into battle. And if
they didn't? He could burn it all down from the inside out.

He could show them.

He could prove to the world not to cross Aidan Belmont.

He could…

…*what the hell was he thinking?*

He tried to take a deep breath and quench the embers in
his chest. He wasn't going to kill his co-commander—even
if he'd screwed his commander and been screwed over in return. He wasn't going to openly rebel against the Guild. He
was still a Hunter. He was still sworn to protect the innocent.

What if they don't deserve protecting?

The voice hissed from the bowels of Fire, a feminine smolder that sent chills down his spine. The same voice that had whispered to him earlier...

What if they are but cattle? Sheep? And you the shepherd. The butcher. The king.

He saw it then, in the fires of the hearth—him on the throne in Edinburgh, the remains of civilization sprawled at his feet, bowed and praying, begging and groveling.

Why do you serve, when they should serve you? Why do you give them power, when you have the might of the eternal flame in your hands?

He looked down, and the blankets were gone, and in his palms sparks like constellations spun and danced. The power thrummed through him, a smoldering chord that lay heavy on his heart. The power. The *power*. To burn or bless, to consume or cauterize. He held life in his hands, and that life pulsed with possibility.

Why do you serve, when you are meant to rule?

The voice changed, melted from feminine to masculine, and from the shadows a figure appeared, flickering from dark to light like an ignited spark. Once, nothing. Then, presence.

And what a presence this man was.

"Why do you grovel, when I can make you king?"

The guy snared Aidan's senses. From head to toe, he breathed sex and sensuality and danger. Tousled black hair that fell past his chiseled jaw; glinting copper eyes and pure white teeth; olive skin that glistened in the firelight. Or maybe it was his own light that made him shine. He wore very little— tight black denim with ripped knees, pointed black shoes, and a smile that sent a thousand terrible thoughts racing through Aidan's head.

That smile said that even the jeans were more than he wanted to be wearing.

Aidan knew the questions he should ask: *Who are you? What are you doing here?*

He knew that the man wasn't a man, not really—he was too otherworldly, too utterly *perfect.* Which meant he was an incubus, a Howl pulled from Fire, a monster craving and crafted for heat and sex and passion.

Aidan knew all of this, but the only question he could ask was, "How?"

The man tilted his head to the side.

"I like you," he mused. The words sent more flame racing through Aidan's chest. Aidan tried to sit up, but the man was at his side, and he pressed Aidan back down with one smoldering, frozen hand. "You are much more...enthusiastic... than the last."

The man knelt. His hand remained on Aidan's chest. This close, only a foot away, and Aidan could see every fleck in the flames of the incubus's eyes. He could smell the musk and cologne, the undercurrent that promised two things: sex and destruction.

Two things he wanted with every inch of him.

"My name, Hunter," the incubus cooed, "is Tomás." The way he bit his lip made Aidan squirm. "And we are going to have *so* much fun."

"How..." Aidan managed. "How will I be king?"

"Shh," Tomás said. He pressed a finger to Aidan's lips. Ice shattered across Aidan's tongue, chills and fever piercing his throat.

Aidan leaned against the touch.

"It matters not how," Tomás said. "Only when. And I can

promise you, Aidan, that your rule will be soon. Together, we will send the whole world to its knees."

"I know what you are," Aidan whispered against Tomás's finger. The Howl's flesh tasted sweet.

Tomás's hand clenched on his chest, and the blossom of pain made him moan with pleasure.

"Do you, now?"

"Yes," Aidan whispered.

"What am I then?"

"What I've been waiting for."

Tomás smiled and removed his finger, pulling down Aidan's bottom lip. "Good answer."

Then Tomás leaned over and kissed his forehead.

Fire raged across Aidan's vision, burning away the flat, the sofa, the city, until it was only the two of them in the flames, the heat and the chaos and bliss, and even as his body ached and writhed and throbbed, he was apart from it, watching it all—him and the incubus, locked in this embrace—but that wasn't what snared his attention. It was the flames. The glorious, pulsating flames that whirled around them, the fire that burned bright with passion and promise.

Because in those flames, he saw his future.

A throne of kraven skulls and a crown of bloodling teeth, a castle of ever-living fire and ash. At his feet, the humans who had scorned him, the Howls who'd hunted him. And at his side, on a throne of ribs and basalt, sat Tomás. His lover. His savior. His king.

"All of this will be ours," Tomás said, reaching over to grip Aidan's thigh. "All I ask is that you submit to me. Obey me. And I will give you everything you desire."

Tomás squeezed, and the castle burned, and around them humans and Howls screamed in agony, in harmony, but he barely heard it as Tomás climbed atop him, took Aidan's face in his hands.

"Be mine," Tomás whispered.

"I already am," Aidan replied, arching his body to be closer to Tomás, to the heat, to the power, to the desire. "I want you."

"Then I am yours."

Tomás pulled their lips together, and Aidan grabbed his hips, pulled himself closer, closer, as the world burned hotter, hotter...

"Damn it, Aidan!" Kianna yelled.

Something soft smacked into the side of his head, knocking the dream away and bringing reality into focus.

The acrid scent of burnt wool filled his nostrils.

"You've set the bloody couch on fire!" she said. She stood by the hearth, hands on her hips and a disgusted look on her face.

"I—" he began, but he couldn't gain his bearings. The sofa smoldered, but it wasn't in flames, thank gods. Just a few patches in the arms and in the wool blanket. But that dream...

Kianna shook her head.

"*And* you have a boner. Is that what this is? Fire acting up because you haven't gotten off in a while?"

"I—"

"Take your time," she said. "I'll give you some privacy."

She chuckled and headed toward the exit, stopping before she left.

"Just make sure you don't burn the place down when you come."

CHAPTER EIGHT

AIDAN DIDN'T JERK OFF.

Not that he even wanted to, but having Kianna draw so much attention to it definitely made it the last thing on his mind. Instead, he sat on the edge of the sofa and coaxed the embers in the hearth with a small thread of Fire.

The dream…

It had been so vivid. So real. He hadn't even realized he was asleep until Kianna woke him up. And yet, he'd only said those things in the dream *because* it was all a fantasy. He didn't actually mean any of them, right?

Not that he thought that Tomás was *real*—the incubus was just some sexed-up fantasy from Aidan's tired imagination. But still… He'd offered Aidan the world on a silver platter, and Aidan had taken it without question.

It made him doubt his sanity.

Maybe Trevor was right. Maybe he *was* a liability.

"All finished?" Kianna asked with a smirk.

He looked over to where she poked her head through the open door. He hadn't even heard her open it.

"Fuck off."

"I'll take that as a no." She plopped wetly down beside him.

"I see the weather hasn't improved," he muttered, staring at her clothes.

"Does it ever?"

He just mumbled under his breath and went back to staring at the flames.

"What are we going to do?" Kianna asked.

We. Not *you.* At least he still had her on his side. For now. He shook his head, and with it, shook off the visions of Tomás and the world on its knees.

"I… I'm not certain."

She nudged him. "I went to spy on the troops. They've begun marching."

He grunted. Of course they had. He'd been trying to get them to march on Edinburgh for months. According to Trevor, the time had never been right—they weren't strong enough, or there was word of a different threat, or some other bullshit excuse. Apparently, the real reason he had been waiting was that he needed Aidan out of the way.

"So, here's the thing," she continued. "We have supplies for about a week here. Two if you aren't a pig like usual. Then we're going to have to move."

"What about taking Edinburgh for ourselves? Are you just suggesting we give up?"

"I know you want to be all mopey right now, Aidan, but it's extremely out of character and it's starting to piss me off. I'm not suggesting we give up. I'm suggesting we don't commit suicide. They'll kill you if you follow them, and you aren't going to get a piece of their glory, no matter how much you whine about it being your idea or how grandiose your dreams of personal power are. Calum is no longer our mark. So. I say we save the little dignity we have—and by that I mean *you*, because I only kill people intentionally—and go somewhere we aren't known. Start over. Find some other Howls to kill. I hear there's a Kin living in Berlin. Always wanted to go to Berghain. Maybe it's still a party?"

He could only stare at her.

"Are you serious?" Fire smoldered and he had to get to his feet, had to pace to keep himself from exploding. "After everything we've done, everything we've sacrificed, you want to just…just…*give up*?"

"You killed a Hunter."

"By mistake!" The hearth fire burned bright with his anger, even though he didn't mean for the power to slip from his fingers. Again. "One mistake and you're willing to walk away from everything we built? We *made* this country, Kianna. And you want to just fucking up and go?"

She watched him, face blank, a slight rise to one eyebrow.

"The country you're now technically exiled from."

"According to who?"

"Whom."

"God, I hate you sometimes. *Whom*, then. According to whom? Last I checked, Trevor doesn't run this country."

"Technically, he does. Well, him and the Kin, and I guess the Church if you want to consider them, but we probably don't want to consider those last two since they're both twats—"

"Shut up!" The fire billowed up and out, and it took all of his self control to quench the flames, to force the Sphere back into submission. In the hearth, the flames sank back to a smolder. But inside, Fire raged. "I'm *not* leaving Scotland. Not until every last Howl is burned off the map. Not until Edinburgh is *mine*. Do you hear me? Edinburgh. Is. *Mine*."

He stood there, panting, his breath hot and his heart racing, while Kianna just smiled up at him.

"About bloody time you showed up to the party," she said.

"What are you talking about?" His voice was gravelly, seared. Fire still wanted to burn the place down.

"If I had to sit for another minute with that *other* you, I was going to kill you myself." She stood and stretched, every movement sinuous. Languid. That was the word. She patted him on the shoulder, the gentle movement enough to nearly buckle his knees. "I still say we check out Berghain someday. Big warehouse party. Days and days of sex and drugs and rock and roll. You'd love it."

He glared at her.

"*After* we kill Calum, of course." She smiled. "Oh, come on, lighten up. You're about to fuck over the Guild a second time. That's exciting! Even if you don't manage to kill Calum, you'll still be a first. Infamy is as good as heroism, right?"

"I don't know why I put up with you."

"Because *I'm* the only one who puts up with *you*." She considered for a moment. "And also probably because you have piss-poor taste in friends. I know I do."

He didn't know where he was going when he left the flat, just knew that he couldn't stay there and couldn't risk trailing after the army just yet. If there were stragglers, he'd be captured or forced to kill again, and that wasn't something he wanted to deal with right now.

Kianna might have thought he was over his slump, but she was wrong. Not that he was broken. Or, to use her word, *mopey.* He just felt...off. Too many dreams ricocheting in his head, drowning his waking life. Too many rugs pulled from under his feet.

He hated to admit that he needed anything or anyone. But as he left to walk out his anxious energy, he realized the truth: now that he was exiled, now that he wasn't waking every single morning with an immutable purpose, he felt adrift.

When he was with the Guild, there'd always been a focus— finding food, defending the innocents, planning the inevitable attack or defense. Now, the only voices telling him what to do were his own and Kianna's. And Fire. And not one of those was a voice he should be listening to.

He *needed* to kill Calum. Needed this victory more than anything else. He needed to prove to Trevor and the rest of the Guild that he wasn't expendable. That he had purpose. Great purpose. With Calum's blood on his hands, he could make his way back to the top. He could lord it over the rest.

He could rule.

For some reason, that thought made his dream hiss back through his mind, but for the life of him he couldn't remember anything beyond a throne. One he very much planned to sit on.

It was still pissing rain outside, and he was still in exile, which meant he shouldn't be using magic. Even the small amounts that would keep him warm and dry would give him away to any Hunter out scouting. He just had to hope all of Trevor's forces were already on the move, and those left to defend the Guild were safely behind the wall, a few miles away. He had to hope he knew the city better than any of them.

That, at least, was a hope he could bank on.

So, rain coursing down his back, he slipped down the street and back into the subway tunnel, his boots slipping on the moss and muck with every step. At least down here it was dry.

He realized a few steps down, however, that he didn't have a torch, and he wasn't about to trudge back through the rain to borrow one of Kianna's.

"Fuck it," he whispered, and opened to Fire. Just a little.

The Sphere unfurled in his chest in a flurry of sparks, a gust of wind in the ashes. Instantly, on reflex, he funneled the heat through his limbs, burning off the rain and drying himself in moments. Just that little bit was a bump to the system.

His heart thudded faster. His brain felt clearer. And as he spiraled sparks of flame around him in a makeshift light, he felt more himself. More empowered. More in control.

With Fire, he would always be in control.

For a moment, he stood there, watching the sparks dance around him, feeling the sparks dance *within* him, and wondered what the fuck had actually happened yesterday. Fire didn't *feel* any different now. It didn't feel stronger. Didn't feel like he was struggling for control.

He laced a tendril of flame around him, making it dart through the air like a dragon. He turned up his palm, let the fire rest in the cup of his fingers as he peered into the red-and-orange light. Felt it as surely as he felt his own heartbeat.

Whatever had happened yesterday—and, to a lesser extent, this morning—was a fluke. He'd been tired. He'd been having weird dreams. *Those* were to blame. Not Fire itself.

If he started doubting his Sphere, he would have a lot greater worries than exile.

"They just don't understand," he whispered to his flame.

Of course Fire got out of control at times. Fire didn't give a shit.

Which was precisely why he and the element worked so well together.

He sent the flame spiraling around him as he walked. Firelight lanced his shadow out like the petals of a black lotus. He fed his doubts and his fears to the flame, and the fire consumed them eagerly. Until all he had left was the low-burning anger, the desire to destroy, to grow brighter. He almost wished he would come across some hungering Howls.

His feet thudded on a body. He glanced at the bloodling he had killed yesterday. Her corpse floated in the calf-deep water, blood long since dispersed. What had her name been?

"What does it matter?" he asked no one, Fire's words burning past his lips. She was dead. He was alive. That was the only thing that mattered in the end.

It wasn't her pallid corpse that kept his attention, however. It was the flier floating atop the film of sludge and rainwater, caught against the track.

REPENT
THE END IS HERE
ALL SINNERS BURN
REPENT, AND BEG
FOR SALVATION

Aidan picked it up, the sodden paper mushing in his hands.

He hadn't seen Church propaganda for the last few years. He'd driven *them* out of Scotland years ago, when it was clear that even though the Church reportedly defied the Dark Lady, they also defied anyone who used magic. Which meant Hunters were lumped in the same category as necromancers.

As far as he knew, the members of the Church had all perished in the wilds as they fled south to England. After all, without magic to keep them safe, what chance did they have?

It's not like any religion had prevented or saved anyone from the apocalypse.

"Who's repenting now?" Aidan asked, and sent a curl of flame through the edges of the paper, watching the words burn.

Something pricked at the back of his awareness, though, something that felt far too much like fear.

If the flier had been floating down here for years, why was it in such good shape? How had it lasted, when there should have been no one to distribute it for ages?

He flipped the smoldering page over.

On the back was the location of a Church, but the flame licked it away before he could make it out. Above it was a name that had become as much of a curse on this land as any Howl: Brother Jeremiah. The priest had come to power in the early days after the Resurrection, and his name had become synonymous—among the Hunters at least—with danger and fear.

Fuck that fear.

Aidan burned the fear like he burned the page. No matter what, the Church wasn't a threat. Even if they had been snooping back in Glasgow. Even if they had thought they could regain the devotion of the masses.

He was the only one who deserved devotion.

The flier disintegrated. He let it crumble, drifting down on the bloodling's face like snow. They would all burn. He would ensure it.

He walked past her. The moment her body sank into the shadows, she and the Church were out of mind.

Fire didn't know the meaning of looking back.

CHAPTER NINE

AND YET, WHEN HE REACHED THE END OF THE TUN-
nel, he realized he *was* looking back. And he hated himself
for it.

The way forward was blocked with rubble and concrete. In
the early days of building the Guild, they'd collapsed this part
of the tunnel to keep the West End safe. Well, safer. Right
before the collapsed wall of dirt was Kelvinbridge Station.
Aidan hopped up onto the platform and stared down at the
water rushing through the tunnel, draining out to who-knew-
where. Technically, the entrance to Kelvinbridge Station was
supposed to be caved in as well, but he'd fought hard against
it, saying that if they ever needed a fast escape, the tunnels
were their best bet. Besides, a single point of entry and exit
was easy enough to guard.

He'd won the argument. As per usual.

He made his way up the steps toward the exit. Halfway
there, he let go of Fire and let darkness fall back around him,
just a faint light and the sound of rain guiding him toward

the outer world. The entrance might not be guarded, but anyone within the Guild would sense someone using magic close to the wall.

The scent of mold and dead earth shifted to something alive and verdant the closer he got to the surface. When he finally exited, he stood beside a park that stretched along the River Kelvin, everything lush and green and wet. Ruined tenement flats lined the street behind him, their red-and-ochre facades spots of color in the otherwise gray-and-green landscape. He'd spent a few days here in the West End in the beginning. This was where the University of Glasgow rested, reaching up past the tenement flats like the towers of Hogwarts. This was where art and history jostled with foreign uni students and hipster locals. He and his mum visited tea houses and cafés and museums, staring at Rennie Mackintosh sketches or just wandering the streets, looking up at the tops of buildings, as that's where they were told all the history and art were displayed.

It was almost possible to still see that past in the landscape. The destruction here was random, like a tornado had torn through. And maybe one had. Some of the flats stood tall— large windows intact and revealing shadowed living rooms— while others were reduced to rubble. She would have hated to see the city like this—to his mum, art was all that mattered. He pushed the thought away. He'd done what he could.

Glasgow had seen hundreds of years of life and battle and despair. He'd managed to keep at least a part of it safe and thriving after the Resurrection. And maybe, when he destroyed Calum, the city would be reborn.

Above him arched an old stone bridge—Kelvinbridge, to

be exact—and on the other side of the river was the wall that kept the remaining humans of Scotland safe. The wall rose four stories tall and looked like a plateau rather than a man-made construct. All worn stone and rubble and dirt. It sliced straight up and ran along the opposite bank of the Kelvin, making a half canyon that stretched for miles in each direction.

He stared at it for a moment, an odd pang in his chest.

The sight of that wall had been the closest thing he'd had to homecoming since he came to this country. The number of missions he'd returned from, bloody and beaten yet alive. The number of times he'd stood atop that very wall, Fire burning in his chest and hellfire raining down on a distant approaching army. He'd defended this place with his life dozens if not hundreds of times. A city that wasn't even his. A country he couldn't leave. He'd given this place everything.

Fat lot of good that had done.

He crept up the covered escalator leading to the top of the bridge and leaned against the wall, just inside the entrance, staring out across the bridge and the wall beyond.

He considered walking out there. Standing at the edge of the thirty-foot gap between the wall and the bridge. Just to see what the guards would do. Just to tempt fate. Instead, he listened to the rain and the rushing river and contemplated what it would take to get this city—*his* city—back. Without Fire burning away the doubt and the weakness, the memories of this place boiled to the surface. Walking through the gardens with Trevor. Plotting their next attack or defense. Lying in bed together, exploring each other's bodies. Or, more often than not, screaming at each other when Aidan flared hot and Trevor turned cold.

Some days, they had been partners. Some days, they were at each other's throats. Fire and Water didn't mix, and when they tried, it was chaos. But it had been a beautiful sort of chaos. Just as the Guild had been a beautiful sort of home.

A home he'd lost.

Just like he'd lost America.

Just like he'd lost his mum.

"Someday soon," Aidan whispered, maybe to her and maybe to Trevor, "this will be mine again."

"What are you doing here, Aidan?"

Trevor's voice echoed up the stairs behind him. On impulse, Aidan opened to Fire and whirled around, but he managed to stop himself before immolating his former co-commander.

"What the hell are *you* doing here?" Aidan asked. Instantly, whatever sadness he'd harbored evaporated.

Trevor stepped slowly up the stairs, a mace in one hand and the other hand shoved in his coat. Water boiled in his stomach. His eyes were sunken and there was a stoop to his shoulders. Maybe Aidan's exile had cost him some sleep. Or maybe Trevor was realizing that organizing an army wasn't as easy as he'd thought. Either way, there was a large part of Aidan that was pleased to see Trevor suffering. Even if only emotionally.

Granted, that tended to be one way Trevor was always suffering.

As always, Aidan was grateful he hadn't attuned to Water.

"I thought you'd be back," Trevor said. Now that he wasn't

angry, his brogue had softened, though his words were still rounded and rolling. "Which I guess answers my first question. You never were good at letting things go. Especially if you didn't get the last laugh."

Trevor stopped a foot away. So close, Aidan could practically feel the warmth of him. Though, with Fire in his veins, everything felt blissfully warm. And he felt blissfully impervious.

"Is that why you stayed around?" Aidan asked. "To rub it in my face?" He shook his head and crossed his arms, turning to stare out at the wall. "If you think I came back to grovel, think again."

"I think you came back because you're scared."

Sparks raced beneath Aidan's skin, and a soft voice whispered within that he never had need to be afraid. Not with Fire in his control.

"Then you know me even less than I thought," Aidan replied. He swallowed. "How did my army take my...leaving?"

"Better than I expected," Trevor said. He almost sounded like he regretted the words. "A few questions, but no one was too surprised. You have a...reputation...among the troops."

Despite everything, Aidan smirked. "Good." Admittedly, he was pissed that no one had revolted. But there was something endearing at the thought of his troops expecting him to be exiled. It was sort of badass. "I hear you've started marching."

Trevor didn't reply right away. The rain hissing down around them quivered at Trevor's agitation.

"Aye," he finally admitted. "The first ranks left this morning." He stepped up beside Aidan. "Frankly, I'm surprised you're not out there trying to beat them to the castle."

"The day's young," Aidan said. "Besides, I need someone to distract Calum so I can sneak in."

"You're really doing it then? You're going against orders and trying to take the Kin by yourself?"

Aidan shrugged. "You never ordered me to stay away from Edinburgh, and now I'm no longer under your jurisdiction, so it's too late to try. I'm a free agent. I can do whatever I please." He glanced to Trevor. "I trained my guys well—they'll have that castle down in minutes. We just better hope they don't get in my way when I go to kill Calum. I can't promise there won't be a repeat of yesterday morning."

"It doesn't have to be this way," Trevor said with a sigh. "Maybe if you stay back, we can talk after Calum is killed—"

Instantly, Fire flared in Aidan's chest.

"Are you fucking kidding me?" he roared. "*You* are the one who just took everything I've worked for away. Do you really think I'm just going to wait around for you to kill Calum? Do you really think I want your pity? Your bloody forgiveness?"

In his mind's eye, Aidan saw the burning castle, the throne of skulls. And he heard the words of Tomás, the faintest memory: *Why do you serve, when you should rule?*

"Calum is mine. This country *will* bow to me. Nobody is going to stop that. Because you know what? I don't feel bad about Vincent's death. He was nothing. And me? I am everything. Soon, I'll make sure the whole world sees it." Aidan looked Trevor in the eyes. "Get in my way, and I swear I'll kill you, too."

Trevor regarded him for a long while. Aidan said nothing,

but he kept the fires within stoked as he turned back to the Guild wall. He refused to sink down to Trevor's melancholy level. He refused to let himself feel bad over what he'd done, and what Trevor had done in return.

Fire only moved forward. Fire only burned, and burned through anyone in its path.

It was about time Aidan did the same.

"I don't know who you are anymore," Trevor finally said.

"Who I've always been," Aidan said. "And who you've always been too scared to see. At least now we know the truth about each other."

He began walking down the street, not caring if anyone else noticed his use of magic. Water hissed and steamed from his skin. He thought it was an apt metaphor. Trevor had drawn the line in the sand, and Aidan had chosen his side. There was no looking back.

No rain or sadness would ever touch him again.

"Just remember," Aidan said. "You did this. You did all of this." He snapped his fingers, and the abandoned shops on the street corners burst into flame, haloing him in harsh light. Trevor stepped back into the safety of the escalator tunnel. Aidan made sure to raise his voice, so Trevor could hear him through the blaze. "You made me choose. And I choose myself."

With that, he brought the fires raging down behind him, blocking himself from Trevor's view.

Trevor wanted to make Aidan out to be a monster?

Aidan would happily comply.

"Britain will ever endure.
We have already faced
the deepest darkness,
and carry the sun
of hope in our hearts.
We. Will. Endure.
We have no other choice."

—Queen's Address, 1 P.R.

PART 2

THE BRIGHTER THE LIGHT

CHAPTER TEN

IT HADN'T TAKEN LONG TO CONVINCE KIANNA
that it was time to move.

Rather, the moment he stepped back in the flat, she was
already geared up and ready. She hadn't asked any questions.
She hadn't needed to. The answer was clear on his face: Aidan
was ready to kill, and thankfully, spilling Howl blood was
their preferred shared activity. It sure as hell beat talking.

Ten minutes and one quick cup of tea later, they were on
the road.

And this time, Trevor be damned, Aidan was using magic
to keep the constant chill and rain of this damnable country
at bay. Maybe that was part of the reason he wanted to kill
Calum so badly—he needed to justify years of misery and
dampness. *Then* he could hop over to somewhere warmer.

"You ran into him, didn't you?" Kianna asked.

Aidan grunted.

Glasgow was an hour behind them, the only thing surrounding them now a few low houses and the remains of the

M8 motorway. Fields and glens stretched out through the heavy gloom, the rain less a downpour and more a constant, irrepressible mist that threatened to settle under his skin and take up residence. Fire burned softly in his chest, a bubble of heat thrown up around them, making rain sizzle and steam against his invisible shield, keeping them dry and warm. Tiny baubles of white danced above their heads as well, guiding their way.

It was more than enough to give them away to the army they trailed. If they were looking. If Trevor was looking. But Aidan knew Trevor would never give the command to kill him, even for this insubordination. Trevor would always avoid a fight, just as Aidan would always seek one out.

Another reason they drove each other insane just as they drove each other to lust.

The last thing he needed was to think of Trevor in any sort of positive light. Thankfully, with Fire filling him, that was easy enough to manage.

"Let me guess, he knows we're following now because your poker face sucks."

"I may have given him that notion, aye." In his mind's eye, he remembered the buildings he'd set on fire, imagined the shocked look in Trevor's eyes. It might have been childish, but damn if that hadn't been a good exit. He glanced at her. "You don't have to follow, you know. As you said, *you* aren't the one who's exiled. You could head back. Take up your old post…"

"And what, die a miserable old cow?" She scoffed. "Please. You may be an arse, but at least you keep things exciting."

"Even though my powers may be uncontrollable in my

sleep and I might burn you alive?" He meant it as a joke, but it was an honest question.

"If your stupid pyrotechnics were enough to scare me off, I would have left you ages ago. Besides—" she gestured to the bubble of steam around them "—you're like a walking space heater. Really, that's pretty useful, especially since I left my hot water bottle at home."

"You're insane."

"Nah. I think that being your mate makes me a saint."

"You have to die to become a saint."

"And I'm following you, so that may happen sooner rather than later. Sainthood achieved. I wonder what they'd make me patron of? Badass bitches?"

He looked at her. Really looked. She was a bloody queen. Shoulders back, head high. Two duffel bags of weapons and food bouncing against her back and a sword and ax strapped to her waist. He knew a bandolier of daggers was across her chest beneath her coat, knew more were sewn into the coat's lining, just as he knew another bandolier crossed it, this one with bullets. Her pistol was sewn into its own pocket in the breast of her coat, just by her heart. Ever at the ready—which he'd always found odd, since no one in this country used guns, especially not anymore.

And those were just the weapons he knew about.

She was a walking arsenal. A one-woman army. If she left him, she would be just fine on her own—a thought that he didn't really apply to anyone else.

Which meant that her answer, glib though it was, hid a deeper truth. She wasn't leaving him because she wanted to be around him. Even though he might be unstable. Even though heading toward Calum was madness. She would rather go out with a bang at his side than die in the ranks of her peers.

Even with Fire burning away his lesser emotions, that was enough to fill him with a small sort of tenderness. And pride.

She looked at him from the corner of her eye.

"Watch where you're going," she said.

Right as he fell into a puddle of muck.

Aidan cursed, hopping about with his boot filled with sludge. Kianna crowed with laughter at his side, and while he undid his boot to drain what looked like a whole loch, he began to feel like maybe, even in exile, things weren't that different from before.

He still had his friend.

He still had his power.

And he still had a shot at immortality.

CHAPTER ELEVEN

HE'D NEVER TRULY APPRECIATED CARS AND PUBLIC transit until the Resurrection.

Even though they passed plenty of electric cars on the road—ones he probably could have jerry-rigged into working, as electricity was, at heart, just another form of Fire energy—there was no way they could make it to Edinburgh in them. The roads had been torn to hell by the necromancers and the ensuing battles. The countryside itself wasn't much better.

He and his mum had taken this route, once, before the necromancers had ruined it all. Back then, it had been lovely—rolling hills and fields of sheep, glistening streams and stone cottages. Now, the landscape had changed entirely, partly from the magic and partly from nature's own frustration.

Tall peaks rose up like talons from the otherwise rolling landscape, their tips dotted white or hidden entirely behind the clouds. Sinkholes appeared out of nowhere, collapsing miles of highway, devouring entire towns. Lochs had boiled to plains and moorland had flooded to endless oceans of murk. Infrastructure

between towns was no longer a priority—especially since Edinburgh was overrun with Howls and Glasgow was one of the few
places in the country actually deemed "safe." There was a Guild
in Inverness and a few smaller compounds dotted throughout the
highlands, but for the most part, Scotland was dead land. And
every single time the remaining humans had tried to rebuild a
road or a rail, it was torn apart by necromancers or Howls.

It was no longer a straight shot. No longer an hour train
ride. They would be lucky to reach Edinburgh by tomorrow night.

Once more, Aidan distantly wished he'd been attuned to
Air, just so he could fly. It sure as hell beat walking everywhere. Even though the trek did mean he had killer legs.

Hours passed in silence. Soon, night hung heavy around
them, the only light coming from a muted moon behind the
clouds and the flickering flames he cast with Fire. The landscape was fully apocalyptic, especially in the dark of night.
No more were the rolling fields dotted with grazing sheep,
no longer were the towns they passed through quaint. It was
hell on earth. And yet, it was home.

A part of him marveled at the destruction. At the heat that
had melted windows and peeled apart foundations, turned
roads to rivers and families to dust. It was beautiful, in the way
that all broken things are beautiful—pure and raw, twisted
and without affectation. It was damaged, destroyed, and it
couldn't pretend to be anything else. Fire smoldered with recognition in his chest, echoing the power and the destruction
that had torn this place apart. That had crafted such beauty.
Fire wanted to continue the terrible art.

All of this will be ours, Tomás had promised.

All of this already is, Fire assured.

"Do you think they'll stick to the plan?" Aidan asked.

Kianna shrugged.

Trevor had wanted to camp outside of Edinburgh before going in to battle, thought everyone should rest. Aidan had insisted they use the element of surprise and attack first thing—not that a fifteen-hour walk was a rushing charge, even if they did have magic to help fuel tired muscles and hasten the trek.

This was their one shot at killing a Kin. At making history. Aidan wouldn't risk anything. Trevor had begrudgingly agreed.

But Aidan did sort of hope Trevor had changed his mind and would allow the troops to sleep. Aidan didn't have an Earth mage to soothe his own tired limbs or embolden his step. Fire was currently a slow burn, and it gave him an energy that meant he could go for hours. But it also meant that, on the other side of it all, he would burn out.

He glanced at Kianna, who still walked as though she'd just stepped out of her flat for an evening stroll. Not even the weight of her bags had slouched her shoulders.

"How do you do it?" he asked.

"What?"

"Be...you..."

"I'm naturally amazing, Aidan," she said. "I thought you would have realized that by now."

"Och, you know what I mean," he said, even though he didn't want to ask. Maybe, under normal circumstances, he would have stayed quiet. But it turned out walking for hours was bloody boring, and their mission was suicidal at best. It was a question he had never pressed, and she had never offered. But the words left his lips anyway. "How are you so strong?"

Kianna trained harder than anyone he knew. She'd studied under every Hunter who knew a martial art, had practiced forms and archery and sniping when everyone else was playing cards or sleeping. He knew skill alone didn't keep her alive. There was no way. But he also knew that, since she never mentioned it, it wasn't something she wanted to talk about.

She didn't answer. He figured that meant the conversation was over.

A few minutes passed.

"It was a side effect," she said. "When I transitioned, the magic they used...it made me stronger. Superhuman. I didn't realize it at first, of course. Not until I accidentally punched through a brick wall. They'd told me the operation was experimental. Don't think they meant turning me into Wonder Woman, though."

"Is that why you hate magic?"

Her eyebrows furrowed, just for a moment, and that told him the conversation was over.

"No," she said.

They didn't speak again until daybreak.

They stopped when the army stopped at sunrise.

He caught sense of magic, maybe an hour or so ahead of them. And since it got closer with every step, he figured it meant the army had called it a day.

Fire burned within him, told him to keep walking, to outpace the army, to go take Edinburgh on his own. Fire promised that he could.

But even if Kianna was Wonder Woman, they were still both human, and the rational part of his mind—not often used, Kianna would argue—told him they needed to rest, as well. And eat. Mostly eat. Using Fire burned calories like nothing else.

They stopped at the next building they came to. The farmhouse was a little off the road and mostly intact, though the field around it was pockmarked with craters as though someone had been gunning down sheep with meteors.

He'd seen it done. Numerous times.

And yes, he might have done it once or twice. Only when drunk, though.

The house's interior was probably the quaintest thing he'd seen in a while. Plush carpets. Cat ceramics on the shelves, decorative plates on the walls beside landscape paintings and still lifes. Hell, the sofa even had doilies. Everything was coated in a thick layer of dust, the floor covered in shards of ceramic cats that hadn't made it through the destruction.

"This place creeps me the fuck out," Kianna said, gingerly poking at a lace cushion. "Practically screams *cannibal*."

"I dunno," Aidan said. He picked up a cat and wagged it at her. "It's kinda cute. Mrow."

She raised an eyebrow. "All I'm saying is, I'm perfectly fine with you accidentally burning this place down in your sleep."

He set down the cat.

"Why'd you have to take it there?"

She shrugged. "Would you expect anything less?"

She had a point.

★ ★ ★

"What will you do?" Kianna asked.

She lounged on the couch under a thick duvet, hearth fire dancing across her features. Aidan curled up on a recliner by the flames. They'd managed to clear out most of the dust and broken china, and a few spare blankets blocked out the morning sun. The Sphere of Fire still smoldered in his chest—he never let go of it, not fully, as it felt like letting go of life itself—but he let it rest there, let it turn to embers. It still drained him slightly, but it was worth it to feel warm.

"What?" he asked dumbly. Their salvaged dinner of rehydrated beans and rice made him want to pass out. Even though a small part of him feared sleeping with so many flammable objects around. Kianna included.

"On the other side of this. When Calum is dead. What will you do?"

Rule.

Aidan bit down the word, the images of him on Calum's throne, of making Scotland bow. Of Tomás at his side. He hadn't given much thought to the dream since they'd left Glasgow. Killing Calum was an overwhelming urge. But, sidled up next to that goal, was the image that still haunted him—Tomás, promising Aidan everything. A throne. A country. A partner.

Tomás isn't real.

And yet, the desire for him was. Aidan didn't know what was worse—wanting to screw a Howl, or wanting to screw a figment of his own imagination. He wasn't one for introspection. Probably for the best—he didn't want to know what it meant that his subconscious had fleshed this out.

"We move on to the next Kin," Aidan said. He looked at her. They'd never really spoken of "after" when they'd spent so long preparing for this. "There's nothing else."

She just nodded, staring into the flames as if they told a future he couldn't see.

Anyone else would have given a speech on there being more to life than killing. Not Kianna. Another reason they got along. They knew the truth about the new world. There was no hope of settling down, of having a home or a family, no chance of love or working toward a brighter future. That was all bullshit.

The only thing left was killing or fleeing.

The two of them knew precisely which side of the line they stood on.

People like Trevor, they thought there was an *after* to all of this. As though one day all the Howls would be dead and the necromancers gone and the world could return to normal. Aidan was smarter than that. He knew there would never be an *after*. There was only this: the rain and the bloodshed, the monsters and the madness. This was the world now.

Dreaming of a world after Howls and magic was as stupid as dreaming of a world where dinosaurs returned.

Things changed.

Just like the dinosaurs, things ended.

In this case, "civilization" had been on the chopping block. Frankly, Aidan thought they'd all earned it for bringing this about. This wasn't some otherworldly plague—the Howls were created by humans. It was humanity's nature to fuck things up. Another reason he didn't really think there was or should be an *after*: humanity didn't really deserve to carry on.

He sure as hell didn't.

Though it would be nice to have a civilization around to remember him.

"Get some sleep," Kianna muttered. She rolled over on the sofa, back to him. "I'll wake you in a few hours." She had an inner alarm that was as good as any clock.

Aidan grunted in response.

"And, Aidan?"

Another grunt.

"Seriously, if you burn this place down, *please* start with the cats."

Despite everything, Aidan grinned.

On the other side of sleep, he was going to make history.

I'm coming for you, Calum, he thought, staring into the flames.

As his vision blurred, he could have sworn he saw Tomás smiling back.

CHAPTER TWELVE

AIDAN DIDN'T DREAM. HE DIDN'T DREAM, AND HE didn't burn the farmhouse down, and when Kianna woke him, his entire body snapped to attention.

It was time to kill.

There was a definite spring in his step as they gathered their things and made their way back on the road. Sure enough, he sensed the army ahead of them, their magic faint and growing fainter. They'd begun moving, as well.

"How far are we?" he asked.

"Few more hours," Kianna said. "We'll be there by dusk."

He glanced to the clouded sky. It was impossible to tell if the sun was even up. Didn't matter, though.

He practically jogged down the road, through ruined fields and glens, a heavy morning mist curled around him and Fire smoking in his bones.

Today was the day he killed Calum.

Today was the day he proved you didn't underestimate Aidan Belmont.

Today was the day he proved once and for all that this country was *his*.

A few hours in, and the faint sense of magic that led him forward changed. Flared. And as nightfall rolled in, the horizon before them burst red and hot with flame.

Aidan and Kianna exchanged a glance. The battle had begun.

"You should be proud," Kianna said as they jogged toward the blaze.

"Why?" he asked. He always was.

"They're following your orders. Immediate attack."

He smiled. If they followed his plan exactly, this might go easier than even he had thought.

Edinburgh roared with hellfire.

Aidan's breath caught in his throat the moment it came into view. It was nothing like the city he had toured with his mother years ago. Nothing quaint or archaic about it, even without the burn in the air. Years ago, only months after the Resurrection, Calum and his necromancers had claimed the city as their own. They didn't just take it over, though. They recreated it.

The old and new towns surrounding the castle had been demolished. Hundreds of years of history, lost to the rumble of Earth mages and the ferocity of Fire. In their place, a wall of slick stone had been raised five stories tall, blocking out whatever now rested within. Aidan had seen the destruction

firsthand, had watched as rows upon rows of tenement buildings were burned to ash and buried beneath stone, as the waters of the Firth of Forth boiled and spilled over, drowning
humans and houses, erasing swathes of land in moments. The
Queen's Palace? Toppled. The great hill called Arthur's Seat
that had guarded the city from the very beginning? Leveled.

All that truly remained of the once-glorious capital was the
castle, sitting high atop a magically raised hill. Stretching out
for miles all around the wall, the soil was smooth and black
and tarnished, glinting obsidian.

And now, in the heat of the attack, that obsidian glim-
mered gold. Something about the carnage pulled at Aidan's
chest, made whispers slither through his heart. Seeing the
castle tugged at him. It was a shadow on his soul, a black hole
dragging him down.

Somehow, deep down in the embers of Fire, the castle
whispered of home.

It's from there that you should rule, the whispers promised,
feminine and forbidden. *This is your destiny. This is your kingdom. From here, you will burn the world.*

He tried to force them down, tried to focus on the battle
in front of him. But every time he looked at the castle, he felt
that hook in his chest, that tug forward. This was where he
was meant to be. Fire knew it. He was beginning to know
it, as well.

They crouched at the top of a hill; Aidan had no idea if
the hill had been there before the Resurrection, or if it was
the work of some pissed-off Earth mage. All that remained
of the town around him was rubble, the ground itself frozen
in burnt waves.

He watched the attack with an odd mix of awe and pride and anger. On the one hand, the black-garbed figures rushing on this side of the wall were his comrades. He'd laughed and trained and killed with all of them, knew most by name. They ran forward with weapons raised, their Spheres blazing like beacons in the night as fire billowed ahead of them, as the ground shook and the wall trembled, as the rains above twisted into icy shards and tornados churned from the skies, lightning illuminating it all in broken strobes. They were doing exactly what he'd trained them to do.

And yet he was supposed to be down there. Not up here, impotent, standing beside Kianna and a cairn of burnt stone, watching the destruction unfold.

Even if the attack had been without warning, Calum's forces were far from unprepared. Shields of Air billowed up and over the castle, blocking it and the city from the worst of the attacks, while the necromancers within flooded the fields without in fire. Aidan could barely see his comrades through the waves of flame, could barely tell where one Hunter's magic ended and a necromancer's began. From here, it all looked the same.

Except for the creatures spilling out through the cracks in the walls.

Calum unleashed his Howls.

Aidan couldn't see them well from here, but he knew without doubt that the black mass swarming from the castle was made up almost entirely of kravens. The bent, misshapen bastard children of Earth were the backbone of the Dark Lady's army. They craved only flesh, were mindless and crazed in that hunger and, as they broke into his comrades, he knew they would be getting more of a feast than they'd had in months.

There was no way to hear the screams of the monsters or the men. Blood and magic bathed the field. He watched them clash. Watched figures fall or burst into flame. Human or Howl, he could barely tell.

Ants. From here, they were just ants. Burning, racing, mindless ants.

A small, distant part of him wanted to feel guilty. For sitting up here, watching other people die, just so he could swoop in and kill Calum later. Instantly, Fire burned up within him, incinerating the thought, the weakness—guilt was an emotion only the pathetic harbored. He wouldn't doubt. With Fire in his veins, he knew he was right. He knew that no matter who died beforehand, the true victory would be his. Killing Calum was all that mattered in the end, no matter the cost in cannon fodder. Fire saw that clearly, and through its burn, so did he.

It wasn't until Kianna physically opened his palm, revealing half moons of bloodied flesh, that he realized he'd been clenching his fists.

"How long?" she asked.

"What?"

"How long until we go in there?"

He chewed on his lip and considered the plan he had laid out months before. The army on this side of the castle was a distraction. The true fight was happening further east, on the shoreline, where a dozen or so Earth mages were en route or already stationed to bring down the wall. Once the wall crumbled, the Water mages—led by Trevor—would flood the town with the waters of the Forth, drowning everyone and everything still within the city walls.

That was the one perk of how dire things had become—there was no one left within the castle to save. Well, there probably were a few hundred humans being kept as food for the Howls, but that was a small price to pay for winning the war.

In his mind, at least.

Aidan almost doubted Trevor would pull the trigger.

"Follow me," Aidan said. He began to jog, staying low and out of sight even though no one would be looking up here. Everyone's focus would be on the battle. "When the wall comes down and the waters subside, we can sneak in. I know a back entrance."

"I bet you say that to all the boys," Kianna said.

"Not the time."

"And I bet that's what they say in response."

CHAPTER THIRTEEN

AIDAN COULD FEEL THE BATTLE IN HIS VEINS AS THEY made their way to the back of the castle. Fire was in tune with the anger and fear, the bloodlust and rage. He'd felt this to an extent before, but never this strongly. It had been years since Scotland had felt this much magic and destruction at once. Years since an event this momentous had taken place.

For better or worse, after tonight, everything would be different.

Either the humans would die, and Calum would rule an empty country. Or they would win, and Aidan would be crowned a king.

Either way, Aidan would blaze in battle. The question was whether or not that blaze would be snuffed out at the end. And frankly, Fire didn't care. His Sphere writhed excitedly within him, scalding his chest as he tried to keep it contained. Not because his Sphere was angry. Not just because people were killing and dying so close to him.

No. His Sphere was restless in its excitement: every step

toward the castle felt like another step toward more than just victory. It felt like coming home.

Soon, this will all be mine.

Aidan guided them closer to the castle wall, staying far away from the main attack and moving nearer to the shore. The transition from ruined city to glass-slick wasteland was razor-sharp, a line that cut a circle all around the castle, as though someone had drawn it with a sextant, the castle at its nexus. On one side, char and rubble, soil and sodden plants. On the other, smooth, glass-black stone that reflected the burning sky above like a mirror.

A testament of Calum's power. His army could melt the world if he so chose.

He never had. The Hunters had always been there to fight him back.

Until now, Aidan thought. *I'll have the balls to do what Calum never could. Rule beyond this circle. Make the whole world kneel.*

Fire smoldered in his chest at the thought, at the rightness of it. He glanced down at his reflection. In the flickering light of the hellfire above, he didn't look entirely human. His face was etched in shadows, and his tattoos seemed to slither over his skin like serpents. He looked demonic.

He smiled.

Let the whole world kneel.

"Do you think we're winning?" Kianna asked absently.

On the far side of the wall, where the battle was taking place, the sky roared with flame and tornadoes, lightning and hail. Any minute now...

"Why do you ask?"

"Because this is taking forever."

He nodded. They should have leveled the wall by now. The initial attack was meant to be a distraction, not the focus. Where the hell was the second unit?

This is why Trevor never should have let you go, Fire purred within him. *Without you, the entire mission will fail. Without you, they are nothing.*

"We can't just wait here," he said. "Something's wrong."

She nodded, as though she'd already figured that out and had been waiting for him to pick up the slack.

The silence back here put his nerves on edge. His mind raced with possibilities of what had gone wrong. For why the wall still stood and why here, closer to the waves and the edge of the wall, everything was silent as a graveyard. He stared ahead, trying to peer through the gloom and darkness while keeping Fire dimmed for fear of giving himself away. All he could see was the towering black wall to his left and the endless expanse of dark waves ahead.

"Is it getting colder to you?" Kianna asked.

He'd thought it was his imagination. Scotland was *always* cold, even with Fire in his veins. But the moment she said it he realized his breath was coming out in puffs. The rain was lighter here, and it was then he noticed it wasn't just misting. It was snowing. The ground beneath his feet crunched with every footstep. Ice.

This wasn't the work of a necromancer, not the work of any magic. No, this cold tugged at his bones, sliced its fingers through his heart and tried to pull out every last drop of heat.

Incubi.

The troops had been ambushed.

"Calum knew," he muttered, and ran faster.

Despite the red sky and flashes of light, everything near the crashing shore was cold and steeped in shadow. He squinted as lightning strobed across the sky, arching far out over the water.

That's when he saw them.

Littered across the shore like some broken Roman palisade were dozens of columns piercing up from the soil. But he knew there weren't columns, not here. There was nothing on the shore but charred earth and crashing waves.

Lightning flashed.

Despite the burn of Fire in his chest, he still found room to be shocked. The columns were the second unit. Scattered and frozen midcharge.

Frozen, save for the few figures still walking among the dead. The figures that had realized they weren't alone.

Kianna was at the ready, a sword in her left hand and a pistol in her right. He didn't think. Fire didn't need to think. Fire just needed to kill.

He pulled deeper through the heat, let the embers roar to life, and gave in to that one immutable need.

Fire flared bright in his chest, hissing power through his limbs and lighting his adrenaline with newfound need. Flames spiraled around his clenched palms. Cast their shadows over the black and the snow like wraiths. The incubi screamed out. The world around them cut colder as the Howls tried to drain their Spheres.

Aidan burned brighter, and as the snow fell around them, they fell upon the Howls.

The incubi and their female counterparts, succubi, were humanoid and beautiful, seductive if not for the blood smeared on their faces and wild looks in their copper eyes. The Howls born of Fire craved human heat and could drain it from their victim from afar. It accounted for the rain-turned-snow, for the frigid cold that ate at his bones, the bite that—had he not been open to Fire—would have sent him to his knees. But with the Sphere burning in his chest, he felt immune. He poured all of himself into the flame, wrapped himself and Kianna in burning heat.

To the incubi, he was a damn buffet.

Good. Let them gorge.

He grabbed the first incubus by the throat and threw him to the side, right in the path of Kianna's blade. Two shots, two flashes of gunfire, and two more Howls fell, bullets piercing right between their eyes, blood bursting behind them in fine mists.

Another Howl tackled him from behind, pinning him to the ground. He rolled and twisted out of the monster's grip. A succubus. Her eyes wide as his dagger lodged in her chest.

Because incubi and succubi were born of Fire, they were immune to it. He could throw every ounce of power he had at the incubi surrounding them, and it wouldn't crisp a hair on their heads. It would probably just make them stronger. But that wasn't why he was open to the Sphere. He just used it to make himself feel alive.

He pushed himself up from his knees in time to see a head fly into the waves, the body dropping at Kianna's feet. He was about to congratulate her when the column beside him lunged, wrapping its arms around his chest and throat, pulling his chin back so he could stare into its cold, pale eyes.

Then, before he could lash out, the Howl inhaled.

Aidan's lungs deflated in a heartbeat, his chest collapsing

as the Howl—a Breathless One—drained the Sphere of Air and the oxygen from his body. Fire snuffed from his chest.

Darkness clouded immediately. His body fell heavy, vision exploding with stars that burned to cinders and ash as his chest screamed and his throat constricted and he knew he would die, knew Kianna wouldn't notice or reach him in time, and he could do nothing to struggle. His thoughts swam. He couldn't move. Couldn't even cry in pain. So much pain. A thousand daggers through his chest as his heart failed to pump, as his lungs pulled in on themselves, a million needles scraping his veins.

Everything he'd done, and he'd die at the hands of a Howl that didn't have a name.

He fell in the darkness.

And there, deep in the abyss, deep in the pain, he saw the spark. A flare of power, a tiny pinprick of red in the black. His imagination. Must be.

The voice, surely.

Your death does not yet serve me, my Hunter.

The spark flickered. Became two. Two red eyes in the dark. The dark, a face. *Her* face.

Your life is not yours to give.

You will serve.

You will burn the world.

The eyes grew redder, bolder, burning hot, burning brighter than the sun, the sun that roared within him. The pain and the heat and the rage.

It flooded him. Filled him. Laced his veins with beautiful agony, a brushfire ignited in the depths of night, a light when there should be only dark. A light. *Her* light. His light.

Fire burned through him, ferocious and raging, a heat he couldn't stand, a heat that threatened to burn him alive.

A heat he never wanted to release.

Distantly, he heard screaming. Choking.

He felt earth beneath his hands and knees. Hot earth. Ashen earth. But all he could see was the fire. The rage. The world burning and ending, the shadows coiling and rising. The light. He was the light that signaled the final flare.

Then he inhaled, and a new pain filled him.

He collapsed to his side as he choked down air, as the burning within him subsided and the Sphere of Fire quietened. Everything was fire and pain, the agony of oxygen returning to his limbs. His lungs burned with hunger. His throat was raw and scratched.

"The hell was that?" Kianna asked.

Her voice sounded distant. So distant.

He tried to push down the pain. Tried to find words to speak as he struggled to kneeling, his hands coated in the ash of the Howl that nearly stole his life away.

No.

Not his life.

He'd thought it was a dream. A nightmare. He thought the voice that hissed within him was a hallucination.

But deep down, in the darkest shadows, he knew the truth. The words he'd been hearing when Fire called loudest. The words he thought were his own.

Those were the words of the Dark Lady.

She had saved him. Somehow.

She wanted him alive.

Your life is not yet yours to give.

CHAPTER FOURTEEN

KIANNA KNELT AT HIS SIDE. SHE DIDN'T TOUCH HIM, didn't try to offer support. He couldn't blame her—every drop of rain and snow dissolved before reaching his flesh.

He couldn't speak. Not that he wanted to; the words stuck in his throat were more than treason. If Kianna knew the Dark Lady was speaking to him… No, that she wanted him *alive* to do Her work, Kianna would kill him on the spot.

He knew this, because he knew he would do the same.

Or so he wanted to tell himself.

"The Howls are dead," Kianna said. "Along with the troops. Jesus, mate. You went up like a bloody bonfire. Nearly lost my eyebrows because of you."

"It nearly killed me," he muttered. His words felt charred. He coughed. Even oxygen hurt.

"Sounds like loser talk to me."

He grunted and pushed himself up to sitting, then shakily stood. His head spun with vertigo; he had to stare at the ground to keep from toppling.

The empty ground.

The Breathless One that tried to kill him had been reduced to less than ash.

Around them, the statues of their former comrades slowly thawed in the deepening gloom. He tried not to look at their faces. The last thing he needed was to put names to the dead. The moment he started doing that was the moment he lost sight of the end goal.

He tried to ignore them. But every single flash of lightning seared their faces into his mind.

Alexander, with whom he'd sparred every Friday.

Felicia, who showed him which of Scotland's few remaining plants were edible.

Mhaire, who taught him how to control Fire's more unstable urges.

He stared at his former friends, his former comrades, and tried to find some sort of sadness. Instead, he could only find relief. Relief that he was still alive, that his painful heart still throbbed, that his burning lungs still pulled in oxygen. He'd been close to death more times than he could count. But that was the first time he'd felt like Death had actively rejected him.

He looked in their faces, at their frozen forms, and could only be grateful that it wasn't him.

And in some sick, twisted way, he felt...better.

Because he was still alive, and that meant he was still worth something. He just tried not to wonder who he was worth something to.

"What do we do now?" Kianna asked.

Aidan grunted, tried to get his thoughts in order. He focused on the waves, their ferocious churning. Trevor had to have realized by now that the attack had gone south and the wall hadn't crumbled. Or maybe he didn't know. Maybe he was too lost to the heat of battle.

Maybe he was dead.

There were two choices: Aidan and Kianna could run back into the battle and try to make their way to Trevor and the other leaders. Warn them of what happened. Try to come up with an alternative attack.

That was the moral thing to do. The *right* thing to do. Even if it meant risking their lives in the process. There was every chance they would be killed by a necromancer or Howl or one of their own before they even made it to Trevor. If he would let Aidan live long enough to give the warning.

The other choice, the one Fire reveled in, was to see this as an opportunity. Trevor was distracted. Calum would think his defense a success. The only way he would have known about the full extent of their attack was if there was a mole within the Guild. Aidan going in and heading straight to Calum would be entirely unexpected.

And *unexpected* meant Aidan had a stronger chance at securing victory for himself. For Scotland.

He pulled deeply through Fire, let the magic flood his limbs, turning the pain that lingered in his lungs into a force he could use.

"We do what we were destined to do," he said, looking to Kianna. He felt the Dark Lady's words twist in the back of his heart. "We make Scotland kneel."

As he'd thought, nothing within Edinburgh had been saved from Calum's destruction. Ages ago, Aidan had his scouts map out the hidden entrances within the wall, and the one nearest hadn't been guarded. Everyone was focused on the frontal attack, just as he'd hoped. Still, it did put him on edge that all it took to break through the most heavily guarded fortress in this country—save his own—was pressing against the right camouflaged panel.

The structures within the wall were clearly never part of the city's original architecture. There were no rising tenement buildings, no historical parks, no cobblestone or sandstone. Years ago, the city had been an architectural marvel, marrying the prestigious past with the neon present. Every vantage had been awe-inspiring. Now the buildings were as slick and black as the wall that guarded them, everything covered in a permanent sheen from mist and magic. But there was no beauty laced through the architecture. The Earth mages who crafted this place hadn't cared for aesthetics.

They'd wanted a prison. And that's what they'd created.

Rather than winding rows of ancient architecture, the city before them was flat and stoic, a grid of two-story barracks with dark windows of twisted iron bars. The stench of death was overpowering; he couldn't tell if this block had been used to house kravens, or the humans kept to feed or be converted into them. Normally, Fire relished in destruction, the offerings of life. But this...this made even Aidan's burning heart turn cold. So much history lost in a heartbeat. So many monuments to great women and men, destroyed. Forgotten.

Replaced by something even more forgettable.

It made his heart race, the absolute feeling of loss that lingered here. But there was more to it. Something else unnerved him, a chill not even Fire could burn through.

Not from the bones scattered like trash on the street. Not from the scraps of clothing fluttering limply against iron spikes. But from the absolute silence.

Thunder boomed and wind howled nearer to the entrance, but over here, at the farthest edge of Calum's kingdom, there was nothing. No screams for help. No growls from the undead. The city was a ghost town, and that made him sick. There had been hundreds of people imprisoned here only months ago; this place should have been brimming with screams for help. In the far-off corner of his mind, he knew the cells were empty because of him. Because of the attack.

There were a few hundred more Howls on the field tonight because Calum had been tipped off that this attack was coming.

Fire whispered that it didn't matter. All that mattered was that he was alive and he was burning. If anything, it meant that there were a few hundred more bodies to incinerate. Even if that meant there were fewer people to save and, thus, worship him for their liberation. At least it meant a more glorious tale.

Fire's urgings should have been enough. But not even Fire could convince him that this place wasn't entirely, horribly wrong. Every step through the empty city tightened his nerves close to snapping. He drew deeper through Fire and Kianna held her weapons at the ready as they made their way closer to the castle. It wasn't hard to track, not when it was the tallest structure in the city, always towering above the imprisoned as a reminder of how bleak the future truly was.

A reminder of who truly ruled mankind.

You, Fire hissed in defiance. *The true ruler is you.*

Thunder rolled overhead, as if the world itself agreed with

the words. The ground heaved with another thunderous boom. Aidan stumbled against Kianna, who held him upright and steady as though she were carved from the stone at their feet.

"That's the wall," she said. She stared down the road to their left, as though she could see through the buildings in their way.

"You sure?"

"Is Scotland on a tectonic rift?"

"We need to hurry," he said.

"Your observations are, as always, illuminating."

He wanted to retort, but she was already off, jogging down the street toward the castle.

"First one there gets immortality!" she called out.

"I really hate you sometimes," he muttered, and followed.

Shouts and roars echoed through the empty streets as the battle poured into the city. He kept expecting to be stopped, for a rogue necromancer or Howl to step into the street and end them. But the focus was entirely on the western entrance. It was eerie, the ease with which he and Kianna reached the great mound of earth that held the castle. Not that he questioned it. Fire sang in his veins with how right this was, how destined this victory. The city was created to be his—why should it not bow to his presence?

The castle towered above the heart of the city, its great pedestal-like hill of molten stone pressing it up to the lightning-streaked heavens. An offering to the gods. An attempt at bridging the gap between mortal and divine. Aidan stared for a moment. The imposing walls, the shadowed windows. Once more, he felt the twinge—before, the castle had stood proudly at the top of the Royal Mile, the great stretch of road layered with shadowed closes and touristy gift shops and pubs carpeted in tartan and decades-old beer stains.

All of that was gone. Melted.

And even though Fire burned in his chest at the might of it all, the more human side of him thought it was a waste. Now, all that existed within a wide arc around the castle was the hill and dead land and, further on, the prisons of the damned. It didn't look like one of the most historic parts of Scotland. With the sharp angles and jutting iron and shadowed, black soil, it looked like a nightmare.

One he intended to make his own.

They raced across the swath of crystalline land, their reflections staring back at them with every curl of flame or flash of lightning in the sky. Aidan didn't let the castle out of sight. Couldn't. He couldn't stop staring at the darkened windows in the towers, the shadowed arrow slits, the ochre stone. Every flash, and he saw shadows shift. He could almost imagine Calum standing from the highest turret, watching the battle unfold. Could almost imagine a dozen necromancers, waiting in the wings with flame and storm at the ready.

And yet, when they reached the top of the pedestal and stood at the castle gates, there wasn't any alarm. There wasn't an attack. Despite the flame within him, despite the rightness that pounded in his ears like a bloody cadence, the stillness here unnerved him, a chill up the back of his spine that his smoke and burn couldn't melt.

He knew taking Glasgow would be easy; his plan had ensured it. But this…this was *too* easy.

This felt like a trap.

There is no trap you cannot overturn, Fire promised, and he let himself burn in that assurance while he surveyed his former army's progress.

The entire western half of the city was chaos, a smear of fire and smoke, gales and lightning. He could barely see through the destruction, but he occasionally glimpsed a figure through the fog of war, someone running or fighting or dying, and Fire ached in his chest every time.

It wanted to be down there, coated in blood. It wanted to burn in the trenches, rather than watch from afar.

His hands clenched as he fought the urge to send down his own flames, to melt the entire city in a breath. He knew he could. He felt the power within his chest. If he wanted Fire to destroy the city, it would. Happily. It seared under his fingertips, ached to get out. So many souls to burn. So many lives to feed to the ever-hungry light.

"Not yet," he whispered to himself. "Not yet."

"Talking to yourself?"

"I'm a better conversationalist than you," he said.

She snorted. "To quote the Scots, *get tae fuck.*" Then she sighed, almost happily, and said, "It looks like we're winning."

"Aye," Aidan replied. He tore his eyes away from the battle. Looked to the castle. "I think we've already won."

CHAPTER FIFTEEN

EDINBURGH CASTLE WAS A FROZEN WASTELAND.

The air dropped a good thirty degrees the moment Kianna and Aidan stepped past the gates. But this wasn't from incubi or any magic. At least, none that Aidan had ever seen before.

Snow blanketed every surface. Whereas outside the world was coated in glistening rain, in here, everything glinted white. Not a beautiful snowscape, however. No. This was no holiday card. Odd statues dotted the undisturbed courtyard, figures Aidan was positive weren't there when he visited with his mum. They were too angular—humanoid, almost, with outstretched limbs coated in snow. Paired with the ice sheening the castle walls, the dark red stone beneath glinting like blood with every flash of light, and the scene looked pulled from a nightmare.

He'd been having too many nightmares lately.

For the first time in this entire attack, Aidan felt the cold twinge of fear. As he stared at the courtyard of ice-rimed statues and perfect snow drifts, watching thick flakes drop from the sky and sizzle against his skin, he wondered how every-thing was so undisturbed. It looked like no one had come through here in days.

"The hell is that?" Kianna whispered. Aidan looked to where her sword pointed.

He thought it was just a statue at first. Propped a few feet away, arms upstretched as though embracing the heavens, icicles dripping from its arms and raised sword like fringe. Then another bolt of lightning shattered the sky, and he re-alized it was human.

Aidan crept closer. "I don't recognize him," he whispered.

The statue was clearly human and clearly dead. And he clearly hadn't been expecting to die so suddenly. His eyes and mouth were open in shock, his tongue blacked with frost-bite and exposure; small flecks of white dotted the tip from where snow had fallen past his teeth. Through the ice rim-ing his young body, Aidan could make out the leather blacks of a Hunter, though it wasn't anyone within his Guild. He had personally trained or trained with every single member of their army. This man wasn't one of his.

Which begged the question…was this man from another Guild? Had London sent up troops unbeknownst to him? Or was this man from a different time altogether? He seemed perfectly preserved in the unending ice. What if he was from before Aidan had even reached Glasgow? Before Glasgow had even been a Guild?

"Aidan," Kianna said. He looked to where she pointed at the top of the wall. More figures, completely frozen. These, however, were facing away from him. Guards? But that didn't make any sense.

He stepped past Kianna, toward one of the more misshapen forms. Lightning flashed, and he nearly jolted back from shock.

It was a kraven.

The Howl stared at him with eyes as bulbous and white as a decaying fish. Like so many of its brethren, it had been broken and torn in the act of being created from Earth—very little of its humanity remained. Its jaw had unhinged, cracking open and expanding to twice the width of its skull, teeth as long and sharp as a tiger's. Its entire spine was bent, its vertebrae pressed through flesh like jagged spines, and its arms and legs had elongated as well, each skeletal finger ending in a fierce talon.

Kravens were grotesque, but—Earth being the heaviest and thus quickest Sphere to tire—they were the backbones of the Dark Lady's army. Aidan had gotten used to the walking nightmares.

As used to a monster as he could be, that is.

"Maybe they were being punished," Aidan mused. He tapped the kraven on the forehead. The ice cracked. Not coated as thickly as the Hunter. Had it been frozen recently? Maybe Calum had killed them as an example, or out of boredom—Calum was an incubus after all, which could account for the frigid air and frozen guards. He was probably insane—who knew how his mind worked?

"They look like guards," Kianna whispered. She crept up to another kraven and poked it with her sword. The blade went through easily. When she pulled it out, a thin stream of black blood dribbled down like sap. "And they haven't been frozen long. An hour or two, tops."

Again, that shard of doubt. Calum wouldn't have killed his own guards when his palace was under attack. Someone had come here before them. Maybe a rogue necromancer, wanting to claim the throne for themselves.

But there weren't any tracks in the deep snow. No sign of struggle. No blood.

Another rumble shook them. The kraven beside him toppled, crashing to the snow with a soft thud. Even though he was accustomed to dead kravens, he still had to look away from the sight of its obsidian blood leaching into the white.

"I don't like this," Kianna muttered.

Aidan didn't like it either, but he wasn't about to tell her that. He pulled deeper through Fire. Burned the fear away.

"Scared?" he asked.

She elbowed him in response, then started walking up the sloped path without him. He rubbed his ribs. One day, she'd learn how to show affection without leaving a bruise. Maybe.

He unsheathed his daggers, curling flame around the blades, and followed her deeper in.

Every step revealed another frozen guard. Every step and the air dropped another degree, until it was only his hold on Fire that kept him from freezing. He glanced at Kianna. She wasn't even shivering.

The castle layout was simple, and the frozen monsters were a veritable breadcrumb trail leading to the heart of the castle. They followed the bodies up and around a few outlying buildings, the world outside practically forgotten in the deep quiet of this place. Aidan kept glancing around, staring at the snow and the abandoned structures, the gargoyle fonts and the old cells and the café. The statues that weren't statues, and the bodies piled up like haystacks. How much of this had just been sitting here, frozen and empty, for the last three years? How much was recent, and why?

Coated in snow and swept of any sign of historical importance, the castle seemed like any other broken structure in this new land. It pissed him off. The castle had once been prestigious. Grand. And just like the city, Calum had bastardized it in his arrogance.

Aidan would restore it, that much he vowed.

When he was on the throne, he would ensure this place of ice and despair would be something better. A light in the dark. A pillar of his power.

It didn't take long to reach the building where Calum waited. Past the barracks and under a high arch, into a courtyard that had once bustled with tourists, he found figures of another sort. More guards. A dozen or so. All of them facing outward. Human necromancers and kravens and probably a few higher-level Howls. All of them dead without a wound. They stood in an arc before the raised entrance to what Aidan thought was once a museum. A stone horse and lion and old regimental guardhouses flanked the tall doors, the etched words above scratched out.

"This is not good," Kianna whispered, echoing Aidan's thoughts.

Aidan squeezed past the guards. Tried not to look any of them in the eye.

"It's either this or retreat," Aidan said, glancing back at her as he put a hand on the door.

"Retreat has never been an option."

She stood next to him. Placed her hand on the other door.

He wanted to have something witty, something assured to say. He'd visualized this moment so many times—bursting or burning the door down, entering in a billow of flame and vengeance, his army at his back as he reclaimed Scotland for the living. Dozens of scenarios, dozens of ways to save the day.

None of them had looked like this—the quiet, frozen courtyard filled with bodies; the distant echo of thunder and magic in a battle he hadn't taken part in; the fear that this was all a trap.

"Let's go," he whispered. Even that was off from his daydreams—he didn't sound reassured or confident in the slightest.

He pushed open the door, and the two of them crept inside.

Frost glistened on every surface, lit by a few candles dripping from sconces, everything ghostly in the glow. Past the small gated foyer, he stood in a long hall stretching far to the left and right. The hall was almost churchlike in appearance, the high ceilings and shimmering windows, the white stone walls and slab floors. Church-like, save for the bodies.

Everywhere—*everywhere*—were more corpses, just like those outside. They crowded before him, a veritable maze. Unlike those outside, though, these weren't random bodies.

These were crafted.

Sculpted.

In front of him was a man, nearly naked save for a cloth wrapped around his waist, his arm raised and his hand holding a caduceus and his back leg extended behind him, as though in flight. His standing foot was nailed to the wooden pedestal he rested on. And there, beside him, a girl in a tutu, frozen in a pirouette, her eyes glassy and staring. A woman kneeling beside a fallen deer, both gazing to the heavens in reverence. Everywhere he looked was another statue, another twisted corpse.

He'd expected an attack. He'd expected Calum to be at their throats. But this room…it was so cold, so silent. So *dead*. He stepped forward, trying to figure out a way to navigate this maze of statuesque corpses, trying to ignore the fear that muted the heat in his chest. Trying to ignore the works of grotesque art. There was a sadism here that made even him blanch. Each of these people had been murdered and shaped, or shaped and then murdered. It was beyond his Sphere's usual need to consume. This was pure, human evil.

"What the hell is this?" Aidan whispered.

Kianna didn't answer him.

Someone else did.

"Amazing what a few years of boredom will do to a man."

Aidan turned on his heel, daggers ready, Fire blazing in his chest.

To see Kianna, crumpled on the ground in the foyer, a man slowly straightening up behind her.

A man in black jeans and polished shoes. A man with dark olive skin and tousled black hair, his shirt unbuttoned and smooth, chiseled chest gleaming in the candlelight. Gleaming like the glint in his perfect white teeth, and his copper-flecked eyes. Gleaming like the spark igniting in Aidan's lungs.

The incubus from Aidan's nightmare smiled. Spread his arms in a half bow.

"Welcome home, my prince."

CHAPTER SIXTEEN

AIDAN'S BRAIN SHORT-CIRCUITED.

He stared between Kianna's prone body and Tomás's glowing eyes, his heart paused midbeat and his thoughts stalled.

He couldn't be—

She couldn't be—

"Don't worry," Tomás said. "She lives. For now."

Tomás stepped over Kianna's body. Every inch closer and the heat between them rose, until sweat beaded across Aidan's skin. So warm. So warm.

Despite everything, Aidan took a small step forward. Fire thrummed wildly in his chest. He knew he should be worried about Kianna. Should be panicking over a nightmare turned flesh. But this man…this *creature*…seemed less nightmare and more promise than Aidan wanted to admit.

"You're real," Aidan whispered. He couldn't tell if his voice was husky from shock or desire.

"Of course I am." That devilish quirk of the lip. That tilted head. That smile sending heat down Aidan's spine. "I'm too perfect for you to dream up."

In the dream, Tomás had been alluring. But here, in the flesh—and he was most assuredly in the flesh—he was intoxicating. He smelled of musk and vetiver, like the wildest, darkest parts of a jungle, the places where sunlight doesn't shine and leopards prey. Everything about him moved with sensuous purpose—even the folds of his sheer shirt curled around him like a cocked finger. Aidan knew it was part of the Howl's design, knew incubi were created to evoke desire.

He also knew that what he felt toward Tomás was more than just carnal want.

When he looked at the incubus, he saw a dream made flesh. Many dreams made flesh. He saw more than just a seductive man; he saw the promises Tomás had made. He saw his place as king.

For a moment, he forgot where he was. Felt himself thrown back in the dream. Him and Tomás in a castle. Him and Tomás, ruling side by side.

Then Tomás stepped past him, gesturing to the frozen corpses around them, and Aidan was firmly back in the present.

"My brother has always had a certain…knack…for eccentricity." Tomás gently caressed the face of a man frozen with a sword upraised. "Personally, I think it's a waste of good flesh. He doesn't even play with them." He patted the side of the statue's face and turned back to Aidan. "At least, not while they're alive."

"What are you doing here?" Aidan asked.

Why hadn't he already attacked Tomás? Why hadn't he run to Kianna's side to ensure she was okay? Why was he standing there, frozen, while one incubus stood at his side, and another lurked somewhere in the shadows?

For that matter, why the hell hadn't Calum attacked?

"Helping you," Tomás said. He circled around Aidan like a panther, looking him up and down. Aidan felt entirely exposed.

He didn't hate it as much as he probably should have.

"Helping me? Why? How?"

Tomás's grin widened. "Come now, my prince. We both know you couldn't have taken Calum on your own." He opened to Air. The Sphere unfurled in the incubus's throat, and of all the things Aidan had seen that day, *that* scared him the most. Normal Howls couldn't use magic—everyone knew that. Which meant...

"You're one of the Kin," Aidan whispered, fear and awe curling in his chest.

Tomás turned and bowed.

"Attractive *and* intelligent. You truly are an upgrade," Tomás said.

"Upgrade?"

But Tomás didn't answer. Instead, he waved a hand, and with a pulse of magic the statues before them parted, blown away in a gust of air.

Revealing a throne in the chamber before them.

Calum strained above it. Crucified and writhing ten feet in the air between the stained-glass windows.

Aidan nearly toppled back.

Blood dripped from the stakes pounded through Calum's hands and feet. Those bloody rivulets turning to icicles that stretched like talons from his outstretched hands, crimson and thick against pale gray stone. Everything about the man seemed gray, bled out. His torn white shirt. The faded black jeans. Even his skin was sallow, a color Aidan had never seen a body go before. Calum looked like he was made of wax. A wax that breathed. Shallowly. Painfully. Every inhalation a curse.

And above the body, written in what could only be Calum's blood, were four words.

MY GIFT, MY KING

"Do you like it?" Tomás asked, walking right past Aidan to nod at Calum. "I thought it was perhaps a bit much. But then I thought..." He looked at Aidan. "For you, too much is barely enough."

Aidan stared at the Kin nailed to the wall. His gut churned with disgust and rage—anger at Calum, for everything he had done to Scotland; angry at himself, for not being the one to torture him so.

"You slit his throat," Aidan whispered, staring at the blood congealing on Calum's neck. How was he still alive?

"Of course," Tomás replied, as though the reasoning was obvious. "I didn't want him to ruin my grand entrance."

"But how..."

Tomás cut him off by placing his hand on Aidan's mouth. Even that move, forceful as it was, made Aidan's chest race with desire.

"Oh, my Hunter. Why waste time with small talk? I have given you my brother on a silver platter. Now, you stand on the edge of greatness. Relish in it."

It shouldn't have been enough to sway Aidan's thoughts, but it was. His mind was sluggish, unable to connect the dots, unable to do anything besides feel. Fire flamed so bright within him, he felt drunk on its power. And when Tomás pulled his hand away, he couldn't feel anything beyond his own unveiled destiny.

"Why did you do it?" Aidan asked. He didn't break his gaze from Calum—the ragged rise and fall of the man's breath, the slow, crystalizing drips of his blood. "All of this." Because he knew, too, that Tomás was the reason the guards outside were frozen. Tomás would have no problem dispatching a castle's worth of minions.

The Kin had carved Aidan's path to victory.

Aidan barely had the brains to wonder what Tomás would want in return.

"Because we seek the same thing," Tomás said.

"And what is that?"

"Something better. Something more exciting than *this*."

He strode forward, eyes locked on Calum. There was something about the way he moved up the aisle of frozen corpses that made Aidan think of a coronation, their bodies all witnesses to his ascension.

"Oh, brother dear," Tomás said, head tilted, a broken marionette, "how far you have fallen."

Aidan followed at his heels, up the row of frozen dead, until they stopped at the foot of Calum's throne. Only then did he realize the throne was made of bodies. Naked and frozen, twined together with faces downturned, arms raised in supplication, the throne back a man and woman wrapped in what seemed like a loving embrace, save for the looks of horror etched into their faces.

In Fire's embrace, the sight didn't disturb him nearly as much as it should have.

"You were given a kingdom," Tomás said to his frozen brother. "And yet you failed to bring the glory of our Mother to this world. You failed her, and she does not take kindly to failures. Or betrayal." He glanced at Aidan, and that one look made Aidan's heart flip with desire, with excitement. "We all reap what we sow, brother dear."

Tomás walked around the throne of corpses and reached up, placing a hand on Calum's ankle. Without the slightest bit of pause or ceremony, he yanked Calum from the wall. The sound of ripping flesh and snapping bones made bile rise in the back of Aidan's throat, as did the thud and muffled groan when Calum hit the floor. Even that disgust was distant, though—he was too busy focusing on the way Tomás's biceps corded with the motion, the flex and strain of his lats. Fire burned off whatever revulsion he might have felt. Fire saw only strength. Fire felt only power.

Tomás stared down at Calum, a sneer on his face, revealing his sharp canines, emphasizing the hard cut of his jaw. There were a dozen battling emotions in that face—sadness and rage and pity, all of it tinted with disgust.

"You deserve to suffer," Tomás whispered, voice rising with every word. "For what you have done. For what you failed to do. You were never her favorite. Never. Never! *I* was the one she cherished! *I* was her perfection!"

Then Tomás shook himself, shuddering violently, and stood straighter. He held out a hand toward Aidan. "Come."

Aidan never took orders. And yet his feet guided him forward, past the twisted throne, Tomás's voice a hook in his heart that he knew he couldn't—and wouldn't—ever defy.

Tomás took his hand when he neared. The Howl's flesh was hot and cold, a wave of fire that pricked Aidan's skin with icicles. But when Tomás's fingers curled around his, everything about that moment felt...*right*. His heart burned and his thoughts swum, his whole body moving as though through warm molasses.

He felt as though every atom in his body had waited for this moment, and now that it was here, he would soak up every molten second.

Even if it wasn't how he'd planned to take down Calum, even though—in the farthest corner of his mind—he knew that accepting the aid of a Kin was borderline treason, this was the moment he had waited for the last three years. This was the moment he had lived and fought and bled and burned for.

And he was more than ready to take on the role of king.

Even if he was doing it hand in hand with a Kin he should have wanted to kill. Fire told him that this was how things were meant to be; Fire was a voice he could always trust.

He stared down at Calum, and perhaps he was only mirroring Tomás, perhaps the feelings were not his own, but he could find nothing but disgust for the creature sprawled and bleeding on the ground.

This close, Aidan could see every wrinkle in the Kin's lined face, every scar on his waxen flesh. Calum was old—older than most humans managed to live. But he also seemed weak, and while Aidan stared down at the man who once was king, he could only think that Calum had failed in every single way.

He'd been content to rule fields of nothing, cities of ruin. He had never strived for greater. He had never dreamed of more.

Calum was nothing, and Aidan could not understand how he had ever viewed the Kin as a threat. As an equal.

When clearly, Calum was subservient.

Tomás squeezed Aidan's hand, searing visions through Aidan's thoughts: burning skies and charred fields, squares of bowing servants and praying Howls, everything, *everything*, praising Aidan's glory. Fire burned in Aidan's chest. And there, in the darkest part of the flame, he heard the voice that had taunted him the last few days, the whispered words of a woman who spoke a deeper truth.

You will be a stronger ruler than Calum ever was, my child, the Dark Lady promised. *You will make the world bend knee.*

"It is time to take your place in history," Tomás said, drawing Aidan from his dreams of destruction. "Fire keeps my brother alive. Destroy the affected Sphere, and you destroy him. Destroy him, and take your rightful place as King."

Fire burned. Aidan knelt at Calum's side.

That's when he noticed the tattoos on the man's abdomen.

In that moment, the world around him seemed to still. Fade out. Even Fire quieted.

He stared at the tattoos that curved over Calum's hips, the sigils and symbols that crisscrossed over his belly. Aidan reached out and gently lifted Calum's shirt. More symbols. No. Not symbols.

Runes.

He knew them. Some from the markings on his own arm. Some from study. And others…others he just…*knew.* Harsh and sinuous, burning black and glowing red, a half light haze that seared into his retinas. They whispered to him, hissing like steam, like serpents, like that internal oceanic whisper that pushed him toward the edge of oblivion. Like the Dark Lady herself inscribed them in his mind.

Entranced, his limbs moving on their own accord, he undid the buttons of Calum's shirt, revealing more tattoos and more runes, lines and symbols that formed constellations over the pale expanse of his skin. And in the center of his chest, right where the Sphere of Fire was meant to be, a dark black circle was inked into his flesh, a black hole around which galaxies of runes danced and spiraled and were consumed. Within the black void, he saw the faint impressions of other markings: brands and burns, scabs and blank spaces of skin. More symbols. Layers and layers of runes, all spelling out words that hissed like poison in his mind.

Distantly, he felt Tomás's hand on his shoulder, the Kin's voice saying Aidan was meant to kill Calum, not undress him. Aidan barely heard it.

Not as the runes repeated in his mind.

Not as they became a language he thought he understood. A language he had known his entire life.

Every word a curse. A promise. Every word uttered by the low, feminine hiss he'd heard through Fire.

Be mine, and be consumed. Be nothing, and be reborn. Death and life are yours to walk between.

He heard Her voice, and it commanded him, moved him, hypnotized him. His hand shook as he traced the runes scarred into Calum's body.

When he placed his hand on the dark mark of Calum's chest, the shadows swallowed him whole.

CHAPTER SEVENTEEN

CLOUDS DRIPPED FROM THE SKY, SEEPING DOWN
to the sodden earth below, long gray streaks of fog and rain.
Dark fog billowed over hills of tombstones, melting with the
sky. Fog pooled at his feet, spilled into the open grave. Fog
and rain and earth, black and gray and white, the whole world
a blot of ink on paper.

Fog curled. And it was no longer just black and white and
gray.

Red seeped through.

Red from rain. Red from rain and blood.

A lot of blood.

Blood from the black-clothed bodies strewn about him,
their faces twisted in horror. Blood from the sky, raindrops
thick and congealing like scenes from Revelations. Blood
that soaked into his clothes, stained his skin. And when he
turned toward the open grave, he realized he wasn't the only
one amid the massacre.

The Dark Lady knelt beside him, staring down into the

grave. Fire burned in her chest, glinting off her golden hair. Her black dress was slicked with rain, but she didn't shiver. Like him, she didn't mind the cold. Not with Fire burning the chill away, making rain sizzle and steam.

She stared down at the black casket, and it was then he saw the shard of crystal she held in one hand. Black as night, curled with pewter and engraved in countless silver symbols that writhed and whispered under her touch. It spoke through his mind, calling like a void, a broken sun he couldn't escape, snaring his chest and pulling him closer to the heart of all darkness. Aidan broke his gaze away. Realized the Dark Lady was whispering something he could barely make out over the thrum of rain, the hiss of steam, the splashes of water in blood.

He stepped forward gingerly, his feet slurping in the blood and mud, until he was right beside the grave. Smoke curled from the casket lid, where the wood had been burned away, the edges glowing red and orange with embers. The corpse within, however, was untouched.

The man's hair was light brown and short, his eyes closed and hands clasped across his chest. He looked like he was in his late forties. But Aidan knew that face, as well. Calum. Looking so much younger here than in life.

"You have fulfilled your end of the bargain," she whispered to Calum's corpse. "And now, I shall fulfill mine."

She opened to Air then, and reached a hand into the grave. Calum floated up from his coffin, his limbs dangling limp like a rag doll. She followed him with her hand, bringing him to hover a few feet from the grave's lip before rotating him to standing. Another curl of her hand, and the suit he wore snapped open, his dress shirt slicing down the middle to reveal lightly tanned flesh. And the countless tattoos that snaked over his body. She smiled at them. Admired her handiwork.

Calum floated closer to her, until she could reach out and touch his dead skin. She did so, trailing a finger over the runes. They curled under her touch, shivering and twisting like insects, like serpents. He heard them hiss in his brain. Their words. *Her* words. Whispers of power, of eternity, of nothingness. Of return.

"Death is but a doorway," she said. "And through that void, that which is fallen may rise again."

She pressed the black crystal to his chest, right in the center of that dark circle. Fire flared in her chest as she twined its magic through her fingertips. Into the shard.

The crystal burned white hot, silvered runes turning black, shadows burned into Aidan's mind. The runes snaked down the crystal, melted against Calum's flesh and spread across his skin, inking themselves beside their brethren, completing phrases that howled in the echoes within Aidan's ears. Calum shook with power. Arcs of energy lashed around him, red and black, shadow and light, all snapping out and back toward the shard in the Dark Lady's hands.

That's when Aidan realized that the crystal wasn't exuding energy—it was stealing it.

He squinted. Calum's Sphere of Fire still smoldered in his chest. Impossible. The Spheres died when the body died. So how was it still active? How was it being drained, when at death it should have just…winked out?

The runes.

Truth shattered through his mind. The runes inked into Calum's skin had kept his Sphere of Fire going even in death. And now, the Dark Lady was draining its final energy. Inverting it.

Turning Calum's corpse into a Howl.

It should have been impossible. Howls could only be born of living hosts. If they could be brought back from the dead...

Aidan felt it in his own chest. The moment when Calum's Sphere tipped over. The moment Fire stopped exuding power. There was a stutter. A skipped heartbeat. An ache of recognition as the crystal pressed to Calum's chest pulled out the very last shred of energy Fire could create. And kept going.

The pause.

The pain.

And then the transformation.

Aidan had never seen a necromancer turn a human into a Howl up close. Only on television, in the aftermath of the Resurrection, when every single station showed the woman before him turning a man into a kraven.

This was worse.

Life leached from the man, his skin freezing in a second as all heat drained from him. Ice shattered over his flesh, turned him white-blue, while deep within, his Sphere turned black. Red swirls of light inverted to shadow, the spiral and swirl switching directions. Even as the shard of crystal burned white-hot and curled with flame, the air around them froze. Rain shattered to ice and snow. Bloody puddles crackled purple and crimson as shards struck from them like lances. The Dark Lady's breath came out in a cloud, and even Aidan—in the grips of the vision—felt his skin freeze, felt the heat rip from his chest. Felt his own heart scream in pain.

Then the ice on Calum's body shattered, his entire body

convulsing, a cloud of crystalline white falling from him like dust.

He fell to the ground. Collapsed to his knees.

But he didn't fall forward.

Instead, he looked up. His movements shaky. His pale eyes rimed red. The moment his eyes locked on the Dark Lady, he smiled.

"It worked," he whispered.

She nodded as she lowered the stone. It still burned red in her grip, sizzling in the rivulets of rain that ran down her snow-flecked skin. She didn't seem to mind.

Calum looked around. At the empty grave. At the bodies scattered about like dominoes, offerings to his resurrection, black and white and bloody. He pushed himself to standing.

"They...they are my family," he said. Was Aidan imagining the tilt in his voice? The tinge of doubt? Of anger?

"Were," the Dark Lady corrected him. "They ceased to be your kin when you turned to me. Consider them offerings to us. To our reign. To your true family. They will not be the last."

"As you say." His face cracked back into a smile. It seemed forced. "In their blood, we will rule."

"Indeed we shall." She pressed the shard to Calum's chest. He held it like a child, fierce and protective. "Behold, your scepter. And soon, you shall have your throne and crown. I will give you Scotland. There, you will spread my truths. There, you will help me rule."

The Dark Lady looked over then, as though she heard a voice in the distance. But her eyes weren't turned to the horizon. They bore straight into Aidan's heart.

"And you, my Hunter, you will help me rule again."

CHAPTER EIGHTEEN

"THE HELL IS THIS?"

Trevor's voice cut through the vision, snapped Aidan back into the bloody, broken present.

Aidan knelt there, besides Calum's seemingly lifeless body, Tomás at his side and Kianna unconscious behind them at Trevor's feet. Aidan looked from his former co-commander to the two Kin before him. He knew what this looked like.

The trouble was, things were exactly the way they seemed.

"Aidan," Trevor said. He hesitated in the doorway, three hunters flanked behind him, their hands on their weapons and Spheres blazing. It was clear they had been ready for anything. Anything but this. Trevor kept looking at Kianna. The flick of a finger, and one of the Hunters broke off to kneel at her side. Earth opened in the man's stomach as he probed Kianna for wounds.

As he did what Aidan should have done.

Why did everything suddenly seem so cold?

"What did you do to her?" Trevor asked, his voice shaking with anger. Then he looked to Tomás. "And what the hell are you doing with *that*?"

Tomás snarled, but he didn't attack like Aidan expected. Instead, he stayed at Aidan's side, hand digging into his shoulder, as though Aidan were the attack dog and Tomás the holder of the lead. Aidan couldn't move; his hand was still pressed to Calum's chest, his fingers frozen and tingling, the rise and fall of Calum's ragged breathing reminding him that he still hadn't done what he had come here to do.

This close to Calum, he felt his Sphere being pulled, felt the Howl vainly struggling to sap out Aidan's heat, his strength. It was barely more than a chill. It didn't account for the cold in Aidan's bones. The feeling that things were going irrevocably to shit. Fire faltered in Aidan's chest.

That was the problem.

Aidan pulled deeper through Fire, and the ache and the doubt burned away. He was the sun to Calum's shadow. To Trevor's disapproving stare. He could burn it all away.

"Aidan…" Trevor said, and though his voice was a warning, Aidan didn't know why.

He stared at Calum. Stared at the runes that whispered through his mind of secrets and succumbing, their words somehow stronger in the wake of the vision. Almost, but not quite, he could read what they were for, could sense the strands that tied Calum to the world of the living, that allowed him to be raised from the dead.

Fire burned through him. And even though Calum had been one of the Dark Lady's creations, he heard her voice in the char of flame. *Kill him. Prove your might.*

Prove yourself to me.

"I'm doing what I promised I would do," Aidan said. To Calum. To Trevor. To the darkest whispers of his soul.

He reached back. Slipped a serrated dagger from his boot. And stabbed straight through Calum's chest.

It wasn't an easy cut. Calum's flesh was thin, but his bones were strong, and even though the Howl didn't fight, his scream echoed through the room as Aidan hacked and sawed, his hands coated with frigid blood. But not just blood. He felt it, as Calum died. He felt the Howl's Sphere fade. No, not *fade*. He felt the power flow, bleeding from Calum's heart to Aidan's hands, sinking deep beneath Aidan's skin. Filling him. Completing him. As Calum died, Aidan felt himself becoming more whole. Felt Fire burn with satiation.

Satiation, and then silence.

Silence, and then the cackle of Tomás's laughter.

Aidan stood, slowly, the dagger embedded in Calum's chest. A flag. A marker that this land was now his.

Trevor and the other Hunters looked on, horror or perhaps awe splashed on their faces as he righted himself, as he curled flame around his fists, blood burning and charring against his skin. It reminded him of Vincent's burning scent. And this time, it didn't turn his stomach.

"Well done, my king," Tomás whispered into Aidan's ear. Heat curled around the two of them. Heat pulled them together as the sun draws in the stars. "Scotland is now yours. Well..." He turned his gaze to the Hunters before him. "It will be, as soon as you get rid of them."

"Aidan—" Trevor began, but he didn't finish the sentence. He knew there was no point.

For the briefest moment, Aidan reconsidered. He had killed Calum. That had to have been enough.

"He commands Glasgow," Tomás said to Aidan. He crossed his arms over his chest, everything in his posture and tone nonchalant. Tomás already knew the outcome. He'd set up his game pieces, and they had fallen in place exactly as he'd wished. "So long as he rules the Guild, you will never have your place as King. So long as he knows you have helped a member of the Kin, you will never walk free. Look. You can see it in their eyes. The doubt. The fear. Well, they *should* fear you. And they should doubt."

Tomás gestured to the throne beside them. When he curled his fingers around Aidan's, Fire roared in Aidan's ears. Fire, and Tomás's words.

"This is all that matters, my prince. My king. This throne. This kingdom. This moment. Your past is but a burden. A shroud. Burn it away, and embrace your new destiny."

Aidan looked to the throne. To Calum. To Kianna. And finally, he looked to Tomás. Guilt should have churned in Aidan's chest. Fear and worry. Dread. But in the light of Tomás's eyes, in the promise of their shared heat, he felt only purpose. He was meant to rule. He was meant to rule it all.

He looked back at his former co-commander, his former lover, and all he could see in Trevor's face was the slam of his office door, the frustration in his eyes as he exiled Aidan from the only home he had left. As Trevor damned Aidan to a life of nothingness.

As Trevor tried to make Aidan less than what he was destined to be.

No more.

Fire burned through Aidan, chased away the doubt, filled him only with anger. With a blinding, blistering destiny.

Scotland was his. *His.* Trevor had tried to take it away. Even after everything Aidan had done, everything he'd sacrificed, everything that had been stolen from him in this damned land, Trevor had declared it wasn't enough.

"Aidan, don't—" Trevor reasoned, his voice softer. He took a step forward, hand raised, weapon lowered, while the other Hunters behind him readied for attack. "Don't listen to him. The war's over. We did it. We won."

"No." Aidan said. His voice rang clear and assured through the hall, burning with Fire's heat. "*I* did it. *I* won."

"Please—"

Yes, Fire hissed. *Bring them to me. Bring them…*

"—Aidan—"

They will defy you. They will turn against you. Again.

"—you don't want—"

Trust no one. Trust no one.

"That's where you're wrong, Trevor," Aidan said. Fire burned brighter in his chest. He barely heard his own words over its incendiary roar, barely felt the cold of the room through the heat that threatened to tear him apart. The heat, and the *power.* The hunger.

Scotland was his. *His.* And he would never let these fools take it from him.

"I *do* want," Aidan continued. "I want it all."

He looked to Tomás.

"And now, I think I will let myself have it."

Tomás smiled. In that smile, Aidan saw his future.

Aidan didn't move a muscle when he lashed out, when Fire

burst from the pores of his three former comrades. Just like Vincent. Just like the unconscious action that had dragged him to this outcome. Only now, he was awake to hear all of their screams. Wanted to hear their screams. Their short screams, as flames filled their throats and stilled their words.

Leaving only Trevor. Trevor, whose eyes ran with tears— from smoke or fear, Aidan didn't know. Or care. Trevor and Kianna, who lay unconscious in the dust of her troop mates.

"Why are you doing this?" Trevor asked. His voice hitched.

"Because…" Aidan began. He pulled through Fire. Squeezed Tomás's hand. The Kin's skin was cold compared to his own. "…I can."

He made it quick.

A burst of fire that filled Trevor's lungs, seared through his heart. No great pyrotechnics, no pillar of flame.

One moment, Trevor stood there. Alive and broken.

The next, he crumpled to the ground beside Kianna, smoke curling like regret from his lips.

CHAPTER NINETEEN

THERE WAS A MOMENT, BRIEFLY, WHEN FIRE LET UP and doubt crept in, when Aidan saw the ash and bodies of his comrades for what they truly were—crimes he'd committed, treason.

Murder.

But with Tomás burning at his side, that moment was barely a flicker in his consciousness. With Tomás, all sins were forgiven.

All sins were encouraged.

With Fire, all sins were glory.

"I underestimated you," Tomás said. "I thought *I* would have to kill them."

Aidan didn't want to think about that. To think on that would be to look back. Fire didn't look back. Fire burned.

Fire burned.

"What do we do now?" He looked away from the bodies. "You've given me the throne—"

"But you want more," Tomás interrupted.

Aidan turned to face him; the heat between them could melt mountains. But Aidan knew he could be stronger. *Should* be stronger. Calum was just the start. *Scotland* was just the start. He knew as much from what he'd seen in the vision— there was more power to be had, power that he couldn't even comprehend.

The power to bring back the dead.

"I want it all," Aidan said.

Tomás just smiled, his canine pulling on his lower lip. Aidan wanted to bite that mouth, to taste every inch of the Kin who called him king. Power rode through his veins, elation at having finally done what he had set out to do years ago. And that power refused to dam itself in the confines of this castle.

"I will give you everything," Tomás replied. He stepped in closer, looked down into Aidan's eyes, traced Aidan's lips with a burning finger. "Everything, and more. But we all have parts to play. And yours, my king, has just begun."

"What do you mean?"

"I mean, I am here to play a bigger game. As are you."

"What game?"

Tomás's smile widened. He leaned in closer. Threatened to burn Aidan alive.

Which was all Aidan truly wanted.

"I have given you what you desired," Tomás said, his lips so close to Aidan's he could taste the Kin's tongue. "And now, you will give me what I seek."

"Which is?" Aidan asked breathily. Fire filled him. Fire promised to give the incubus anything he so asked.

"I want the key to my brother's creation." His words a bedroom purr. His eyes sparking prophecies. Aidan leaned in.

And Tomás stepped back. Pointed to the corpse at their feet. Even that distance made cold and need ache in Aidan's chest.

"Bring me the shard that brought him back to life," Tomás said, "and I will grant you the world."

Visions flashed through Aidan's mind—the flames, the power, the bloody graveyard. The Dark Lady and Calum's corpse. The impossible resurrection.

"Yes," Tomás whispered. "I know you have seen it. I know her words speak to you. You have seen the truth."

Aidan shook the visions from his mind. Everything tumbled in his head, puzzle pieces without a board. Fire's hum didn't help; he was drunk on the power, and any direction felt futile.

"Where is it?"

"If I knew that, why would I ask you?" Tomás snapped.

Aidan jolted at the anger in Tomás's voice. Then Tomás shivered. Regained composure. Ran a hand through his hair with an elfish grin.

"I would apologize," he said. "But I feel you know what it is like to experience things…fiercely."

Aidan nodded, felt the curtains draw back over his fear, hiding the doubt and rationality.

"Find me the shard," Tomás continued, his voice dropping back to its purr. "Rule your kingdom. Then you will learn the rest of our game."

He wanted so badly to reach out to Tomás, to pull the incubus closer, to celebrate his victory with all the passion and pleasure Fire promised them. But Tomás took another step away, toward the shadows, toward the statues, and Aidan stayed rooted in place.

He wouldn't pine.

He would make the Kin come to him.

"I will be watching," Tomás said.

"I'm counting on it."

Tomás paused. As though that were not the response he'd expected. As though he didn't think Aidan could be an equal.

Then his eyes flickered to Kianna's body.

"I wouldn't tell her about me, were I you. I don't think she would approve."

Aidan laughed and looked back at his only friend. "She doesn't approve of anything."

Tomás nodded.

Then he opened to Air, a flicker of pale blue in his throat. The next moment, he was gone.

Emptiness settled on Aidan's shoulders the moment the Kin disappeared. It sank though his bones, curled in his gut. Emptiness, and cold, and purpose. He reached into his flame and forced it through his bones. He would not let Tomás's absence sadden him.

He refused to need the Kin for anything.

He refused to need anyone for anything. Not anymore.

Aidan looked around at the frozen sculptures, the humans Calum had twisted into some otherworldly art. At the blood-smeared wall—*my gift, my king*—and the broken body bleeding out beneath it.

This was his home.

His castle.

He had earned it.

And as he stared at the corpses, as he looked up into the shadows and cobwebs on the rafters, as he let his senses stretch out to the firestorm above, the battle slowly dying down in the city, he realized that he didn't want this.

The castle was too small.

Scotland was too small.

Calum had been content to contain his rule here. But not Aidan. This was a mausoleum.

Calum ruled only the dead.

Aidan would rule the world.

He reached down and yanked the dagger from Calum's chest, and set about the gruesome task of sawing off Calum's head. He would need more than his word to make his fellow Hunters follow him. And what was a revolution without a little decapitation?

Maybe he'd even get some cake.

When finished, he walked down the aisle, gripping Calum's hair in one hand, Fire burning with purpose in his chest.

He would spread.

He would devour.

He would find the shard that Tomás desired, and he would in turn take everything the incubus could offer.

And more.

He pulled through his Sphere. The statues beside him burst into flame. One by one, he set the corpses alight. Their rising embers a swirling crown above him. The only crown he needed. A baptism of Fire was the only coronation that suited.

When he reached Kianna, he gently looped her arm over his shoulder and carried her away from his comrades. Out the great doors into the frozen courtyard beyond.

The Sphere of Fire smoldered in his chest. Guided him forward. Ever forward. Ever hungry.

The moment the door closed behind them, he reached through that poisonous power and let the castle feel the weight of his might. Fire burst through the stained-glass windows, snaked its way over stone and frozen skin. He felt Fire feed, felt it devour the statues of Hunters long past, the support beams of the hall, the corpse of Calum.

The throne too small for him to occupy.

He fed it all to the flames, and Fire delighted in the feast.

That's when Kianna woke up. Startled from the thunderous boom as the roof caved in and the sky burned bright with his power.

"What..." she mumbled. She stood straighter. "What happened?"

"It's over," he lied. He held up Calum's head. "We won."

He knew it wouldn't be explanation enough forever. But for now, it was.

She stopped. Pushed herself off of Aidan to look back at the inferno.

"We won," she repeated, a whisper. A single tear slid down her face. "You bloody bastard. You did it."

"Aye," he said. "I did."

There was a moment, watching the tears of pride and who-knew-what-else fall down her face, that he felt the twinge of shame. He had lied to her. He had killed his co-commander, his lover. He had agreed to help Tomás, and had promised to never tell Kianna about it. He was no better than the monster he had just ended.

Kianna looked to him. Sniffed at the tears.

"Less than ten minutes in command, and everything's already gone up in flames. I guess I expected nothing less."

Aidan broke out in laughter, Fire curling back into his chest, burning the doubt and the shame away.

"What can I say?" he asked. "I wanted to redecorate."

"You're going to tell me everything," Kianna said, turning away from the blaze. "But first, I need a fecking drink."

"Done."

Together, they walked down the path while Edinburgh Castle and all of its terrible secrets burned behind them.

Behold, the reign of Aidan, he thought. He looked down to Calum's head.

Aidan smiled.

"There is no perfect magic, no pure power.
Only nature is perfect, only the gods
are pure. We have toyed with both.
And so
we have damned ourselves twice over."

—Diary of the Violet Sage,
5 Oct, 3 P.R.

PART 3

THE DEEPER THE SHADOW

CHAPTER TWENTY

AIDAN AND KIANNA SAT AROUND THE BONFIRE, far away from the castle walls and the destruction they'd left behind, the city smoldering on the horizon, painting the night as red as the blood they'd spilled. Even from here, Aidan's chest ached with the call of Fire.

After Calum had fallen, it had been a pretty quick job sweeping up the rest of the Howls and necromancers that hadn't died in the first few minutes of the attack. Without their leader, and with the Guild's morale boosted, Calum's forces fell like cards.

The Guild had been hit heavily, but victory was all that mattered.

Fire told him as much, and if he began to doubt that, he would need to doubt a whole hell of a lot of other things.

Aidan had expected Kianna to grill him about what happened in the castle. His lie had come swiftly and succinctly— she'd been struck by a hidden guard, gotten knocked out.

Trevor and a few others came in and helped take Calum down, but had sadly died in the process.

He made sure to make his voice catch when he mentioned the last part.

The surprising thing wasn't the ease with which he came up with the lie, but the ease with which she accepted it. And when they came back down from the hill and helped destroy the last of the necromancers and Howls still fighting back, the troops had accepted the news, as well.

It was a shame that Trevor had fallen in battle. But falling in battle was the name of the game, and to die killing Calum was the greatest of honors. Or so Aidan had reminded the troops.

He hadn't mentioned that he was—ignoring that whole "exile" thing—now in command. He didn't need to.

The moment he held up Calum's head and claimed the title of King as his, his comrades had erupted in cheer. He was swept up in the tide. Regaled as a hero.

As he should have been all along.

Around them, the remaining troops laughed and drank. Aidan wasn't certain which of them had decided to bring the victory booze, or maybe someone had found a wellspring of whiskey in a ruined house. They had set up camp about a mile from Edinburgh, in what seemed to be an old football field. A myriad of tents were scattered about, their colors sharp and shadowed in the firelight. The surviving Hunters had been healed by Earth mages, who were now mostly fast asleep, which meant everyone awake was celebrating. Somewhere in the camp, Calum's head was being paraded around on a pike. What was left of it, at least.

Turned out, there were quite a few people with a lot of

unspent aggression toward the Kin, and bashing his head in was as satisfactory postmortem as pre.

Even better, for the first time in what felt like months, it wasn't raining.

Maybe Aidan's luck was finally improving.

He took another drink of whisky and looked to a guy sitting across the fire from him. Pale Irish skin, curly black hair and beard, an angular face covered in dirt and recently healed scars. Aidan barely remembered the dude's name. Gregory or something. It didn't matter. All that mattered was the fact that the guy kept looking over. A different fire sparked through Aidan's chest every time he did. He fought down the blush that rose in his cheeks and turned it to something he could use, an anticipation, a desire to hunt in a different way.

His luck was *definitely* improving.

"I think he wants you," Kianna said, following Aidan's not-very-hidden stare.

Aidan just took a swig of whisky and found solace in the fire that burned down his throat. "That doesn't matter. The question is whether or not I want *him*."

He knew he should have felt bad about Trevor. For lying to Kianna. For making his own friend an unknowing accomplice. But that voice was small, and suffocating, and the more he fed his doubt to the flames, the less he feared retribution.

He had killed Calum.

Liberated Scotland.

What did it matter, the casualties along the way?

He stared over at Gregory and fed all the uncertainty into the fire, let the heat inside him grow with a different need.

A different sort of victory. In that moment, he realized that yes, yes—he wanted, and would have, Gregory.

"What about you?" he asked her. "Any lads or lassies you want to bone?"

"Please never say 'lad' or 'lassie' again. You sound like a tourist."

He laughed and nudged her in the side. Gregory looked over at the sound. Aidan grinned at him, his heart flipping over with excitement. After his time with Tomás, he was horny as hell. If he couldn't take the incubus, Gregory would be a fair consolation prize.

"You didn't answer my question," Aidan said.

Kianna glanced over her shoulder, to another Hunter-ringed fire. "Maybe," was all she said.

"Och, c'mon. You deserve a victory shag."

"I deserve many victory shags," she said. "Especially since I know this will only inflate your ego. I can't even imagine how terrible dealing with you will be from here on out."

Aidan winked. "You flatter me."

She bit her lip, and her face shifted to concern. "Are you sure you're okay?" It wasn't a question she often asked him—it got too close to prodding, which they'd sworn against years ago. The first time he'd tried to get her to admit that she was upset, she'd broken his arm. Thankfully, they'd been near an Earth mage at the time. He told himself she had known that when she did it, but he wasn't exactly convinced. "I know you pretend you're a hard-ass, but I know Trevor meant a lot to you."

He looked to the fire. And even though that should have

made him feel better, should have made his Sphere burn with recognition, all he could see was Trevor's face in the flames.

He had to convince himself that this had been the only way. Trevor had seen too much. They all had. Aidan would have been questioned, or tortured, or worse. It was either him or them.

When it came down to it, he would always put himself first. Him, and Kianna.

He had to.

"I will be," he said. "It's…it's going to take some time."

She nodded. Leaned in a little closer. "You know…you know you can always talk to me, right? I'm your mate. I love the hell out of you." She paused, and he looked over, watched her expression change in the flames. For the first time in all the years he had known her, she actually looked vulnerable. Maybe it was because this was the first time he'd ever seen her tipsy; she didn't like the thought of being impaired, when an attack could happen at any moment. "You got me out of there. You saved my life. I should have thanked you. Just know…just know I'll always be there for you. Always."

Guilt twisted in Aidan's chest, and he had to look away. He hoped she would think it was because he was bad at dealing with emotions.

Not because he was lying through his teeth.

"Thank you," he replied. "I've got your back, too." That, at least, would always be true. For everything she'd done for him—for not abandoning him when everyone else had—he would always have her back.

He just had to convince himself that right now, having her

back involved lying. To save her from the harsh truth that her best friend was a monster.

She leaned over then, and hugged him awkwardly. He flinched under her touch in spite of himself. He'd known her since the Resurrection, and this was probably only the fourth or fifth time they'd hugged. In that moment, he was reminded that she was just like him—young and fucked up and scared. Only she didn't have magic to take off the edge.

She didn't have Fire telling her that weakness was death.

He wondered what inner voice was.

"Okay, arsehole," she said, leaning back. "Enough of this shite. I'm gonna go get laid." She looked over to Gregory, who was making a great show of not paying them any attention. "Looks like you're going to have your hands full."

"Hope so," Aidan replied.

Kianna stood, using his shoulder as a prop, and looked over to Gregory. "You treat this boy right," she said. "He owns your ass now."

Gregory smiled, a blush rising in his cheeks, and before Aidan could yell at Kianna to shut up, she turned from the fire and went to join another. Aidan watched her stumble off.

"Think she'll be okay?" Gregory asked.

Aidan started. He looked over to Gregory, who had moved close enough that their elbows nearly touched. Aidan tried to turn the guilt and the fear into desire.

He had won. He had gotten away with everything.

He ruled Scotland.

And now, he needed to claim his prize.

One of many prizes.

"She'll be okay," Aidan said.

"Good," Gregory said, his words a lilting brogue. He held up his mug. "So, em, congratulations."

Aidan clinked mugs. Took a sip. But he didn't take his eyes off of Gregory.

In the back of his mind, he knew that if he stalled, his thoughts would get the better of him. Already, he could smell the burn of Trevor's flesh, could hear the echo of his comrades' screams. Try as he might, those weren't images that Fire could consume.

He needed a distraction. And he knew just how to get it.

"I have a few ideas of how you could help celebrate my victory," Aidan said.

"Oh?" Gregory asked. He cocked his head to the tent. "Maybe you could tell me in private. Or better yet…" He leaned in, pressed a hand against Aidan's thigh, sending heat coursing through his chest. "Maybe you could show me."

Aidan didn't think. He just leaned forward, closed the gap between them, and pressed his lips to Gregory's. There wasn't a spark, not like with Tomás, but he found a flame. A hunger. One that could make even Trevor's screams fade away. And when Gregory shifted and sat on Aidan's lap, straddling him in one swift motion, Aidan let Fire out to play.

CHAPTER TWENTY-ONE

"YOU'RE GOING TO LOVE IT HERE," HIS MOTHER SAID.

The plane had just touched down and Aidan wanted nothing more than to pass out and sleep for a week. Overnight flights were apparently not his forte. The four-hour layover in New York hadn't helped.

But his mum looked excitedly out the window, more energized than he'd seen her in months. Maybe years.

"I haven't been here since I was a little girl," she said, staring out at the tarmac and distant fields past Glasgow Airport. "But it's just as green as I remember."

Frankly, Aidan was already over this trip. He'd been excited in theory to get out of class, to take two weeks off and explore a foreign country. But he stared out the window at the gray and the rain, exhaustion lying heavy in his bones and a strange sickness in his chest, and he wanted nothing more than to be back in his bedroom. He was already cold, but it beat being in Vermont for the start of winter. Wait, did it snow in Scotland?

Someday, he would move somewhere tropical. Until then, he would do this because it made his mum happy. Because right now, she needed this happiness more than anything. And because this was a free trip, and she promised it would change his life, and even though he would much rather be back with his friends, he'd agreed to go. For her. This trip was for her.

He'd heard her talking to his dad in the weeks and months prior, worried that Aidan was growing distant. That this might be her last chance to reconnect with him before he got too old to want to hang out with his mom.

Just the thought made his chest clench. He stared at her as she stared out the window, tried to find some excitement, if only for her.

He'd do anything to make her happy. Because he knew that, in a few years, he would leave for college and break her heart. He knew that she already reeled from the loss of her own parents. The pain of it was almost too much to bear.

"Why did you do it?"

Aidan turned to the aisle, but he was no longer on the plane.

He was back in the throne room. Back in the room with the frozen bodies. But these weren't the nameless corpses he'd seen. No. As reality and history crashed around him, he saw them for who they were—Vincent and Jessica and Matthew and Kent. The four Hunters he'd killed at Fire's command.

They stood poised around him, ashen and frozen, but their eyes…their eyes followed him, glistening with terror, their mouths twisted in screams they couldn't shed.

And there, above the throne, was Trevor. Nailed to the wall as Calum had been.

Only Trevor was much more alive.

He struggled against the nails in his hands and his feet, and Aidan took a step forward to help him.

One step. And Matthew burst into flame beside him. The moment the fire started, Matthew was able to scream.

Another step, and Jessica went up in smoke.

Aidan took another step forward—he had to save Trevor, he had to—and Kent turned to fire.

When Vincent went up in flame, filling the hall with smoke and the terrible smell of burning flesh, Trevor screamed. "Please! Please stop. You're killing them. You're killing everyone."

The words were a lance to Aidan's chest. He looked to the burning pillars around him, to the people he had killed without pause.

"No," came a voice beside him. "You are saving them."

Aidan's heart fell to his feet at the sound of his mother's voice.

He looked over, saw her standing there at his side. Just as she'd been when he'd seen her last—her purple raincoat ripped and dirty, cuts on her hands and face. Blood caking her skin.

She didn't look sad, though. Not like when she'd forced him away from her, when she'd flung herself in front of the kravens that had threatened to rip him apart.

No. She was smiling.

That smile made his chest hurt worse than any pain he'd known.

He crumpled to his knees.

"Mom?"

She stepped in front of him, half blocking his view of

Trevor, the man still crucified and writhing. Shadows curled at her feet. Beckoning like fingers.

His mother smiled. Placed a hand on his forehead as tears rolled down his cheeks.

He blinked, and she shifted, becoming someone else—a woman with long blond hair and pale skin, a woman who seemed more shadow than flesh. Then he blinked again, and his mother was back.

Were her eyes always that dark?

Her hand was heavy on his head, her touch cold, colder than ice.

"Do not fear what you are becoming, my child," she said. "Do not mourn those who burn along the way. They are nothing. Nothing but fuel for your victory march. Nothing, compared to what you will become."

She pressed her palm harder to his forehead, and behind her, Trevor burst into flame, filling the cathedral with his screams, with the scent of burning flesh. But as her hand pushed into him, through him, he felt no pity.

No regret.

He stared up into his mother's abyssal black eyes and felt only purpose.

CHAPTER TWENTY-TWO

NOT FOR THE FIRST TIME, AIDAN WOKE CURLED against a stranger's chest.

Not for the first time, he woke with a gasp, struggling against the nightmares that tried to drag him back under. His breath burned and his skin was slicked with sweat. But the dream was fading, and nothing save for his pulse seemed to be on fire.

For a moment, he let himself lie there, let himself try to find comfort in the slow, steady rhythm of Gregory's breath against the back of his neck. At the pressure of Gregory's arm against his stomach and chest.

Then Fire smoked its way through his consciousness, reminding him that this was dangerous. This was weakness. And even though Calum was dead, Aidan could never afford to be weak again.

Before Gregory could wake up and ruin it all by talking, Aidan slipped from under the guy's arm and pulled on his clothes, then walked out of the tent. A part of him considered staying by the cooling fire, coaxing the embers back to life, but there was an anxiety in his bones that not even magic would burn out. So he kept walking. Out through the tents, toward the field beyond. A few comrades still sat around their fires, drinking or drunk, singing or asleep. Those awake nodded at him groggily when he passed, raising glasses or cheering softly. One of them raised Calum's head. Definitely not much left. Aidan smiled at them in return.

He didn't feel it.

His thoughts reeled from the dream. How long had it been since he'd dreamed of home? Of his mother? Those were two paths he never let himself tread and, thankfully, ever since he'd become attuned to Fire, his dreams had followed suit.

It's just stress, he tried to tell himself. But what did he have to be stressed about? He'd liberated Scotland. He was, for all intents and purposes, King. He just shagged a really hot guy.

For some reason, though, he couldn't shake his dream from his mind. Already, it was nearly lost to the fog of forgetting. He remembered being on the plane. He remembered watching his mother watch the plane land, the excitement on her face. And then…

He shook his head. It was already gone.

So why did it latch in his heart like a rusted hook?

He shivered and pulled deeper through Fire, wrapping himself in warmth. The rest of his doubt and dreams faded in the heat.

He passed the last tents. Kept walking. And when he was a few hundred yards away, he finally stopped. He hadn't realized he was walking straight back toward Edinburgh.

The sight of it made his breath catch.

Smoke curled from the burning castle, snaking up into the heavy gray dawn like the shades of those who'd met their end within its walls. Once more, he felt that pull in his heart, as though the castle were a part of him. As though it had always been his destiny. To come here. To triumph. To rule.

Not for the first time, he felt the twist of disgust within himself. Not for what he had done. No—he couldn't let himself think about that, couldn't let regret or doubt sneak back in—not for that, but for what the castle had become. He had wanted to rule. He had wanted a grand coronation. To ascend the throne with pomp and circumstance. To have some relic as a crown. To have a seat of power.

Instead, he was given the shell of a castle and the ruins of a country.

After all his hard work, it still wasn't enough.

It wasn't fair.

"What are you thinking?"

Aidan jumped. But before he could pull through Fire, the voice registered, and he forced the adrenaline down.

"What did I tell you about sneaking up on me?" Aidan asked, looking back to Kianna.

"That I'm damn good at it."

She stood beside him, hands in her pockets, staring up at the castle. Even though they had won, even though there was truly no threat to be seen, she still had a few weapons on her. A katana at her waist. A pistol on her thigh. Undoubtedly a few throwing knives in the inner folds of her coat. And a length of chain wrapped across her chest.

"Why do you always carry those?" he asked, even though he already knew the answer.

"Same reason you're always open to Fire."

"Because I'm addicted?" Her words. Not his.

"No. Well, in your case, yes. But in mine, because I refuse to be caught off guard." She fondled the pistol. "Besides, years ago, I named this one Kindness. So I always carry it with me."

That was a new one. Though she did always seem to have a gun on hand. He just never realized it was the same one. Or that it had a name.

"Kindness?"

"Yeah," she said. "Mum always taught me to kill my enemies with kindness. So I do."

Aidan snorted in spite of himself. "That's a terrible pun," he muttered.

"Whatever. You laughed."

Silence lingered for a moment while they watched the smoke curl. At least, Aidan tried to. The mention of Kianna's mother brought his dreams back to mind, the tiniest spark in the ashes of his thoughts. He let go of Fire, just for a moment, and let the dream smolder.

"What are you doing out here?" she asked. "And up so early, too?"

"Thinking."

"Dangerous."

He nudged her. Thankfully, she didn't nudge back.

He wondered if she remembered what she said last night. About always being there for him. He wondered if she would still mean that, if she knew what he had done.

She didn't let him wonder too long.

"I always thought that when we destroyed Calum, we'd find a way to get it back."

"What?" he asked.

She gestured to the field. "This. I dunno. Like there'd be a switch. But here we are. Day after victory and nothing's changed. Scotland's still a pile of shite."

"I'll make sure to complain to the landscapers. You sound depressed. Did you not get laid last night?"

When she did nudge him back, he stumbled to the side. Slightly.

"They were quite amazing, thank you," she said. "All three of them. But you know what I mean. I guess I wanted to believe we would wake up and it would feel different. All that's changed is that there are a few less Howls for us to kill."

He shrugged. "At least we woke up."

"Aye. I guess."

He considered telling her about his dream. But that would open a door neither of them wanted to peer through, victory or no. They didn't talk about their pasts. Ever. Hell, he barely gave himself room to *think* about his. So why was it coming up now, when he should have been elated with the promise of a future?

"So what do we do?" she asked.

"What we were trained to do," he replied. "Kill the undead."

"I never understood why we call them that. I mean, they're not raised from the dead or anything."

Aidan shrugged, remembering the vision of Calum. *One of them was, and I have to find the secret to it.* Kianna continued.

"Do you think they're going to let you back in?"

His heart stopped.

"What? Why wouldn't they?"

"Because you were exiled." As though he could have forgotten.

"I killed Calum."

"I know," she said. "But it might be difficult to convince the council that's enough. They still might see you as a threat."

Little do they know... he thought, visions of Trevor and the rest flashing through his mind. He squashed the images down.

"I've redeemed myself," he said, his words flat.

"I know, love. I'm just saying we might have a bit of difficulty convincing everyone else that." She looked over at him, and her serious expression faded into a grin. "You're going to have to be on your best arse-kissing behavior. And I know that's hard for you. Licking, however..."

He nudged her again.

"How was Gregory, anyway?" she asked. Just as nonchalant as if she were asking what he thought dinner was.

"Fine," he replied.

"That bad, huh?"

He just shrugged.

They stood there for a bit, staring out at the ruins of Edinburgh, the silence between them heavy and mostly comfortable. Aidan refused to worry about returning to Glasgow. He had worked too hard and sacrificed too much to let Trevor's sentence of exile get in the way of further victory. He'd earned his place.

Even if the rest of the country didn't know it, he *was* King. And they would learn that soon enough.

"Strange, innit?"

"What?"

"I'd thought that I'd feel more relaxed once this Calum business was over with. If anything, I feel more stressed."

"Worried someone's going to come after us?"

"Nah. I *know* that's going to happen. It's more..." She tapped her lips with a finger. "It's more like, what do we do when there's no one else to fight? Do we just live? With this?" She gestured to the field, to the ruins beyond.

He knew what she meant. He told others that he fought to rid the world of Howls, but he and Kianna, they knew the truth.

They fought because the alternative was boring.

They killed because anything less felt worse than death.

"Don't worry, love," he said, mimicking her accent. Poorly. "We'll be dead long before that happens."

"I hope you're right," she said.

Trouble was, he could tell she meant it.

So did he.

CHAPTER TWENTY-THREE

THE TROOPS MADE IT BACK TO GLASGOW THE FOL-
lowing afternoon. The slow, two-day trudge was one he
hoped he never had to repeat. If only the Howls hadn't eaten
all the damned horses. If only the necromancers hadn't destroyed the roads.

If only it hadn't started raining after the first hour, and
hadn't let up since.

Aidan had expected cheering from the amassed crowds
when they made their way through Glasgow's gate. After all,
the army would only return if victorious. There was no option for failure.

Instead, the moment the drawbridge opened and he and
his army marched into the waiting city, there was silence.

He walked at the front of the troops. Made sure everyone
within Glasgow saw him for who he truly was—a leader.
Victorious. Loved. He would have held Calum's head, but it
had "accidentally" been dropped in a fire the night before.

It didn't matter. No one was there to see it. At least, not the crowds he'd expected.

They walked past the high black walls of magically crafted stone, a heavy rain falling around them, making everything gray and black and green in the pallid light. At once, the familiar smells of the city wafted over him—the scent of baking bread, the tang of stone, the undercurrent of excrement. Above them, high on the wall, the guards left to man the city watched them pass, hands to their foreheads in salute.

But the city itself—the wide boulevard, the winding side roads that stretched up into the rolling hills of the West End— was nearly deserted.

"Not exactly the hero's welcome," Aidan muttered to Kianna.

She grunted. Watched a small child run off into a nearby building.

Was it the rain?

Normally, he'd feel his hackles rise, but the city didn't seem abandoned or off. It just seemed...blasé. They walked deeper in, making their way toward the University. The architecture here had been mostly salvaged. The long sandstone tenement flats that housed all of Glasgow's residents. The winding cobbled and concrete streets.

Just like before, the tenements facing the main road had shops on the ground floor. But they had changed drastically in the past few years, cafés and chippies and barbers giving way to more important vestiges of humanity. Like open-air grocers. Seamstresses.

And pubs.

There was still a pub on every corner, if not more. They were the only things that had truly survived and thrived post-

Resurrection. There was always a reason to drink your troubles away. And in this country, there was always a need for a warm place in which to do it.

A few civilians stared from windows as they passed, holding pints or small children before them like shields. Before, Glasgow had been fairly chic. But now, with all clothing passed down and recycled and restitched, the emphasis was on warmth rather than fashion. There were still peacoats and cardigans and hints of tartan, but they had all been layered and repurposed. And soiled.

It made Aidan's blood boil, seeing them cower within the walls that he and his troops kept safe. Acting as though he were part of the problem. Fire roared within him, told him to show them just what they should be afraid of—set a flat on fire, turn the rain to embers. The rest of him knew it wasn't personal. Commoners treated every mage like a boil-covered witch.

To the civilians, he and the rest of the Guild were a necessity, but a terrible one. Using magic, they were no better than the monsters and necromancers that prowled outside. He'd always thought that Scotland would be more receptive to magic, that maybe somewhere up in the highlands they still believed in the Fair Folk and other worlds and all the rest. But the truth was, humanity was all the same.

The people here didn't trust what they didn't understand, same as everyone else.

Which meant that even though Aidan and the rest of the troops were the only reason any of them were alive, they were regarded with the same hatred as Howls and necromancers. At least the civilians tried to keep that hatred concealed behind layers of drunkenness and fear.

Aidan made sure to look each and every person he saw in the eye. To remind them who was in power.

Who it was that paid for their new freedom in blood.

He wondered if that freedom would be enough to change the council's mind.

They cut through Kelvingrove Park, which had been converted into magically fueled greenhouses and grazing grounds. Fields of barley and hops and wheat stretched along the River Kelvin, bowing under the weight of rain, while glasshouses brimmed with vegetables. Distantly, he heard the bleating of sheep. And a bagpipe. Of bloody course. He *hated* bagpipes.

Above it all, peeking up over the few remaining trees, was the building the Guild had taken as its own: Glasgow University.

Even after everything that had happened—the buildings lost, the cities destroyed—there was a magic to the University that belied the turn of years. Its tallest tower still stretched up to the graying sky like a castle turret, as it had when Aidan first visited. Umber stone, intricate latticework in the upper windows, slate-tiled roofs. Castle-like. Majestic. Sprawling. The other University buildings might have fallen, but this one endured.

It filled him with pride just as it filled him with dread.

This had been his home. Not even a week ago, it had been torn from him. Now, like a scorned lover, he had to hope that it would accept him back.

No, Fire seethed. *You should never feel the need to grovel. It is they who should beg for forgiveness.*

He curled that confidence around himself. They would beg to have him back, and he would allow it. So long as being there served him.

CHAPTER TWENTY-FOUR

AIDAN WASN'T ALLOWED IN THE COUNCIL CHAMBER.

That was his second clue this homecoming wasn't going to plan. The lack of cheering crowds he could forgive, but this? He was forced to wait in the hall outside. The meeting took place in one of the old lecture halls, and where the exterior of Glasgow Uni was grand and archaic, the interior—here, at least—was modernized, an anachronism in its own right. Blue carpets, fluorescent lights that hadn't seen electricity in years, makeshift lantern sconces carved into the walls.

He sat on a wooden stool and stared out the window at the deepening gloom. All he could hear was the pounding rain and the occasional rumble of voices deeper in the hall.

He couldn't even try to spy. A burly guard had been stationed outside the door. The guard stared straight ahead, arms crossed at his chest and a wicked mace resting against his hip. He looked like he could crush Aidan with a single hand—and Aidan knew he could, seeing as he'd trained with Markus many times. Normally, he'd have tried to chat.

Now Aidan just sat in silence, fuming, unable to even play with Fire for fear it would be seen as a threat.

He must have been waiting for at least an hour. The sky deepened to pitch-black, and a lone Fire mage came around to light the lanterns. Even that small act of magic made his Sphere twitch and anger flare—not that he wanted to be the one lighting lamps, but he sure as hell hated that he was being told not to. He kept his Sphere slightly open in his chest, soothing it like a kicked dog, waiting for the time he could let it out to play. By the time the door opened and Kianna stormed out, he was ready to burn the whole place down from agitation.

"What did they say?" he asked, standing.

She glanced at him. She didn't stop walking.

He looked back once to the open door, hoping to see the council members, hoping to get a sense of what had happened. Kianna grabbed him by the shoulder and yanked.

"They aren't exiling me again, are they?" he asked. He'd tried to make it sound like a joke but realized the moment the words left his lips that it sounded more serious than not.

Especially since she didn't answer right away.

"Kianna—" He had to jog to keep up with her. "Kianna, they aren't exiling me. Right?"

"No." She looked back to the council chambers. Walked faster. "But also yes."

His heart dropped to his feet. He desperately itched to open to Fire, to burn off the anxiety. He held out. "What the hell does that mean?"

"It means they're letting you stay," she said, not meeting his eyes, "but they aren't letting you lead. You've been demoted." She paused. "Basically, you're a new recruit. They're assigning you to a squadron tomorrow."

It was worse than exile.

It was anonymity.

"You're shitting me," he whispered.

"I wish. I had to fight for that, too, so you can thank me later. They were going to throw you out."

"Even after all I did for them? I killed Calum. I'm the first person to kill one of the Kin! Those sorry mother—"

"Actually..."

Somehow, the way she said it made him feel like whatever she was about to deliver was worse than his demotion.

"What?"

She hesitated. Looked back to the door, though they weren't being followed.

"You weren't the first," she said. "They've had word from the Voice of the Prophets. Back in America. Someone else killed one of the Kin."

"What?" Aidan stopped dead in his tracks. His question hung in the air above them, a guillotine ready to slice through the last remaining shred of pride he had. In the back of his mind, he had thought he would always have this. They could take away his title. They could take away his home. But no one could take away his victory. His place in the halls of history as being the *first*. His name in the immortal list of deeds that had changed the world.

And yet, some prick over in America apparently had.

He didn't even realize Fire had opened within him until Kianna cocked an eyebrow at the flames twisting around his clenched fists. She didn't seem frightened. She just looked frustrated.

"Aye." Her voice was heavy with regret. "I'm sorry, Aidan. But apparently Leanna was killed over there a few days ago."

"And we're just now hearing about it?"

"In case you hadn't noticed, we don't have the internet anymore. And pigeons tend to get lost over the Atlantic."

"This isn't funny," Aidan said. His teeth ground so tight a small part of him worried about chipping a tooth. Again.

"Never said it was. But look—these are the cards we're dealt. You're allowed back into the Guild. You still killed Calum. *We* know what you've done. And everyone important knows it, too. It will filter out that you were the one who liberated Scotland. You'll still get your place in history."

He knew she was trying to make him feel better, but the truth was, she *didn't* know what he'd done. Not the half of it. Fire burned away the little voice inside saying that without this victory, he was nothing, and the lives he sacrificed to get here were sins staining his soul. Fire burned it away, but not fast enough.

"So what do you suggest we do?" He tried to force down the rage that threatened to burn over. Tried to keep himself from running out of the Guild and setting someone else on fire.

Again.

"I told them we needed to take this opportunity to cleanse Scotland," she said. "That if we hesitated, the necromancers would regroup and retaliate. So tomorrow, they're going to be sending out a few parties to scour the rest of the country. They still haven't decided what they're going to do with you.

But if it makes you feel any better—which I know it won't—
I told them I wouldn't go anywhere without you. For now,
though, we wait."

It was a punch to the gut. He'd come here to be celebrated.
To rule. And now, the best he could do was be relegated to
cleanup crew. Fire seethed. It refused for this to be the answer. Even Kianna's small offer of friendship burned up in
the inferno.

"I thought you wanted to go to Europe," he said. "Go kill
the rest of the Kin. Fuck orders and all that."

"I do." She placed a hand on his shoulder and leaned in.
For her, that meant leaning down quite a bit. "But Aidan…
we gotta play this smart. Everything is in an uproar. Two
Kin are dead, and there's rumors the guy who did it over in
America could read the runes. Maybe even create new ones."

Aidan glanced to his arm at that. He could feel the burn
of the runes against his forearm, his Hunter's mark. But he
also felt a whisper, the barest breath of memory as the runes
and sigils etched into Calum's skin drifted through his brain.
Somehow, he knew the ones on Calum were different from
the ones on his own arm. Like a different language altogether.

The marks on his arm never made sense to him, but the
ones on Calum…those, he felt, were like a language he had
read in a dream. Perceptible, but just barely.

"So?" he asked. *I can, too. Sort of.*

She studied him for a moment, her expression frustrated.
"I ain't about to give you a lesson in magic," she finally said.
"Or what it means that someone out there could make new
runes. The important thing is us. This. There are two ways
you can play this, Aidan. Either you get huffy and storm off

again and get kicked out for good, or we play it smart and bide our time." She glanced around. There was no one in the hall. Not that it meant they weren't being spied on. "Eventually they're going to want to send troops to Europe. They're excited. They think we might finally be able to start gaining back territory, and if America can send over reinforcements, we could really turn the tide."

Despite everything, a thin note of hope curled through him. "You honestly think America would send troops over here? They don't give a shit about us."

Right after the Resurrection, it had been every man for himself. No foreign aid or relief funds or marches for solidarity. The whole world had gone dark, communication cut off, transportation ended. Nothing but silence. Well, silence and the screams of the dying.

She stood and began walking down the hall. "They want this over like the rest of us. So yeah, I'd imagine that once they get themselves sorted, they'll be on their way. They have the numbers. More than we do, at least."

Aidan had written America off long ago. But if they were sending reinforcements, that might mean he could get back. He could go home.

Home.

Flashes of his mother, torn apart by Howls, and his father, waving from the airport lobby, played through his mind. He did his best to stomp them down. Along with the disappointment that none of this was going the way he'd planned.

"The council will see reason soon enough," she said. "You've led us to victory once, and they'll need that foresight again if they want to keep going. But it's going to take them time to see it, and the best way for them to *get* to see it is for you to play by their rules. For now."

He hated it. He hated that he had worked his ass off to get thrown back to the bottom. He hated that he was trapped here once more, waiting for orders to die, when a week ago he could do whatever the hell he wanted.

He hated that he had built this place, and here he was, a prisoner within its walls.

"Come on," Kianna said. "I'll take you to your room. You need sleep. Rather, *I* need sleep, and I can't deal with your whinging right now."

"I know how to get to my room."

"No. They assigned you a new one." The hint of a smirk returned to her face. "Did you forget? Your old one had fire damage."

CHAPTER TWENTY-FIVE

HIS NEW ROOM WAS DEFINITELY A DOWNGRADE.

Most of the Hunters' barracks had been hidden below-ground, the logic being that if a necromancer attacked the Guild, they'd go for the top bits first. Aidan personally thought it was stupid, and any Earth mage with half a brain would just collapse the warren of tunnels beneath the Guild and be done with it, but he hadn't been high enough in rank for his opinion to matter at that point in the planning process.

In any case, this had clearly been one of the first rooms created. The walls and floor and ceiling were all the same flat stone, melded from the earth by magic. A single lantern sat in a nook carved into the wall, and the bed was a twin.

His last room had been in an upper level, an old office. There had been an armchair and Persian rugs and heavy throws. King-size bed. A fireplace and small liquor table. Perfect for entertaining guests.

This was basically a casket with some extra leg room.

He stared up at the ceiling, freshly showered and in pajama

bottoms, Fire burning in his chest and small flames dancing through the air around him, sparkling like stars or dust motes. He didn't know how late it was and told himself it didn't matter. Nothing seemed to matter right now.

It wasn't a morose thought, honestly. It filled him with anger. He should have been on a throne right now. He should have at least had a room with a window.

For a while, he considered leaving. Just packing up his shit and going back to the flat Kianna had prepared for them. Telling the whole Guild to fuck off—he'd done his time, Scotland was free and he could do what he damn well pleased.

But Kianna was right.

If he did that, he would die of boredom. He'd killed one of the Kin. He couldn't settle for going around mopping up a few starved Howls. Where was the fun in that?

Frankly, he'd peaked. And the only way to find a new pinnacle was to head to Europe and find the next Kin. And the only way to do *that* was to have the support of the Guild. Once more, bureaucracy was a pain in the arse. Frustrate him though it did, he knew he couldn't make it over there on his own. Neither he nor Kianna knew how to sail, for one thing, and the Chunnel between England and France was collapsed. And no doubt the borders were heavily guarded, to prevent more Howls or necromancers from coming over.

Kianna was right, damn her. He needed to play it smart. Needed to bow to whatever whims the Guild had for now. If only so he could influence them later.

He would get what he wanted.

He just had to be patient.

And Fire was horrible at being patient.

After a while, he became aware that he wasn't alone in the room, but he didn't make any movements, not right away. He recognized the feeling of eyes on his body. The shift in temperature. The delightful shiver that told him he wasn't just being watched, he was being admired.

He toyed with the flares above him, made them dance over his chest, highlighting his darkened skin, the swirling tattoos, the rise and fall of his muscles. Beads of sweat pricked over his skin, but he enjoyed the heat. Just as he enjoyed the effect he knew it had on his guest.

"I was hoping you'd show up," Aidan said eventually, sending sparks dancing around his fingertips.

"I was hoping you'd be wearing less clothing," Tomás replied. He stood just behind and to the side of Aidan, against the wall and mostly out of sight. But when Aidan spoke, he stepped forward and let Aidan devour his presence.

Like Aidan, he was shirtless. Like Aidan, the firelight seemed to worship Tomás's olive skin, the peaks and valleys of his flesh, the sharp white of his smile. Unlike Aidan, he didn't seem to mind the cramped quarters.

"That can be arranged." Aidan didn't bother sitting up. Instead, he curled one arm behind his head and let the other rest over his stomach. He kept his Sphere open. Not for defense, but for effect. Proper lighting was everything.

Besides, he knew Tomás wouldn't hurt him.

It was a dumb assumption, yes. But it didn't make it any less true. Especially when Tomás smiled like that. He knew he had the Kin on a short leash. The incubus may have been created to evoke desire, but Aidan had many years of playing with Fire to know a few tricks of his own.

"What are you doing here?" Aidan asked. He cocked an eyebrow, trailed his free hand down to the waistline of his pajamas. "You don't strike me as the type of guy who just likes to watch."

Tomás chuckled. "He thinks he is so cute," he muttered. Then growled in the back of his throat. "The trouble is, he is right."

Tomás knelt at the bedside in one smooth motion, folding his arms under his chin and tilting his head to the side, staring at Aidan through thick eyelashes, his hair a beautiful tangle.

"You don't strike me as the type to watch, either. And yet here you wait, while the Guild does your dirty work." Tomás's eyes narrowed. "I didn't help you kill my brother so you could hide away and rot." There was a fierceness in Tomás's voice that made Aidan worry, just for a moment, that his assumptions of safety were wrong.

"Plans changed," Aidan said smoothly. He waved his hand and curled more flame around it, watched the threads of fire dance between his cracked knuckles.

Tomás reached out trailed his finger along the knuckles of Aidan's other hand.

"And you plan on letting them control you?" Tomás said. "Perhaps I chose the wrong man as my king. Perhaps he is not strong enough to rule."

Aidan clenched his fist and the fire turned blue. "What would you have me do?" he seethed. "I can't just incinerate them all."

Tomás reached out and took Aidan's fist. Flames spiraled around the two of them. Anyone else, the fire should have burned. But it licked against Tomás's skin without leaving a mark, and even though they were Aidan's flames, something about the way the fire curled over Tomás made him think the incubus controlled it as much as he did.

Aidan couldn't help but feel like that exchange was the most erotic thing he'd ever seen.

Tomás watched the flames dance. Then he turned his gaze back to Aidan, his expression serious.

"Who says you cannot?"

And for a moment, Aidan could see it.

He knew the weaknesses of this place, knew where one well-placed explosion could bring down a wall, or which hall to burn to snuff out the lives of the most of his brethren. He could do it. He could bring all of Glasgow down—city and Guild and all—just as he'd done with Edinburgh. In his mind's eye, he saw the Guild on fire, saw the chaos he could bring, saw himself walking through the flames...

"Yes," Tomás whispered, his voice a soothing temptation. "There is the man who would be king."

Aidan yanked his hand away and forced Fire and the dreams of its conquest into submission. He didn't let go of the Sphere, though. "I'm not killing other Hunters."

"Why not? You have before. Five times, in fact. No need to stop now."

"I'm not a monster."

Tomás's eyes narrowed, but his lips curled into a smile.

"Perhaps not like me. But in your own way..."

"I don't think you're a monster," Aidan said, the words drawn from his lips. He knew it was what Tomás wanted him to say. He found himself trapped in Tomás's gaze, those copper-flecked irises pulling him in.

"And that is why you might be one," Tomás whispered. "It is also why I like you."

Despite the heat running in his veins and the actual sparks that could set the bed ablaze, Aidan chuckled at the corny line. "You? You *like* me?" Howls didn't *like* anyone. Not even the Kin.

Right?

Tomás's other hand reached over and gently caressed Aidan's cheek. "I like you very much," Tomás whispered, his eyes flickering from Aidan's eyes, across his face and down his chest. "In a way...in a way you remind me of myself. The passion. The anger. The lust for power."

"That's not all I lust for," Aidan said. And drew his free hand up along Tomás's naked torso, resting it on Tomás's face. Tomás practically purred at the touch, and the intensity of being this close had narrowed Aidan's focus to acquiring only one thing.

But when he pulled Tomás's head toward his, the incubus broke away.

In a flash, he stood back against the shadows of the wall. Aidan wondered if he might be the only man in history to be turned down by a literal sex demon.

"No, no, not yet," Tomás said. His voice was breathy, his chest heaving. He ran a hand through his hair, staring at Aidan all the while with a mix of desire and confusion. "You are an interesting one, my king. For you, I think, I would burn down the world."

Aidan pushed himself to sitting. Tomás seemed to be wrestling with himself, and Aidan enjoyed watching the struggle.

"I've already done the same for you," Aidan said.

"He has, yes. But he must prove himself again."

"How am I supposed to prove myself when I'm locked up here?" Aidan asked, gesturing to the walls around him. "I'm not going to kill my own Guild, no matter what you offer. I can't exactly just run off to find your brother's shard when I don't know where it is. I don't work for you."

Tomás smiled. Aidan had thought the statement would set him off, but if anything, the Kin seemed to like it. "I know, my king. You are in control. You are always in control. But there is much you must yet do. My brother was but the first—"

"No, he wasn't," Aidan said. He sat up straighter. "Another one of you was killed. Leanna."

He hadn't known if he would bring it up with Tomás, but the moment the words left his lips, he knew it was the right—and wrong—thing to say. A dozen different emotions seemed to burn behind Tomás's copper-flecked eyes. Chief among them: regret.

"How did you know?" Tomás asked quietly.

Aidan shrugged. "Prophets. Sometimes we get word from the temple in America for big things. Like losing the Kin that ruled the country." He leaned forward. "Why didn't you tell me?"

"Because," Tomás said. "You should have been the first to feel that victory. The blood of a Kin on your hands. The taste of immortality. You deserved it more."

"More than who?"

Aidan could tell he had Tomás trapped then, and it filled him with a sort of power, one he hadn't felt when he killed Calum. Now he felt in control.

"Who killed Leanna?" Aidan pressed. His eyes narrowed. "Or did you do it? Like you did with Calum?"

The room grew cold, yet sweat dripped from Aidan's skin.

"I did not kill my sister," Tomás whispered. "Nor did I kill my brother. I merely made them ready. Presented them. To those who needed to secure their place in history."

"Who?"

"His name is Tenn. And if you are not careful, he will come and kill you, too." Tomás knelt at Aidan's side, took his hand. "We cannot let that happen," Tomás whispered. "I couldn't bear losing you. My prince. My king. That is why you must trust me. Why you must secure your power here. For when Tenn comes for you, he will surely try to kill you."

"I won't let that happen," Aidan said. Leaned in closer.

"Nor will I," Tomás replied. He reached out, gently cupped the side of Aidan's face. Aidan curled against the hot and cold of the Kin's palm. "While you rest, I am seeking the heart of my brother's power. The shard that pulled him from the grave. When I find it, I will send you for it. And when you hold the secret of his resurrection in your hands, even death will cower at your feet. Then, and only then, will you secure your place in history."

Tomás's breath was hot against Aidan's lips. Aidan could see it, could *feel* it—the power of immortality, the spark of life he could snuff or enflame.

"And the boy?"

"Means nothing, in the end. Not compared to you, my king. Nothing compared to you."

Aidan leaned forward. Pressed his lips to Tomás's. His vision exploded in heat and desire.

But a second later, the Kin was gone.

CHAPTER TWENTY-SIX

IT PISSED RAIN, BUT NEVERTHELESS, HIS MOTHER
wanted to see the Isle of Skye.

They'd taken the ferry over. Even though there was a perfectly
good bridge. His mother said this was part of the experience.

Apparently, the experience she wanted to have was patting
his back for half an hour while he vomited over the side rail.

In the rain.

In December.

By the time they reached Armadale, Aidan was colder and
more miserable than he'd been in his entire life. Less than four
days in this country, and he wanted to go back to Vermont.
Not something he ever thought he'd crave.

He wanted to say the island was beautiful. Something about
the rows of houses and winding cobbled roads and gnarled
trees made him think of home. Not that Vermont had the
tenement flats, and the hills in Vermont were more mountains, but something about the smell triggered memories. The
wet earth and decaying leaves. The fresh rain.

Or maybe it just reminded him of home because he was finally on dry—ish—land.

They were safely in their B&B. Aidan had showered and put on warm clothes. His mother was reading a guide book by the window, and when he looked at her, his heart ached. Every single second she was in this country, she appeared younger. He felt the opposite, but it was nice to see her feeling better. It had been a hell year for her—her mum had passed away of cancer earlier that year, and her dad of a broken heart a few months after.

It didn't help that magic was discovered a week or so after her mom's death.

Magic could have saved her. Both of them.

It just hadn't been fast enough.

Aidan and his dad had put the trip together for the two of them. A way to get Aidan's mum away from everything. And a way to get Aidan and her to reconnect.

Seeing as he'd just spent the last thirty minutes vomiting in front of her, it seemed to be going swimmingly.

At least she got to mother him again, something she often said she missed being able to do now that he thought he was too old for it.

"What do you feel like doing first?" she asked.

"Staying dry," Aidan said. He flopped down on his tiny bed and wrapped his arms around his knees. Everything in this country seemed miniature—the tiny rooms and tiny beds and tiny tea sets. Outside, rain kept pouring down. Didn't the sky ever run out of water?

His mother looked at him and smiled sadly. "Oh, come

on, Aidan. It's just a little rain. Besides, everything we have is waterproof."

"I hate being cold," he replied. "And *waterproof* is an over-statement." His coat and pants were currently draped over the heater, though whether they were drying or just making the windows fog was up for debate.

"Why don't we go for a hike?" she asked, as though she hadn't heard his complaint. She'd gotten really good at ignoring them over the last few years. "You can wear my extra sweater. And then we can come back and have hot chocolate."

"I'd rather just watch TV. You know, British television is so fascinating."

He made his voice as deadpan as possible. And he hated himself for it. A tiny voice inside of him was screaming to stop being an asshole, to stop adding to her pain, but he couldn't control himself. That part of him *wanted* to go out and hike with her. It wanted to connect, to talk about his boyfriend and what he wanted to do with his life and daydream about the future.

Instead, he grabbed the remote and turned on the TV.

He hated himself for it.

Hated himself.

Especially when she sighed and put her guidebook down.

"Well, I'm not going to waste what little daylight we have sitting in here," his mum said. "I can watch TV at home."

She stood from the alcove and began putting on her layers. Slowly. He watched from the corner of his eye. Knew he should turn off the TV and give in and go with her. But it was like every second that ticked by was a grain of salt in the wound, a rub against his pride. If he had agreed earlier, he could have gone. But he'd put it off too long and now he couldn't let himself change his mind.

She sighed a lot.

Every time he hated himself more.

"Okay, well," she said. She stood by the door. Looked at him sadly. "You sure you don't want to come along? Just a little walk. Maybe go see some sheep. Baaaah."

He just shook his head. Ignored her hopeful grin at making the sheep noise.

"Okay," she said again. Shuffled about. Pulled her hood up over her long black hair. "I'll be off then. I'll bring you a hot cocoa on my way back. Would you like that?"

He shrugged.

Fuck, you ass! Why are you being like this?

"Okay. Bye then."

He didn't watch her go.

But when the door latched behind her, he jumped from the bed and went to the window. A minute later, she stepped outside into the rain, her back turned to the B&B, and walked up the cobbled road beneath the dead trees. He watched her go, a purple smudge against the rain. And when she was out of sight, he thudded his head against the window frame, hating himself for doing this. Again.

That was the point of this trip. To make him stop being a selfish ass. To reconnect. To stop pushing everyone away.

Tears welled up in the corners of his eyes, and not from the pain.

He could still jump into his rain gear and run outside to catch her. He could still make this right.

But he wouldn't.

Because he was a coward.

Because he was an asshole.

He deserved for his heart to hurt like this. But she didn't. He wasn't supposed to be hurting her. Just himself. He was the only one who deserved it.

"Damn you," he whispered to himself. That, and a dozen other horrible things. Not one of them made him go and put his boots on. Not one of them would push him from this room.

He knew it. And he hated himself more for it.

No.

No, he could change this. He had to.

He turned from the window to go put on his boots, to run out and say he was sorry, to go join her for an evening of staring at sheep and laughing and drinking hot chocolate in some little café somewhere.

And there, standing between him and the door, was a woman.

Not just any woman. But *her*.

She stood there, wearing a long black dress that seemed sewn from shadows, her blond hair spilling across her back and shoulders like moonlight through poisonous smog.

"I wouldn't go out there, were I you," she said. Her voice was a hook against his heart.

He heard it, and he knew he would follow.

"You know what you will find outside that door if you go," she continued. Took a step forward.

And he knew. He knew, because this was a dream, and he had already lived this. He knew he would try to make things right—he would put on his shoes and run out the door and it would be raining but he would find her. He would find her in her silly purple parka beside a field watching the sheep and when she saw him, she would smile. Then something would flicker in the field. Something fast—something from a nightmare. The sheep would scream and bleat and run, and she would look between him and the monsters approaching on the field, creatures neither of them had seen before, and she would know. Somehow, she would know. Mother's intuition. And she would scream at him to run.

Run, as she ran the opposite direction. Away from him. Toward the monsters in the field.

He would scream after her.

He would watch as the monsters overcame her, as her screams for him to flee turned into something else.

And he would hate himself. But he would run.

From her. As she died to save him.

"I could save her," the Dark Lady said, pulling him from his memories.

"Save her?" He couldn't save her. He couldn't save anyone. That wasn't what he was good at. He was only good at hurting. At destroying. At killing.

After he'd watched his mother sacrifice herself for him—something he would and could never have done for someone else—he had turned to that. To doing only that.

He wasn't here to save. He was only here to ruin.

"Yes," the Dark Lady said. Closer now, so close she could reach out and touch his face. "I am the ruler of Death, my child. And those who worship at my feet need never fear Death's cold embrace."

"She's gone. She's already dead." The words fell too easily from his lips. Heartless. Heartless. He was always heartless.

"No, my child. She waits here. In my embrace." She brought Aidan's hand to her heart.

Her dress changed in that movement, rippled out to become a purple poncho, slick with rain, and then he was staring into his mother's eyes, and had she not been holding his hand, he would have crumpled.

"Mum?"

His mother smiled. Nodded.

Then her eyes widened in fear, and between one blink and the next, she was gone, replaced by the woman in shadow.

"Serve me," the Dark Lady said. "Help me return, and I will return her to you. Whole. I will help you mend the relationship you wish you'd always had."

There should have been a voice telling him not to. There should have been a whisper in his heart that this was wrong, so wrong. This was the Dark Lady, the woman who'd created the Howls and bastardized magic and destroyed the world.

This was the Dark Lady, and in this moment, she was the only one who could give him what his heart truly wanted.

"Promise me," he whispered. "Promise me you'll bring her back. Promise me she'll be whole."

"I promise, my child." She reached out, stroked the side of his face. It felt like his mother's hand, her warmth, that small tremble of love. "I will give you everything. All you need do is serve."

"Then I'll serve you," he whispered. He felt something coil through his heart, binding as iron. "If it gets my mother back, I'll do whatever you want."

She smiled. Patted his cheek lightly.

"I know," she replied.

Then, before he could ask what she meant, she—and the dream—were gone.

CHAPTER TWENTY-SEVEN

AIDAN EXPECTED LIFE TO FEEL DIFFERENT.

He thought he would wake up to a sunny sky and birds in the trees and a cheerfulness in the streets. Instead, he woke up to Kianna barging in with a tray of tea and a scowl. "I have good news and bad news."

"Good morning to you, too," he muttered. He pulled through Fire and lit the one lantern in his room. Whatever he'd been dreaming faded in that movement, burning away with reality. All he knew was that it felt important. All he knew was that it made him feel like shit, and he was more than happy to forget it.

"Which do you want first?"

"Tea," he responded.

She snorted and set the tray on his bed. "Who says that wasn't the good news?"

"Tea is never good news," he replied. "Because it means there isn't coffee."

"Americans," she muttered. She flopped down on the bed

beside the tea tray. There were biscuits on it, as well. Damn. Maybe this *was* the good news.

"Okay, shoot. What's the good news?"

"Good news is, we've been stationed together."

"You're certain that's not the bad news?" He tried to grin; he knew, however, that that was the type of joke she would usually make. The fact that she hadn't put him on edge.

"The bad news is that they're keeping us here."

"What?"

"They say it's because we've earned a break," she said, rolling her eyes. "Truth is, I can tell they don't trust us out there. Well, *you*. I don't run the risk of immolating my troop mates."

For a brief moment, he worried they had found out. That the Prophets in all their erratic wisdom had seen what he'd done to Trevor and the rest. But no. He reminded himself this was still about Vincent. He was still being punished for the lesser of his sins.

"I can't just sit around while everyone else fights for us," Aidan said. Even now, with Fire a low hum in his veins, he felt the pull. The draw to kill, to screw, to burn.

"I know," she replied. "But I've put word in that we want to be deployed as soon as possible. Hopefully, in a few days, they'll realize you aren't going to burn down everything around you, and we'll be free to go. Just…don't burn down everything around you, okay?"

"I make no promises," he muttered.

Honestly, he kind of meant it.

The next few days passed by in a blur. Without the thrill of battle to tell the time, Aidan's life condensed to great swathes of gray. The empty black of morning in his windowless room. The dull tint of his tea. The endless rain while he and Kianna trained in the courtyard. She wouldn't let him use magic in those training sessions. She never did. Said he needed to rely on more than the Spheres to survive. He hated it. Mostly because she kicked his ass every time.

At night, they would take their dinners in the corners of the mess hall, discussing all the boring drudgery Aidan was glad he got to skip. Kianna didn't like anyone, which meant everyone tried to get on her good side with gossip and rumors. Of which there were plenty. Reports from up north of the smaller Guilds rallying. Reports of a small Guild in the Hebrides that had been overthrown and burned to the ground by the Church.

Reports of movement in the south. Of Churches attracting more followers.

After all, the Kin in Britain had been killed. A servant of the Dark Lady was dead. To the zealots, that meant the time was ripe to kill the rest of them, Hunters and Howls alike.

Once more, Aidan was smug in having had the foresight to kick them out of Glasgow before they could be a true threat. If he ever saw a Sept, he would feel no shame in burning it to the ground.

Hopefully, though, he would never have to.

It wasn't the never-ending cold or rain or rumors that got to him, however. If he cared to admit it, it was the lack of Tomás. After all the promises of power, he hadn't seen a hint of the incubus since that first night. He was starting to think it had all been in his head. The silence. The fact that nothing had changed. At least, not for the better.

He watched the Guild slowly expand. On the fourth day, when the surrounding countryside was definitively cleared of the Dark Lady's forces, the gates of Glasgow were opened. At least during the day. People were allowed to return to their old lives, to find their old homes. What was left of them.

Perhaps to the surprise of no one, very few people actually left the city. There was still too much risk. From the wall that kept everyone safe, Aidan watched the drawbridge open and the dozen or so civilians walk cautiously out. Some carried bundles, as if they'd hoped to discover their old homes were intact, and settling back into their life would be easy.

No one had been let outside the walls since Glasgow had been barricaded. Not necessarily just for the protection of the civilians—unarmed humans meant easy prey, which meant a greater draw for wandering Howls or necromancers out to convert. Which meant no one truly knew the extent of the damage in the world beyond, save the Hunters who died to keep it safe. Soon they'd all learn the truth. There was nothing to go back to. Nothing to repair. They would need to start from the ground up, and it would be a long time before they managed to return to the world they'd left behind. If ever.

Anger churned in Aidan's gut.

How fitting, that—after Calum's death—the civilians were allowed to go free, and here he sat, barricaded, waiting for someone else to decide when he was allowed to go back into the world he alone had liberated.

"It's not fair," he muttered to himself.

Fire burned in his chest. Guiding him forward, ever forward. He stared out to the east, to where Edinburgh probably still smoked. To the throne that should have been his.

Kianna told him to wait. To bide his time. Patience wasn't his virtue.

If it was true that someone had killed Leanna, he had to work harder to secure his place in history. He had to find that stupid shard Tomás had mentioned. Because as he waited here, that prick back in America was still making waves. And Aidan had no doubt that soon, he would land here.

Aidan refused to share his country with someone like that. Aidan refused to let anyone else believe they were his equal.

"I have found it."

Aidan jolted. Looked over to see Tomás standing beside him. The incubus radiated heat, and it made Aidan wonder which of his troop mates or civilians would be found frozen later that evening, but he didn't have the heart to care who Tomás had fed on. Not really.

With Tomás at his side, it was hard to care about anything but power.

"Found what?" Aidan's heart raced and his breath caught. He didn't try to hide it, though—Tomás knew the effect he had on him. Aidan fully intended to use that observation to his advantage.

"The shard."

It sounded so funny, the way Tomás said it, like this was some magical quest and not a fight for survival.

"Why do you need it?" Aidan asked. The last few days had made him doubt everything. Some mystical shard that could bring back the dead was top among them.

"I don't. But you do." He took a step closer. "I know what lies in your heart, Aidan Belmont. I know you wish to rule, to burn the world down. But to do so, you will need more strength than you currently have."

Aidan bristled with the statement. "I'm strong enough," he said. "I killed Calum."

"With *my* help," Tomás reminded him. "But I may not always be at your side to assist." He leaned in, whispered in to Aidan's ear. "Besides, my king, I *want* you to grow in power. I want to see what you can do when you truly take control."

"I have no problem taking control," Aidan said.

Tomás purred in the back of his throat. A second later, he stood a few feet away, and Aidan's hand clasped thin air.

"Perhaps not," Tomás said, head cocked to the side. "But you still are not the man you could be. The shard holds more than power, my prince. It holds secrets. Secrets that could prove very useful for us in the months to come."

"What sort of secrets?"

Tomás chuckled, burning away the hints of the dream that tried to surface in Aidan's mind. "If I told you that, they wouldn't be secrets, now, would they?"

Another second, and then Tomás was at Aidan's back again. This time the Howl's hand was around Aidan's throat, the other pinning Aidan's arms behind him. Pain lanced through Aidan's shoulders.

"This is not a negotiation," Tomás growled into his ear. "I handed you Calum, and now you will do as I wish. I could threaten those you love. I could promise to rip your whole world away. But I know what scares you most, Aidan Belmont. I know I need only promise you a lifetime of *this*, and you will bend to my will. And that is the future you will have without my blessing. Get. Me. The. Shard. Or I promise you, no one will ever remember your name."

"I thought I was your king," Aidan grunted, his lungs hot.

"Kings can be replaced. Tenn may not be my first choice, but he will do should you fail me."

Aidan choked as Tomás's grip tightened.

"Get me the shard."

Then Tomás was once more a few feet away. Aidan tried not to stagger, not to collapse. The incubus was too strong. But he would find a way to make himself stronger.

"Where is it?"

"London," Tomás said. He smiled wickedly. "Good luck."

Then, with a flicker of Air, the Howl was gone.

Aidan let himself lean against the wall. Stared down at the peasants below. The ants. Tomás's words rippled through his mind.

He would never be like one of them. He would never be common.

He would be remembered.

And if that meant getting a stupid crystal, so be it. London was the biggest Guild in the UK. All he had to do was walk in there and ask for it.

In a small corner of his mind, he wondered why Tomás hadn't done something similar. Clearly, the man had no problem appearing wherever he pleased.

Whatever. He needed a reason to leave.

"I'm coming for you," he whispered to the three remaining Kin. "For all of you."

And Tomás? But that wasn't a question he had an answer

for. Not yet. Not until he knew whether he wanted to screw the incubus or rip him apart.

Then he thought of Leanna. Of Tenn. The boy who thought he could usurp Aidan's place in history.

He wasn't about to let that prick steal his thunder. *He* was the ruler. *He* was the one for whom the world would kneel.

And if Tenn decided to get in his way, well… Aidan would kill him, too.

CHAPTER TWENTY-EIGHT

HE DIDN'T SEE KIANNA UNTIL AFTER DINNER.

She had been in meetings all day, apparently, and since he wasn't being informed of what was going on, he couldn't imagine the meetings were good. All he knew was that two thirds of the Guild had been deployed, some north, the rest south to alert the Guild in London of their success and help in the eradication of any remaining Howls.

He knew, because he'd watched the troops march while he had been stationed inside. He'd trained most of those warriors.

The hypocrisy made him sick.

He wandered down the hall that led to Kianna's room. She lived in an aboveground room just like he once had. Though she had made sure to request one not by his; apparently he was too loud when he had boys over. Outside the hall windows, the sky was dark and flooded with rain, only the occasional flares of light from passing Hunters or civilians breaking the gloom. It was easy to imagine that the rest of humanity had just broken away and sunk into the abyss, leaving only this: the rain and the cold and the dark.

The very elements he felt he would spend his entire life fighting back against. Vainly.

He stared out, saw his reflection staring back. Blinked.

And he wasn't alone in the hall. A woman stood behind him, her pale hair glowing in her own unearthly light, her lips dark red with spilt blood, her hand on his shoulder, claiming him…

Aidan turned, but there was no one there. Just the closed door to Kianna's room and the frantic thud of his heart in his rib cage.

Just like that, his dreams spilled back into consciousness. Him and his mother in the field. The frantic cries of the sheep and her own mangled screams as the kravens tore her apart.

And then the Dark Lady. Promising him she would grant more than power. Swearing she could bring Aidan's mother back from the dead.

The thought was a jagged shard to his chest.

He could have her back. He could right his wrongs.

But just as quickly as the hope flared, it burned to a crisp as Fire's harsh embrace enveloped it. Even though he'd seen the Dark Lady resurrect Calum, even though he'd seen life after death, he couldn't let himself believe it was possible. Couldn't let himself believe anything the Dark Lady said was true. She was the shadow, the lie. If he let himself think *she* could help him, he'd be no better than the necromancers.

Besides, there wasn't anything of his mother to bring back. Calum had been whole. Prepared.

The thought sickened him, and so did Fire's anger. He had

almost let himself be weak. Had almost let himself get tricked into following the Dark Lady. He wouldn't be so stupid.

He was going to get the shard not for her, not for Tomás, but for himself. He would unlock its secrets, and he would keep every single one of them for himself. He would harness its power and more, until he had the whole world begging for forgiveness. Including the Dark Lady and all her minions. She had cost him everything. He would never let himself think that she could bring it back.

He knocked on Kianna's door. It wasn't latched, and opened slightly after the first knock. He peered through, wondering if she had left or…

"Are you a perv or did you just forget how doors work?" Kianna asked, her voice flat.

Aidan fought down the blush and pushed the door open.

Kianna sat at a desk inside, back facing him, the room lit by a few oil lamps and a fire roaring in the hearth. It was warm and comforting despite the wind and rain crashing against the large windows. But the heat didn't stop his blood from going cold the moment he saw what she was doing.

"Shut the door, will ya?" Kianna said, not looking toward him. "I swear to Christ you were raised in a bloody barn."

Aidan did so, but he didn't look back at the door. His stare was transfixed on the great wooden desk before Kianna, on the rows and rows of bullets set up in perfect lines, glinting silver soldiers in the lamplight.

Silver, save for the ones dripping crimson.

"Kianna, what are you—"

But he knew perfectly well what she was doing. Her arm raised over the desk, slowly dripping blood from a fresh slit in her forearm. Imbuing the bullets with her blood. Ensuring no necromancer could turn them against her.

She was preparing for war.

Her eyes flickered to him before she looked back to her work. "Already did 'em once," she muttered. "But I like a second coat for good luck."

He stepped into the room. Tried to seem nonchalant as he plopped down on her unmade bed—a king. Nicer even than his old one.

Truth be told, even though he knew she had to imbue her weapons and bullets with blood—seeing as she didn't use the Spheres to keep them bound to her—he'd never caught her in the act. She was highly secretive. About everything.

"Looks like spreading kindness requires a big sacrifice," he said, nodding to her pistol.

"That was a stretch," she said. "I hope you weren't working on that one long."

He grunted.

"Put the kettle on, would you?" she asked. "I'm always a bit woozy after this."

He watched the blood drip down her arm, transfixed by the red as it glinted warmly in the lamplight. So transfixed that she had to ask him a second time. He shook his head and went to the hearth, then hung the filled copper kettle from a hook over the fire. He didn't bother mentioning he could boil the water with magic. She had refused that offer a hundred times in the past. Said she could taste magic in the water. That it spoiled tea, just like it spoiled everything else.

"They say this is older than magic," Kianna whispered, watching the blood drip down her forearm. Her voice filled his head like amber. Crimson blood. Honeyed words. "Blood magic. The power of sacrifice, of offering. They say that when we offer our flesh to the gods, the gods grant us immortality." She scoffed. "Rubbish. I don't offer anything. I just know it works."

It was about as close to esoteric talk as she'd ever come, and when she reached over to grab a wet rag from a bucket steaming with the scent of herbs, he knew it was the last.

"Gaining immortality, though..." she continued. She looked back to him. "That's something I think I've finally gotten sorted."

"What do you mean?"

"There's a problem," she said. "But I think we can make it an opportunity."

"What's the problem?"

"London isn't responding."

His blood went cold as Tomás's smirk cut through his thoughts. *Good luck.* What had the Kin known? "What?"

Despite the direness of her words, she seemed nonchalant about it all as she wrapped the rag around her forearm and used her teeth to tie it tight. Her movements were well practiced. He couldn't even imagine the number of times she'd done it. And without letting an Earth mage heal her after...

"The troops that left...none of them have returned."

It was general protocol—whenever troops were deployed, at least one Air mage was sent back to report to the main Guild once the destination was reached, to give updates or ask for reinforcements. Short-wave radio was too easily intercepted and didn't reach that far anyway. As the mage flies, London should have been a short return trip.

"What do you think it means?" he asked.

"Either they got lost on the Underground, or the Guild's been jeopardized."

"And what do our overlords want to do about it?"

She chuckled. "You used to be an overlord."

"And I relished in it." He leaned forward. "Please tell me you convinced them to let us go investigate."

Her lips twitched into a grin. "I didn't fight my way up through layers of British bureaucracy without learning how to get what I want." She gestured to the bullets. "Thus, the arsenal. They're sending us out tomorrow morning. Low-key operation. Small command."

"Speaking of command—"

"No such luck. You'll be taking orders from me, wee man."

He slumped back. He tried to convince himself it didn't matter—he was still getting out to the field and down to London. Once he got the shard, the rulings of the Glasgow council wouldn't matter anymore. He just had to be patient. Which was never a virtue he held dear.

Kianna stood and pulled the kettle from the stove, muttering to herself about how Americans sucked at making tea, then poured the steaming water into a teapot.

"I thought you'd be more excited," she said. She set the kettle back by the hearth.

"I am," he said. He pushed through Fire, just enough so he could truly mean it. "I was starting to go crazy."

"You were already there," she said. Looked down at her bandage. Red seeped through the cloth. "Damn it. Cut deeper than I thought." She reached over and grabbed a fresh bandage—

dry this time. He watched with morbid fascination as she redid her work.

"Why do you do this to yourself?" he asked.

He hadn't actually meant to voice the words floating through his head, words he'd thought countless times before. Why not let someone heal her? Why not get attuned? Why live in this world of magic and monsters and intentionally deny yourself the best part of it?

Without magic, Aidan couldn't see much point to life. So where had her drive come from?

He hadn't meant to ask it, and he hadn't expected her to answer. She never had in the past.

"Because magic makes everything worse." She glanced up to him. Then her eyes flickered to the bullets. "And I'm already bathed in blood. Might as well use what I'm used to."

He didn't press her for more. He'd tried, once, when they met at the abandoned hostel up north. He'd tried, and she'd nearly walked out the door on him, leaving him to die, without magic and without family, by Loch Lomond.

He'd come to her without any more tears to shed, and she had at least given him the dignity of never asking why that was.

"My parents were killed a few days before the Resurrection," she said. Her words were heavy. Thick as the blood congealing on her workbench. "By magic."

"I'm sorry," he said. Necromancers had taken so many, it was almost like saying your family member had died of cancer. Common, but no less heartbreaking.

"It's not what you're thinking." She stared at the bloody rag in her hand, and he knew that she wasn't seeing the cloth. "It wasn't a necromancer. And we didn't know about the Howls yet. No. This was some dumbass, high on power, and we were in the wrong place at the wrong time."

She glanced at him before looking away. For the first time in the years that he'd known her, she actually looked lost.

"That's the worst of it, you know? They didn't die because of monsters. They didn't die because of evil, or a war, or anything that we fight against. They died become some arsehole wanted them to die. I watched them go up in flames," she said. "By the time I was able to snap the bastard's neck, my family was dead."

She sniffed. Tossed the wet rag into the flames, where it hissed and steamed and filled the room with smoke that reminded him way too strongly of Trevor and Vincent's burning bodies.

"That's why I don't use magic. Magic stole my parents away from me, and my strength was the only thing that kept me alive after. If I had known better, if I had thought myself strong in the face of magic, I would have saved them. Now I know—even magic is no match against me. And I plan on keeping it that way."

The rags hissed. She sipped her tea.

"I'm sorry," Aidan said again. This time, it sounded more like he meant it.

"Don't be," she said. "Sadness doesn't change anything. Just makes you slow."

He sat there in silence, watching her drink, watching the flames crackle, not knowing if he should comfort her or leave.

"I know what you did in there," she said.

"What?"

His attention snapped right back to her. But there wasn't the slightest hint of mockery or threat on her face.

"I know you killed them. I heard Trevor begging you, when I was coming to."

"I don't know—"

"Playing stupid doesn't suit you," she said. "Neither does playing weak."

Her eyes bored holes through his heart, and he had no idea what to say.

"I'm not telling you my life history because I want to share a good sob story. I'm telling you because I worry about you. Good people can do terrible things, Aidan. Often when they think their motives are altruistic. You're a bastard, but you're a good person. Don't let anything burn that away."

It didn't sound like she was threatening him, but that didn't make him feel any better.

She knew.

"What did you see?" he asked. Did she know about Tomás as well? Were all his secrets hidden behind her eyes? Fire had winked out long ago, and now his heart hammered somewhere deep in his gut.

"Nothing," she replied. "I didn't wake up until you grabbed me. But I had heard things. Screaming. Begging. Took a few days for it to come together, and you owe me for some really shite dreams."

"I don't—"

"Then don't," she said. Her next words were low, but razor sharp. "I will trust that you did what had to be done. But I swear to every god listening, Aidan Belmont, if you ever turn

on me, I will put a bullet between your eyes before you so
much as make a spark."

He swallowed. Hard.

"Good," she said cheerily, leaning back in her chair as
though she hadn't just threatened his life. "I need to rest, and
so do you. We leave at first light."

He stood awkwardly, torn between interrogating her and
running straight out the Guild and never stopping. He settled
for just nodding and turning for the door.

"Sweet dreams," she said.

She sounded like she meant it.

By the next morning, Aidan was going mental with frustration.

He hadn't been able to sleep. Not after that. Kianna knew
he had killed Trevor. She knew Fire had taken over once
more—or, worse, that it hadn't, and Aidan had killed his former lover in cold blood. He lay there all night, staring at the
black ceiling, for the first time in his life not wanting to open
to Fire to ease away the darkness and the cold.

For the first time, Fire and passion scared him.

Had he been acting solely under its spell?

Was he a threat to the ones he loved?

Without the flame whispering that he was safe, that everyone was safe so long as they didn't get in the way, he couldn't
be sure.

But a small voice inside of him—one that had been silenced
years ago, one that sounded way too much like his old Sun-
day school teacher—whispered that he was getting exactly
what he'd earned. For some reason, the flier he'd seen in the

Underground flickered through his mind again. *All sinners burn*. Just the thought made him shudder. He didn't put any faith in faith, but that didn't mean the rhetoric didn't resonate.

If there was a god, he hoped he never met them. For everything he'd done, there was no way in hell he'd go anywhere but, well, Hell. He closed his eyes and tried to convince himself it was all rubbish. Even though he was hearing the words of a figure most people thought of as a god.

Even though he had been told outright he could become one himself.

Kianna knocked on his door after what felt like days, bearing a pot of tea and some warm biscuits. He had been dressed and ready since lying down.

"We leave in an hour. Gear up." She set the tea on the tiny-ass bedside table and left. No mention of their conversation hours ago. No further threats for him to be on his best behavior. And he knew then, like all other things in their past, this was dead and behind them.

He opened to Fire and burned the last shreds of his doubt away. He was fed and out the door in moments.

Their small troop assembled in the cloisters. When he'd first visited the University, he'd thought the passage looked straight out of Harry Potter—a covered hall between court-yards and buildings, supported by columns that stretched up to arched domes like miniature cathedrals. Back then, students raced between the pillars to their next class, or chatted on benches in the green courtyard beyond. Now, the cloisters were filled with racked weapons and the clangs of sparring Hunters. Frankly, he thought the metallic din of war suited the space much better.

His small team—no, *Kianna's* team—waited impatiently at the edge, staring out at the misting rain. Only three others, total. An Earth and Air mage named Margaret who had a bow and sword strapped to her back. Kianna.

And Gregory.

The guy turned around the moment Aidan laid eyes on him. Shite.

Aidan had a rule: never serve at the side of someone you're screwing. It was fine when he was a commander. The power dynamic always worked in his favor—he could be aloof and pull strings from afar. But to serve side by side...that felt like a recipe for disaster.

And by disaster, he meant emotion. Mostly grief.

It didn't help that when Gregory spotted him, the guy smiled. And not one of those cocky *oh it's you* smiles, but a genuine *I'm happy you're here and maybe I even volunteered to do this because I'm secretly in love with you* smile. At least he didn't try to muck things up further with small talk.

Aidan didn't meet Margaret's eye. The last time they'd worked together, he'd been in charge. At least she had the decency to nod in a sort of half bow.

"Fancy seeing you on this mission," Gregory said, effectively dropping from Aidan's graces. Small talk was his biggest pet peeve. "Didn't think I'd see you again. After you ghosted me and all."

Aidan knew the correct response was some sort of apology or lie. But it was early and he hadn't slept and he wanted to start killing things ASAP so he could finally make his situation bearable. "Aye, well, I was drunk and you were available." He looked over at Gregory, just enough to see that his words hit home. "Don't take it personal."

Then, before Gregory could respond, Aidan grabbed one of Kianna's duffel bags and headed for the drawbridge.

Less than a minute in, and this mission was already going to shit.

CHAPTER TWENTY-NINE

THE LAST THING AIDAN WANTED WAS TO WALK THE entire way to London. Thankfully, he didn't have to.

The Guild had maintained a few small electric SUVs, though they were rarely used—the vehicles could go over a fair bit of terrain, sure, but there was something to be said about riding into battle in a tiny metal box that could, at any time, be collapsed in on itself by a necromancer. That was another problem with vehicles, from planes to tanks to submarines. All it would take is one Earth mage, and you'd be screwed.

This time, though, there was little chance of that. And, with electricity being just a manifestation of Fire energy, Aidan was like a walking battery. He could keep the vehicle going for days.

It still wouldn't necessarily make the much trip faster—without cleared highways, there would be a lot of off-roading and detours—but it saved them from walking all the way to

London. The thought of that made Aidan's legs ache. One day, he would attune to Air so he could fly. One day.

The vehicle was pretty average—a boxy mini-SUV that was still smaller than a sedan back in America. Dark green. Battered to hell. Missing a headlight. It wasn't some apocalypse-chic murder machine. No monstrous grill or spikes or flamethrowers because, again, pretty pointless against magic. But it would get them there. Hopefully.

Kianna hopped in the driver's seat and he called shotgun— a small blessing—and Margaret and Gregory jumped in the back.

Aidan glanced over at Kianna. He kept expecting the bomb to drop. Kept expecting her to make some snide comment about not catching them all on fire. *He* knew she wouldn't do that, but he couldn't convince his murderous Sphere she would stay on his side.

"Barely a week back from battle and we're sent to the field again. No rest for the wicked, eh?" Gregory asked from the back.

"Shut up, Gregory," Aidan replied. He closed his eyes. Pressed his forehead to the side window.

This was going to be a long trip.

Hours passed.

The ride down was far from smooth. They navigated around craters blown through concrete and cities melted to glass. Occasionally, Margaret would pull through Earth and smooth out the terrain, but it wasn't her strongest Sphere, and the acts left her drained and scrambling for the food supplies they'd brought along.

Kianna cycled through the CDs left over in the vehicle. Some electro mixes, some folk, some fluty new age shit he had her turn off after the first thirty seconds...then had her play, a few hours later, because he couldn't remember the last time he'd heard music through a stereo and anything was better than nothing.

They'd gone on a few short missions in vehicles, but this felt strange. He stared at the rushing rain, at the shadows of buildings and hills and rolling fields, at the slice of their headlight through the gloom. He wanted to talk to Kianna, but he didn't know about what. Didn't know what he *could* talk about with Margaret and Gregory in the back. Occasionally they'd pull over for snacks or a pee break, but for the most part they drove in silence, him with his forehead pressed against the window and Kianna focusing on the road ahead. No one slept, either. Not with the bone-crunching jolts every few yards, or the quick swerves while Kianna avoided cars or potholes or sheer cliff faces in the middle of the road. Well, he supposed Kianna, at least, *was* speaking, if the constant stream of cursing counted.

On the plus side, there weren't any bodies in the road to avoid or crunch over. The Howls weren't known for leaving anything behind.

Every once in a while, Gregory would speak up from the back, asking a question or making a statement that he probably thought would get the conversation going. Every time, his words were met with silence. Most of the questions had to do with history, or the future. *"Remember what it was like when—" "What do you think will happen after—"*

This wasn't the car for hypotheticals or reminiscing. Even

Margaret, who probably had more of a heart than he or Kianna did, kept silent.

Eventually, Gregory stopped trying. Thank gods.

About the only things worth staring at on the ride down were the road signs. More numerous the farther on they went. And more ravaged. Adverts for the New Church of Our Salvation.

REPENT OR BURN

THE END IS COME

MAGIC IS THE DEVIL'S WORK

And, his favorite: WE KNOW YOUR SINS

"If that was true," he said, nodding to the bullet-pocked sign, "I better hope I'm never caught. They'd die of old age before pulling all my sins out."

Kianna's knuckles were pale on the steering wheel. She didn't chuckle. A quick glance in the rearview told him that his joke hadn't been any better received back there.

It wasn't a laughing matter, not really. Everyone had heard tales of the Church and the Inquisition, the bloodthirsty arm dedicated to the historical creed from which it stole its name: to seek out and atone the sins of anyone linked to magic.

Which always meant torture.

Sometimes, it meant death. If they were feeling merciful after making you beg and bleed for it.

Another reason Aidan had kicked the Church and all its zealots from Glasgow: they were as dangerous as the necromancers if you were a Hunter. Hell, they were dangerous even if you'd never touched magic in your life. So long as you screamed at the right times, they seemed to think it reached their God all the same.

Let them come, Fire hissed within him, *and we will see who burns.*

He let the confidence wrap around him. Even the Inquisitors were mortal. Fire had been around from the very beginning and would burn long past the Church's final sermon.

Though, right now, heat and flame and sparks seemed the furthest things from reality, even as he fed small amounts of magic into the engine.

He stared out at the water streaming down outside, listening to the flutes and some woman singing wordlessly, and for some reason, he thought of Tenn. In that moment, he felt a thread pulled taught between them, heart to heart, and even though he didn't have any clue what the guy looked like or what Spheres he used or anything, he felt connected. Not in some stupid romantic way. This was cosmic. A shared bench before the table of the gods. Tenn had killed one of the Kin and here Aidan was, paving the way to kill his second. Even though he refused to let Tenn get in the way, he wondered—briefly—whether the boy had ever felt like this.

Did Tenn know Aidan existed? That he had liberated Scotland?

America had put up its walls long before the Kin took control. Even while the rest of the world cried for help, America remained ambivalent—if not entirely averse to—the rest of the world's problems. But Aidan had a hunch that Tenn would know about Aidan's triumph. He had to. It would almost be unfair if he didn't.

Even if Aidan's name hadn't spread overseas, there was always Tomás to tell him of Aidan's existence. It seemed like the Howl was playing the two of them, and Aidan wondered what the game was. Jealousy flared within him for a moment, Fire hissing that Tomás shouldn't be with someone else, but he burned it away before it could fester. He wanted the incubus, yes. But only to use him.

Aidan was a king. And that meant everyone else was just a peasant. Including the Howl who thought himself a god.

Aidan thought, and Kianna drove, and around midnight he realized there was a glow on the horizon.

"What's that?" Gregory asked, shifting up in his seat.

The glow was harsh and white, electric. Faint at first, barely a haze through the rain, but it spilled above the dilapidated buildings before them in a corona, a curse. Aidan hadn't seen that much electric light in years.

"London," Kianna said. Her words were dull. Depressed.

Aidan couldn't even imagine what sort of homecoming this was for her—the street tangled with cars, the cityscapes melted and transformed. He could see the clench of her jaw in the light of the dash and the glow of the horizon. If he was any other guy, and she any other girl, he would have reached over and put a hand on her shoulder or thigh to let her know that he was there for her, and he cared.

Since it was the two of them, though, he did nothing but rap his fingers on the door, staring idly at the accumulated dirt under his chipped nails. He needed a spa day.

The thought made him chuckle, and Kianna stared daggers at him.

"Sorry," he muttered. "So." He shifted in his seat, leaning against the door to look at her. "What's the plan?"

"We should probably stop soon." Kianna yawned.

"Sounds good to me."

The London glow was still miles away, and the road was getting worse the closer they got. That was the trouble with cities—for the Howls and necromancers, cities were smorgasbords. Especially since—with a few well-placed necromancers—all exits could be destroyed. It didn't take long to suck the breath or the heat out of a congested street. Just as it didn't take much to burn a crowd and leave the bones to the beasts.

Or turn them all *into* beasts.

Another reason why Aidan tried to avoid the big cities when he could. They just felt like graveyards.

He wanted to tell her to keep going, keep calm and carry on and all that, but the truth of it was, he was ready to sleep. Preferably somewhere that wasn't jostled every five seconds. Preferably without Kianna's curses a grating lullaby in his ears.

Around them, whatever borough this had been was completely demolished. He could see for miles over the rubble. Rows of flats and shops reduced to piles of charred stone, cars turned and toppled, small bits of flora poking between the debris. He wondered idly just how many people had been killed here, and how quickly it had come about.

"Shite," Kianna said.

"What?"

She nodded, and he looked forward.

The road ahead was completely clogged. All of the cars pointed directly at him, all of them trying to leave the city. Clearly, none had made it. Not with the gaping crater taking out a full swath of road and half the surrounding flats. There was no way around it—the rubble on each side of the street was too high to drive over, and it traced all the way behind them like a half pipe.

Kianna grunted and shifted into Park. "Looks like we're walking," she said, killing the engine. "Either that, or we reverse and hope there's another route."

"Walking? I thought you wanted to sleep."

Kianna shrugged off Aidan's question. "We're exposed out here, and I don't see any places nearby to rest up. Unless you want to take your chances sleeping in the open?"

She didn't wait for an answer. She hopped out of the vehicle and began walking. Aidan was right after her, though the others hesitated a moment before joining. He couldn't really blame them.

Theoretically, it should have been safe. The Guild ahead should have cleared the nearby land of Howls. Especially a Guild as large as London's. But the fact was there—if scouts had gone missing, something was wrong. And that meant they couldn't take any chances.

"Lead on then," Aidan said. His foot caught on a flier. SINNERS REPENT. Chills raced down his spine, despite Fire's constant caress. "Just get us sinners somewhere warm."

"Hell's warm," Kianna said.

"Clearly not," Aidan said, and spread out his arms like a crucifix.

CHAPTER THIRTY

IT FELT LIKE THEY WANDERED FOR HOURS.

Through deserted streets. Jumping at shadows. Margaret was open to Air and scanning, but she never once sounded an alarm. Civilization was still ages away, and with it, any chance of human contact. Aidan clutched Fire as tightly as he held on to his daggers. Kianna had Kindness in one hand and a vicious ax in the other. Even Gregory seemed serious, his eyes shadowed and his sword held tight as Earth hummed in his gut. They trekked closer to the glowing white of the Guild, scouring the land for a flat that at least had a roof.

Honestly, though—he didn't want to stay here any longer than he had to.

He couldn't put his finger on it. He'd been over all of Scotland, had seen more ruined or battle-stained or bloody places than he could recount. But this felt different. London didn't just feel abandoned. It felt hollow. Hungry.

Like in Edinburgh, there was an emptiness here that tugged at his Sphere, made chills race down his spine despite the flames flickering around his body. But unlike Edinburgh, this didn't feel like the creation of a Howl. It felt…unnatural. In a way that even the Kin never did.

"Do you feel that?" Gregory asked.

Aidan nodded.

"Feel what?" Kianna asked from ahead.

"The emptiness," Margaret said. Her eyebrows were furrowed, pale blue light from her throat glowing against her skin. "I can't feel anything out there."

"The Guild is still further on," Kianna said.

"That's not what I mean. There's nothing. No people. No animals. No…" She trailed off, biting her lip with worry.

"What?" Aidan asked.

She didn't answer right away. They had all paused, rubble spread out around them in a field of despair, the only sound the click as Kianna turned off the safety on her gun.

"It feels like this place eats magic," Margaret finally said. She shuddered and shook her head. "I don't know. It's not right, whatever it is. And whatever it is, it doesn't want us here."

"Sounds like London," Kianna said. "Never really liked tourists, even before the Resurrection. Now you know why I don't go home."

She looked to Aidan, as though daring him to say the real reason.

Obviously, he didn't.

She turned and led them away from the road, toward a row of buildings that didn't look as derelict as the rest. At least these appeared to have roofs. And seeing as the rain had followed them, that alone was a godsend.

★ ★ ★

Aidan sat on the front stoop, Fire a low burn in his chest and his comrades sound asleep in the room behind him. It hadn't been a flat like they'd hoped. Rather, it was a corner store that had been thoroughly raided in the previous years— no crisps or snacks on the shelves, shattered glass everywhere. The flats above had been blown clean off, and parts of the ceiling let in the drizzling sky. But it was dry. Ish. And covered. Ish. There might not have been beds, but after they'd blown the glass away and settled in with some blankets from the car, Aidan feeding a small fire in the middle of the shop, it would act as a fair base. For now.

Aidan was antsy.

He wasn't used to being cooped up in a car all day. He wasn't used to sitting still, to not training. Or killing. He wanted more than anything to uncurl Fire and burn through his frustration. Start a wildfire and see just how far he could make it spread. That sort of thing. The sort of thing that would make Kianna doubt his ability to keep the damned Sphere under control.

So instead, he sat, legs tight to his chest, watching London glow just as he had watched Edinburgh a few nights before. Another potential conquest. Another chance to fight. To burn. To rule. To die.

Fire whispered through his thoughts, dreaming up the sort of strength he could gain from this strange shard. Tomás said it would make even death bow to him. Not that he took the Howl at his word, but still. If it had brought Calum back, it had to be powerful. No matter what, it would help him rule. And when Tenn appeared, it would keep the boy in his place.

But it wasn't just thoughts of magic that made his lips twitch into the occasional grin. It was the thought of how it would feel to rule from London itself. After all, if the Guild here was compromised, overrun with necromancers or something, there would be no one to stop him from claiming it for his own after the threat was eradicated.

Fire told him that of course the threat would be eradicated.

The rubble beyond shifted. Aidan jerked to awareness, a dagger in hand and Fire glowing bright, tendrils of flame curled around his fist. Light flared bright enough to see the intruder.

Aidan let out a sigh and collapsed back against the door.

"What the hell are you doing out here?" he asked the fox. The beast was tiny, fur glimmering orange and red in the light of Aidan's flame. It didn't seem at all put off by Aidan's glow. Instead, it took a few steps closer, its eyes calm and unwavering, ribs slatted and shadowed with hunger.

It was rare to see animals anymore, especially in cities. The Howls had fucked up the entire ecosystem with their hunger. Aidan had overheard more than one conversation about how the world would collapse even if the Howls were banished—everything was out of sync, whole ecosystems destroyed, weather patterns shifted, the world collapsing. The only creatures that survived anymore were the small scavengers. The ones that could hide. But this guy…he wasn't hiding at all.

"Aren't you supposed to be scared of me?"

But the fox just stepped closer. Aidan stayed still. Let the fires around him fade, until there was just a small sphere of light hanging above him. They locked eyes, and there was an intelligence there that startled him.

For some reason, those eyes made him think of his mother.

The fox blurred as tears formed in his eyes. Aidan blinked them away. He couldn't think that about her. He couldn't let regret overtake him. He'd done all he could. And now, he was doing what he could to avenge her. He had to tell himself that—ending the Howls was all he could do. He sniffed and pulled through Fire, let it burn through his veins, let it boil away the depression. His tears turned to puffs of steam.

Still, the fox watched him. Examining him.

Your hatred will destroy us.

Aidan jolted and looked around.

The voice was feminine, but not the oceanic hum of the Dark Lady. No, this was different, lilting. Innocent.

There was no one nearby. No one but the fox.

"Jesus," Aidan whispered. "Get a hold of yourself."

The fox cocked its head to the side. Licked its lips. Aidan wondered if maybe he had a snack he could give it.

Then the door opened behind him, and Margaret stepped out. The fox disappeared into the shadows like it was made of them. "Who are you talking to?" Margaret asked.

Aidan grunted and burned away the last of his weakness. "Just myself," he said. "No one important."

She gave him a slight smile. "Your shift is up. Go get some sleep."

He nodded and stood. Stared out at the shadows.

The fox didn't return. Why did he want it to return?

"Something out there?" Margaret asked.

He thought about the way it stared at him. At the intelligence in its eyes. And the voice…

He shook his head. He was just tired. Delusional. Too much time in a car.

"Nothing," he told her, heading indoors. "Just my imagination."

CHAPTER THIRTY-ONE

HE WAS LOST.

Two days of fleeing north through the midlands, trying to find his way along deserted roads, trying to avoid any sign of humans. He'd crossed over on the ferry—a nightmare of jostling waves, crowded people, and far-off explosions—and had abandoned the group as soon as they hit land. He knew crowds were dangerous. Crowds attracted monsters. Crowds meant he couldn't run.

And he had been running for days.

Partly to stay alive, partly to stay away from the bloody memory that haunted him. First, to Glasgow, trying to escape. But all flights had been grounded. No one was going anywhere. So, he'd come here.

He was soaked to the bone and freezing, the sky above relentless in its quest to make him as miserable as possible. At least he hadn't run across any more monsters. What were they calling them? Howls. He'd heard it on the radio. Seen it on the television, all channels playing the same clip over and over, as though hijacked: a woman in black with blond hair, turning a man chained to a chair into a nightmarish monster.

Howls. For the noise they made when they attacked.

Shorthand for how hollow they'd become in the process of conversion.

Magic had done this. Had done all of this. And yet he knew in the back of his mind that he would need magic to survive.

He crouched by the entrance of the abandoned hostel. He was far from the beaten path, next to Loch Lomond and surrounded by trees. It felt safe. Nothing should feel safe. He hadn't slept a goddamned night since…since… He shook his head and fought back the tears. He couldn't think about her. Not anymore. He couldn't change it, either.

He just wished he could get the sound of screams and bleating from his ears.

He stared out at the rain, at the darkening night. Then at the shattered windows of the hostel. He'd been standing there for the last twenty minutes, too afraid to go in, too cold to move on. It was too easy to remember the screams in the houses and flats he'd passed along the way, the blood-splattered windows, the burning doors, the thick smoke that hung heavy over everything, clogging his lungs and filling the streets with hungry phantoms. He didn't want to be a voice never heard from again. He didn't want to be a number in the list of casualties claimed by all this madness.

He looked back out at the gravel path that had led him here. Maybe it would be safer out there…

"Are you coming in or not?"

He nearly pissed himself.

The question came from a girl about his age. Maybe sixteen. But even though she was young, she looked…old. Shoulders back, chin high. Eyes that had definitely seen shit. She held a lacrosse stick in one hand, a butcher knife in the other. Her hair was long and in locs, black and pink, just like the pink T-shirt and tight black jeans. Stylish, in a way. Save for the rips on her clothes that were clearly not part of the original design. Not if the splotches of blood were any indication.

"Who are you?" Aidan asked. He took a step backward. She looked like some crazy-cool zombie-killer chick who could rip his head off without blinking. Whereas he… He looked at his muddy jeans, his soggy clothes. The chunk of wood he'd been using as a weapon.

He looked like he should have been eaten ages ago.

"Kianna," she said. She eyed him up and down. Again, he was struck by her mannerisms. She played it cool. Collected. Like she'd been prepared for this all along. And there was a darkness in her eyes that told him preparation hadn't been kind.

"Aidan."

"You one of them?" she asked.

No use asking what she meant. "No."

"Use magic?"

"No."

"Good." She opened the door wider.

"Do you?" he asked. What if *she* was a Howl? One of the more humanoid ones? Someone who could steal his breath or his heat or drain his blood like a vampire? If she was a necromancer, he couldn't imagine her just sitting here, waiting for victims. Then again, he couldn't imagine a Howl waiting in the middle of nowhere, either. Unless she was keeping her victims locked away in the hostel...

"No," she replied. "Magic got us into this mess."

He bit his lip. Looked out at the rain. He hadn't come up here for no reason.

"I was going to attune," he said. "I heard there's a place up here that will do it."

"There was," she replied. "Are you coming in or not? You're not exactly helping keep the warm air in."

"What do you mean, *was?*"

She groaned and looked at the ceiling. "They're dead. Just like pretty much everyone else in this world. Thanks to magic."

"How do you know?" It wasn't a very brave response; inside, he felt his hope deflate, his words falling flat.

"Because I was there," she said. "Saw the place for myself. I've been seeking out survivors. Go figure that you'd be the first."

He looked past her, into the darkened hostel. Maybe his hostel-prison idea was correct. Maybe she was worse than a necromancer or Howl. Maybe she was some psycho killer.

He'd seen the movies.

"Look," she said, impatience clear in her voice. "If I was a Howl I'd have killed you already. And if I was a necromancer I'd have turned you into a monster. Clearly, you're too stupid to be either, so are you coming in or not?"

He hated to admit it, but she had a point. Not about him being stupid. But the rest.

He nodded and stepped inside. She locked all three dead bolts behind him.

She guided him deeper into the hostel. Past the foyer filled with forgotten backpacks and the reception desk littered with paper and a lounge filled with sofas and a fireplace long-since gone cold. He shivered. Now that they were inside and rain wasn't pouring over him, he was reminded how damn cold he was.

"We'll get you changed," she said. "Afraid I don't trust having a fire going, but there are dry clothes left over in some of the guest rooms." She looked him up and down, and her face cracked into a wicked grin. "I think a few toddlers stayed here last. They should have left clothes that will fit you."

Despite everything—despite the blood and the tears and the ache in his body—he actually chuckled. "You're a bitch."

She shrugged. "I'm a survivor. They go hand in hand."

In the back, in the kitchen, was a makeshift cot and a few bags, their contents splayed out over the floor. Clothes. A few bits of food. Mostly, the space was taken up with weapons.

"You know, this *is* a hostel," he said. "Which means there are actual rooms with actual beds."

"I hadn't noticed," Kianna said, plopping down on the cot. "Though I *had* noticed they're all upstairs, and that—last I checked—I hadn't grown wings to fly in case I was attacked. A kitchen is the perfect place to hide out. Plenty of weapons on hand, very few obstacles in the way, and—" she pointed to the barricaded back door "—an easy escape route if I need it."

That's when he noticed the crates along the wall by the entrance he'd stepped through. Another little barricade. It was no wonder she'd lived as long as she had. She was smart. Smarter than he was.

Not that he'd admit that.

"Go," she said, pointing to the hallway. "There are towels and the like upstairs. And clothes. And before you even think of making some quip about me joining you to warm you up, just know I've already killed three men this week. Two by cutting off their balls."

"I'm gay," Aidan said. Of all things to worry about or admit right now, that seemed to be the least of them.

"And I'm not interested in any case. Go. Change."

He didn't move, though. He stood there for a moment, watching her organize her weapons, feeling the weight of everything settle on his shoulders. He wasn't going to get attuned. Which meant he couldn't fight back. Which meant he couldn't get home. Which meant he would die here, unable to avenge his mom or go back and tell his dad he loved him. He'd die here, and no one would know.

"What?" Kianna asked. Her eyebrows furrowed. "Please tell me you aren't about to start crying."

He sniffed, realized he *had* been about to start crying. He pulled himself together. Or tried to. "I'm just wondering what we do next."

"We? Who says this is a *we* thing? I'm just giving you a dry place for the night." She paused, let her words sink in. "I work better alone."

"You said you were looking for survivors."

"Ones who can fight," she corrected him.

"I can fight."

She cackled. "How?" She nodded to the stake in his hands. "Planning on stabbing some vampires with that thing? Doesn't quite work like the stories, love. You're not a fighter—you're a liability."

His heart pounded. Not out of fear, but desperation. He couldn't let her turn him away. He knew she didn't need him. But he knew he wouldn't last without her help.

Clearly, she knew it, too.

"I'm heading toward Inverness in the morning," she said. "I've heard they're mobilizing there. Putting some sort of resistance together. You can come with, but you're not my responsibility. You die, you die. I ain't risking myself to save your sorry arse. If you make it there, we part ways. Got it?"

He nodded slowly. "Thanks."

"Don't thank me," she said. "Not yet."

He wasn't exactly heartened when he turned and walked up the dark staircase to the bedrooms. But at least he had a plan. At least he had a companion.

He had a chance.

"Oh, Aidan," came a voice. Feminine, but older. Familiar. It chilled him, speared his heart in place. "You never had a chance."

He turned.

There, pouring from the shadows, was a woman molded from nightmare. He knew her in an instant. Just as he knew in that moment that he was dreaming. And that he wasn't waking up.

"Every step you've taken," she said, gliding forward. She touched his cheek with a hand that glowed like St. Elmo's Fire. "Every choice you've made. All of it has been by my design. All of it to bring you closer to me."

She leaned in, breathing against his ear. He wanted her to smell terrible, like graveyards or dead things. Instead, the Dark Lady smelled of incense, frankincense. Holy. Pure.

"You could never escape me," she said. "Not when I am the game board on which you play. You are mine, dear Hunter. Even now."

She kissed his cheek. Fire flooded his vision. The world burning, innocents screaming. His mother and father, once more at his side. Alive. Whole.

"I will give you everything," she promised, a burning whisper in his ear. "As soon as you have found the shard. You will aid me, and in return, I will bring back your family."

"Why do you need it? I thought it was for Tomás."

"Tomás is mine. As you are mine."

"I'm not yours," he hissed. He couldn't move. Couldn't push her away. Couldn't stab her in the chest or burn her to cinders. He realized then that it wasn't because she was forcing him to stillness.

He didn't want to do any of those things.

He felt her smile against his cheek.

"You already promised yourself to me. Your words have bound you, body and soul. But keep the spark, my dear. I am afraid you are going to need it."

Then she pressed her hand into his chest, curled her fingers around his heart.

His nightmare burned in a choir of ecstasy.

CHAPTER THIRTY-TWO

BURNING.

Everything burning. White and hot. Searing fire. But not the Fire Aidan knew.

Pain burned through him, wrenched screams from his lungs as the world spun and seared and he dragged himself out of the darkness. Out into a cold room, and a blinding heat. And the scent and pop of bubbling flesh.

He tried to struggle. Tried to wrench free from the awful nightmare. From the pain that dug into his arm. Through his arm. Searing down to the bone and deeper. Fire and lightning shattered down his spine as he convulsed on concrete, as strong hands pressed him down.

He screamed.

He couldn't scream. Not against the pain that choked him.

He couldn't scream, but that didn't quiet the screams inside. The rage of Fire. The howls of anger and betrayal. They screamed louder than he ever could.

And when they reached their apex, when he thought his soul would rip apart from agony, the pain stopped.

He slumped against the floor. Broken.

And then, before he could speak, he turned his head to the side and vomited.

"There, there, my son," came a voice. "The worst is now over. Your body recognizes this. It, too, desires purification."

A face came into the light. An old man. Face lined and weathered, beard more gray than not. Black and purple robes. A bent bronze cross around his neck. Aidan knew him. How did he know him?

The stranger put his hand on Aidan's forehead. The faintest touch. Yet it still made Aidan jerk back in anticipation of pain.

He reached toward Fire.

He reached.

But—

No.

No no no *no*!

His eyes went wide as he struggled, tried to reach for the power that had filled and fueled him the last three years.

"What..." he gasped. "What have—"

"Shh," the man said. "Do not fight. Rejoice in your victory, my child. Rejoice, for you are nearly free."

He reached down and grazed a finger across Aidan's forearm, over the tattoo that bound him to the Spheres. The mark that could never, should never, be corrupted or undone. The tattoo that was now crossed by a terrible, smoking welt. Another man held a scalding red brand at his side. Similar to the cross around the man's neck. Angular, sharp. More than a cross.

A sigil.

A curse.

No. A rune.

He reached to Fire again. He wanted to burn the man alive. Wanted him to suffer for what he had done. But no matter how hard he fought, inside, he found nothing.

Tears welled in his eyes. From the emptiness in his chest. From the cold that leeched through his heart. Cracked against his bones.

Fire wasn't there.

Fire.

Wasn't.

There.

"Now you see," the man said. He caressed Aidan's brow again. "Let your tears flow. Cleanse yourself in their waters. And rejoice—never again will you feel the touch of the Dark Lady. Never again will you feel the taint of her power."

Then the man leaned forward, peering deep into Aidan's eyes. His mouth cracked into a smile. It was then that Aidan recognized him; the serpent he'd chased from Glasgow. The man he'd hoped to never see again. And when that recognition dawned, so too did a cold deeper than any ocean.

He was as good as dead.

"We know who you are, Aidan Belmont," Brother Jeremiah whispered. "We know of your sins. And your pain—your salvation—has only just begun."

"We have fallen far, my brothers, and yet
the Lord still speaks. The Word
rings clear. We must cleanse
the world of magic, lest we fall
even deeper
into the bowels of Hell."

—Sermon of Brother Jeremiah, 3 P.R.

PART 4

WHAT MAN HATH WROUGHT

CHAPTER THIRTY-THREE

AIDAN BLACKED OUT.

He didn't dream. Didn't hallucinate. He swam in midnight and felt the Dark Lady's eyes on his back. His world jostled and crashed. Pain was a constant ebb and flow, a pulse along with his heartbeat. And with it all was the greatest sense of emptiness, of loss. He couldn't place it, couldn't grasp the sensation long enough to understand. But as he swam in the darkness, he knew the void without was nothing compared to the gaping nothingness within.

A part of him wanted to drift away forever, to vanish into the abyss. He knew what it would spell, but death seemed far more comfortable than an eternity of *this*.

Then his body slammed against concrete, and he jolted from his darkness with a gasp. Just in time to hear a door slam shut. A lock slide into place.

The shivers started a second later. And with them, the dull, throbbing pain in his arm that made him cry out once more.

He curled over to his side. Tried to hold off the tears as he held on to his wrist.

He didn't know what was worse: the cold, the pain in his arm or the emptiness that clawed at his chest. He curled tighter and tried to find some sort of heat. Tried to reach for the power that had kept him alive for so many years.

He couldn't find it. He couldn't hold back the tears. There, alone in the dark and the cold and the emptiness, he started to sob.

He couldn't actually remember the last time he'd cried, and it surprised him so much, he laughed. Snot dripped from his nose and tears ran down his cheeks and he couldn't tell if he was still crying or just laughing or if it even made a difference.

Of course it didn't make a difference.

He was royally fucked.

The pain of absence was immense. He kept reaching for Fire, the reflex so ingrained in his mind it felt like breathing. Kept waiting to feel the heat blossom in his heart and rush down his fingertips, filling his veins with purpose. With life. And every attempt was a missed breath, a broken heartbeat. Every time he reached for it, he felt like he was dying all over again, his fingers clenching and unclenching as though they could claw flame from the air.

"Eventually," came a voice, "you'll realize there's no point fighting it."

Aidan jolted upright, tried to shut down his emotions. He sniffed and rubbed his face, but it didn't matter if he was covered in snot and tears—it was too dark in here to see. Besides, it's not like his cell mate would have missed hearing him sob.

"Who are you?" He sounded pathetic. He tried to steel his

voice as he sat up. Pressed his back to the wall behind him. Told himself he wasn't cowering. Tried, but without Fire backing him up, there wasn't much fight left.

"Name's Lukas," came the voice. "I'd, um, I'd shake your hand, but I don't quite know where you are."

A thousand questions warred in Aidan's mind. The only one that came out was, "What the hell is this place?"

There was a pause.

"Hell."

Aidan didn't respond. He heard the guy sigh and shift, the creak of a cot frame.

"We're in London," Lukas finally said. "Home sweet home."

The words made Aidan's gut sink even further. "What do you mean, London? London is a Guild."

"*Was.* Until the Church took it over."

Aidan's thoughts were slow. As if, without Fire, they were freezing in his mind. "When—"

"A few days ago," Lukas replied. "We got word Calum had fallen. Everyone started celebrating." A pause. "I wish I could say that the Church attacked us. Came in the night. But they didn't have to. They were already here. There was a coup the moment the Guild let their guard down. Half the Guild was murdered in their sleep by civilians who'd been brainwashed into thinking they were doing God's work. The rest were captured. Branded by the Church. Now, they're—I mean, we're—being tortured. Though as you're finding out, the brand is torture enough.

"Turns out, all those horror stories about the Inquisition were real."

Aidan wanted to vomit. He wasn't certain if it was from what Lukas was saying or the pain that throbbed in his arm and skull. "The others I came with. Are they—"

"Dead? Probably not." Despite the words, Lukas's statement didn't make Aidan feel any better. For one thing, Lukas said it like it was a bad thing.

"Where are they?"

"How the hell should I know? I've been locked in here since the coup. If they're lucky, they're down here with the rest of us. If not, they're upstairs."

"What's upstairs?"

Lukas didn't answer.

Aidan reached down, gingerly touched the skin where his tattoo rested. It hurt like hell, but he didn't let up. The flesh was hot and welted. The moment he touched it, he felt... wrong. His head swam like he was spinning, falling, spiraling down into a pit. It emptied every emotion from his heart, a vacuum, a cavern he couldn't escape. It hurt worse than the physical pain. It was something beyond hurt. Something beyond even death. It was absence. Absence of what it meant to be alive.

He hissed and drew back his hand.

What the hell had they done to him? Or, better question: How the hell could he undo it?

"I'd say it gets easier, but I don't like lying. Once you're branded, you ain't getting your magic back."

It should have been impossible. Aidan had seen Hunters get entire arms blown or hacked or eaten off. They could still wield magic. The ability went deeper than the mark of the runes. It branded itself into your soul, attuned you to a frequency you could never forget.

Apparently, he had been wrong.

"Why are they doing this?" Aidan asked.

"Don't quite know," Lukas said. "Glory of God? Spreading the good word? Good ol' witch burning? It's hard to say. That's the thing about Inquisitors. When you're being tortured, it's usually them doing the questioning. Goes with the name. If I had to guess, though, it's because—without Calum as a threat—they figured now was the time to take over England. Wouldn't surprise me if they'd already done the same up in Scotland."

It didn't explain why they'd suddenly decided to abandon their truce with the Hunters and start overthrowing Guilds. At the end of the day, they were all supposed to be on the same side.

Sure, he'd heard stories of Hunters getting pulled in for questioning. Hunters who had never made it out to tell their tale. But for the Church to mobilize like this, to take over a Guild…it felt like an act of war. Especially when led by Brother Jeremiah. Aidan had thought the man dead. Was this some petty act of revenge?

They came after Calum fell.

Something snaked through Aidan's chest. An emotion he could barely place until the weight of it dragged him down.

Guilt.

The Church had overtaken London because Calum fell. Because *he* had killed the Kin. Because his victory had made everyone cocky. Because he had kicked Brother Jeremiah and his followers out into the streets to die.

This was the price of his pride.

"What's your name, by the way?" Lukas's voice made Aidan jolt.

Aidan considered lying. Not that he could see telling the truth making things any worse.

"Aidan," he said. "Aidan Belmont."

Lukas hissed in a breath. "*The* Aidan Belmont?"

Even the awe in Lukas's voice did nothing to make him feel better. Nothing would make him feel better.

His silence must have said enough.

"Did you really do it?" Lukas asked.

"What?" Aidan replied, trying to keep his words steady. He hated that he was shaking. Hated that he could be scared. Hated that without Fire, he was nothing. Nothing. He'd always been nothing.

"Defeat Calum."

"Aye," Aidan replied. "I did."

"What was it like?" Lukas asked. His words were soft and heavy with excitement.

For a moment, Aidan considered telling the truth. The full truth. After all, he might as well start practicing his confessions now. Why not admit that he'd stormed into the castle to see Calum pinned to the wall? That he had only won because another Kin had come in to do most of the dirty work? That *that* very Kin was the only reason Aidan had pushed to come down here? He considered sharing every dark secret of his soul, and without Fire to tell him otherwise, he nearly did.

His soul was a very dark place.

Instead, he grunted, "Not what I thought it would be. Do you have any idea how many Church members there are?"

"No idea. We never counted." Lukas paused. Sighed. "Not that it matters, really. All it takes is a few of them to get into the people's heads, and you have a whole new Sept. Their faith is a plague."

Aidan felt it then—that note of anger, of rage. Not over being trapped, but over how easily the very people he'd liberated had turned against him.

"Shit," Lukas said, and that's when Aidan heard it: a shuffle outside the door, the thud of footsteps.

Aidan had just enough time to get to his feet before the door opened. Warm light poured in, flickering and orange, and just the sight of a flame made Aidan's chest ache. He stumbled and reached out, steadied himself on the wall.

So much for not looking weak in front of the enemy.

There were three of them. Two maybe in their twenties, with shaved heads and strange angular tattoos on their scalps. The third, the man in the middle holding the lantern, was Brother Jeremiah.

Aidan found himself flinching at the memory of hot metal on his skin, at the sensation of emptiness when everything else consumed. "You," he whispered to the man who had done this to him.

Old Aidan would have leaped forward and wrung Jeremiah's neck with his bare hands. No matter the guards holding clubbed staves. He would have gone down fighting. Rather, he wouldn't have gone down at all. Now it was all he could do to keep upright. To stare the bastard in the eyes rather than cower like he wanted.

"Me, indeed," the man said. He smiled and bowed graciously, acting all the world like he was entertaining a guest and not holding him prisoner.

"It is good to see you again, Aidan." Even though the man sounded like a grandfather, blood laced through his words. "Ever since we were forcefully removed from our home, I have prayed that we would cross paths once more. It seems my prayers have been answered. I hope you slept well on your journey; we have a great deal of work at hand. The road to salvation is long and arduous, especially for one such as you. But tonight is a night for rejoicing. For here, you are found. And with our help, we will guide you from the darkness, back into the heart of the light." His smile made Aidan's blood run even colder. "Let us begin."

He gestured to the guards. They grabbed Aidan by the arms, yanking him out the door and into the hall. He didn't even have the strength to fight. Especially when one of them grasped his burnt forearm. Aidan bit back a scream and tasted blood. They shoved him out. Jeremiah locked the door behind him.

Aidan knew Lukas's expression all too well.

He didn't expect Aidan to return.

CHAPTER THIRTY-FOUR

"YOU CAN'T DO THIS."

Aidan's words echoed in the too-empty room. Too empty, too white, too sterile. Maybe this place had once been an office. No longer. Candles dripped like blood from the shelves, casting flickering light over the laminate table and the silver tools glittering there.

The table dripped, too, but not *like* blood. With blood. A thick, heavy sap staining the tiles at Aidan's feet.

Not all of it his.

Aidan's head swam as he tried vainly to stay awake. Conscious. He'd given up struggling against the ropes holding him to the chair long ago.

"It is my charge, my son," Jeremiah said sagely. "I must cleanse the world of evil. I must cleanse *you* of evil, and to do that, you must pay for your sins in blood."

He paced back and forth before Aidan's chair, scalpel loose in one hand, his fingers tipped crimson.

"I didn't realize your God condoned torture."

Aidan couldn't tell if the warm liquid dribbling from his lips was saliva or blood. What did it matter? The guards had punched him a few times to get him to settle down; Jeremiah's touch was far less blunt, but all the more painful for its precision.

Now, the guards were gone. Just him and Jeremiah and all of Jeremiah's toys and a dozen candles reminding him of the power no longer his to control. The power that had, in a way, been the cause of all this pain.

"This is not torture. This is salvation. You may be free of magic, but it will take conviction and strength to bleed the last remnants of the Dark Lady's sin from your soul."

For a moment, Aidan tore his eyes away from Jeremiah, focusing instead on the welt covering his Hunter's mark. A cross in a circle, its points crossed by arcing lines. It scrawled red and raw over the looping circles and sigils of his tattoo. Breaking it. Disconnecting him from something that should have been as close to him as breathing.

A sob caught in the back of his throat. No matter what Jeremiah did to his body, he'd already done the worst thing possible.

Aidan couldn't even find the rage to hate the man for taking Fire away.

Jeremiah stepped closer then. And when he gently pressed his thumb to the scar, Aidan cried out as lightning burned his vision white.

"What I could do and have done to your physical body is nothing compared to what awaits you in the afterlife," he said through Aidan's pain. "I am saving you, my son. Magic has brought Hell to this earth. In renouncing magic, you give in to divine mercy. In bleeding out your sins, you prove your love to our God. Only there will you find mercy. Only in His embrace will you find forgiveness for all you have done. For all the sin you brought into our world."

Jeremiah let go of Aidan's forearm; the pain subsided and the room inked back into focus.

"I don't believe in God," Aidan managed. He'd been raised atheist, and if anything, the last few years had taught him that the gods—if they were real—didn't give a damn about humanity. No caring god would have let the Resurrection happen.

"God is very real," Jeremiah said. "As are the many false idols who oppose him. One of whom, I believe, has chosen you to bring her shadow into the light."

"What are you talking about?"

Aidan's head lolled. Yep. Definitely blood trickling from his lips.

"The Dark Lady works through you," Jeremiah whispered. "She has chosen you, Aidan Belmont. She has chosen you, but you are not past saving. Not yet."

Truth echoed in Jeremiah's words, a fear whispered into life.

The Dark Lady *had* chosen him.

Did Jeremiah know? Or was this his usual tirade?

That was as far as Aidan's thoughts could go. The further he pressed them, the further they contracted, sinking back to the sensation he would never voice.

Jeremiah was right.

Jeremiah was wrong.

The Dark Lady *had* chosen him. He had sinned. Gladly.

And even if he believed in the Church or a God, he knew

in the pit of his bloodied heart that no amount of pain or repenting would ever save his soul.

"I have waited a long time for you to fall into our care,
Aidan Belmont. We have followed you for years, and we know
what you have done." Calum's throne room flashed through
Aidan's mind, the throne and the blood and the burn of his
comrades, the screams and the fear in Trevor's eyes. The sins
racking up, one by one. "You've tasted her power. You've
heard her words. She speaks to you, doesn't she?"

Aidan didn't answer, but the stutter in his heart spoke the
truth. *How does he know?*

"This is why you are here, my child. You serve a greater
purpose than those around you. If the Dark Lady speaks to
you, *through* you, then perhaps, by purifying her from your
veins, we may find her source. We may find a way to purify
our entire world."

"You're mental," Aidan said. Coughed blood. *How does
he know?*

How does he know?

If Jeremiah was right about the Dark Lady, what if he was
right about the rest? The damnation and sin and… *Get a hold
of yourself!*

"If you want to know about the Dark Lady," Aidan managed, forcing the fear away, "why not interrogate a necromancer?"

Jeremiah smiled.

"Because she hasn't spoken to them since the Resurrection.
Not since she was killed by our illustrious order. Even her
followers thought her dead. Until you came along. You have
heard her voice. Of all people in the world, you are the one

she has chosen to continue her work. It is my charge to discover why you are her conduit, and how to end her for good."

"She *is* dead."

It had to be true. She couldn't be speaking to him. He couldn't be chosen for anything, let alone *this*.

"Evil never dies. It merely changes form. And now, it seems, it has chosen you."

"I liberated Scotland. I can't be evil. I can't be hers."

"You liberated Scotland with magic," Jeremiah said. "And with her orders simmering in your veins, those victories were never for the glory of God. You are not an altruistic man, Aidan Belmont. Pride, perhaps, is your greatest sin of all."

He placed his free hand on Aidan's forehead, as though blessing him. Or preparing to drown him.

"The road to salvation is long and fraught with terrors," he said. "It is not with pleasure that I wield these tools against you. But it is God's will. And I am but a pawn. Together, we will learn why the Dark Lady has placed her mark upon you. Together, we will walk through the valley of the shadow of death. Perhaps, if your soul is strong, and your heart pure, you will reach salvation on the other side. After all, my own road was long and shadowed, but I endured. It is only fitting you pass the same test."

Jeremiah smiled. Aidan's heart stopped in that gaze. Whatever charade of righteousness Jeremiah paraded under vanished. He wasn't a pawn of some benevolent God. He was a maniac hell-bent on revenge.

The trouble was, he seemed to be right. The Dark Lady had chosen Aidan. She'd spoken to him. Commanded him. And he'd agreed without question. He'd convinced himself it was so he could get his family back. So he could see his mother again. So he could make everything right. When that was done, he'd defy the Dark Lady and punish her for causing this hell.

But without Fire burning away his doubts, he knew the truth.

He'd agreed to help her because he wanted to rule, no matter the cost.

Jeremiah's blade dug a channel through Aidan's arm, and as his world went red, as the room filled with Aidan's screams, Aidan knew no amount of repenting would save him.

Not when the Dark Lady had already taken him as her own.

No matter the reason, his soul was hers.

CHAPTER THIRTY-FIVE

AIDAN WOKE WITH A SLAP ACROSS HIS FACE. IT wasn't the pain that woke him, but the jolt.

Every inch of him hurt, a dull, throbbing ache that stretched from his toes to his fingertips. Jeremiah hadn't been stingy in his methods; he'd used every instrument at his disposal. Multiple times. Aidan quickly learned that Jeremiah wasn't interested in a confession. At least, not right away.

Aidan couldn't have spoken through his screams if his life depended on it.

Apparently, tonight, it hadn't. He was still alive, but that didn't mean he was grateful for it.

He'd blacked out halfway through round two of an awl jammed beneath his fingernail. He had never read it, but he was pretty certain that wasn't in the Bible.

"Hey," came a voice in the flickering dark. Thankfully not Jeremiah's. "Are you alive?"

Aidan groaned. It was about the only response he could muster.

"Good," Lukas said. "I didn't want to share a cell with a corpse."

Slowly, the room came into view, the space lit by a single tiny candle. Aidan blinked multiple times, tried to force down the nausea rising in his throat, tried to ignore the frozen emptiness of his chest. For a moment, he thought he was in a hall of mirrors. The walls were crystalline smooth, carved by magic and glimmering wetly in the candlelight, reflecting the flame a thousand-fold.

The moment he saw that flame, he ached for the warmth that had always been a part of him. The assurance. The strength. He barely even registered the rest of the room. It was a holding cell, clearly, similar to the ones they'd constructed in Glasgow—tiny, with two small cots and a chamber pot in the corner.

A definitively full chamber pot.

Lukas sat on the bed beside him, his pale face lined with worry and his red hair sparking like fire in the light.

Aidan pushed himself to sitting. Or tried. The moment he shifted weight, a new glittering wave of pain crashed over him, sending him back to the hard bed. His eyes fluttered as darkness pulled at his many raw and bloody edges.

"Hey, no, no." Lukas put a hand on Aidan's shoulder. Patted the side of his face. "Stay with me."

Lukas's face swam. Blurred. *Tomás?*

"What…" Aidan managed. His mouth tasted like blood and his jaw hurt. He ran his tongue over his teeth, over the lip ring Jeremiah had nearly ripped out. Another tooth was chipped. Kianna would shit herself laughing if she knew he'd broken another one.

The thought made him laugh, which made him wince, and a moment later he was sobbing for the second time in front of this stranger, every convulsion making him hurt more and cry harder. And through that pain was a single, terrible question: Was Kianna even alive?

Lukas didn't say anything, nor did he retreat. His hand stayed on Aidan's shoulder as Aidan tried to get himself under control. Everything hurt. Inside and out. And when he instinctually tried to open to Fire to burn the weakness and pain away, he gasped. The pain of absence struck him like a hammer, a blow to the ribs. He curled in on himself, felt more shudders trace down his body. Heard, at the very edges of his consciousness, his mother screaming his name.

No, no. He couldn't go back. He couldn't look back.

He took a deep breath. Forced the blood and the screams back into the shadows where they belonged. Even there, he could still hear the cries echoing in his own hurt.

"Sorry," Aidan eventually managed. He forced his eyes open, forced the memory away. He coughed. Red splattered across the sheets.

"Don't apologize," Lukas said. "You were just tortured half to death. I think you're allowed a breakdown or two."

Aidan tried to sit up again, slower this time, and Lukas helped guide him. His help didn't lessen the pain. If anything, it made him want to scream in frustration. He wasn't supposed to feel this hurt. This *mortal*.

The moment he was up, another shudder wracked him, this time from cold, and Lukas pulled a blanket over Aidan's shoulders. The harsh wool scratched Aidan's skin, and it was then he remembered he was shirtless. Jeremiah hadn't kept his torture to Aidan's limbs. Nowhere had been safe.

Nowhere had been sacred.

Lukas didn't shuffle away, just sat there, so close Aidan could practically feel his heat. Gods, he wished he could truly feel heat.

"Why are you being nice to me?" Aidan asked. It wasn't the most pressing question in his mind, but it was the one that escaped his lips. He hated it. He sounded pathetic.

"Because I'd like to think you'd do the same if roles were reversed." Lukas raised an eyebrow. He had a sharp, aquiline face, almost statuesque, though that arched eyebrow was adorably expressive. "Your silence is making me think otherwise."

Aidan swallowed the blood pooling in his mouth and wondered when he'd bitten his tongue, and how much blood he could ingest before vomiting. Or passing out. He didn't think it was much for the first. He'd already thrown up a few times under Jeremiah's care.

"Aye," Aidan muttered. "I'm not known for being nice."

"I gathered." Still, he lingered at Aidan's side. Aidan refused to admit it was comforting. It was just the warmth. The only real warmth in this frozen room. He wanted to draw it closer, but he refused to lean in. Refused to let himself need Lukas's embrace. Even if he desperately wanted it. Even if the empty cavity within froze worse than ice. He would use the candle to set himself on fire first.

"He's like that with everyone," Lukas continued. He pulled back the sleeves of his sweater. Bandages wrapped every inch of his flesh, stained with old blood. "Jeremiah's a bit of a dick."

"A bit," Aidan said with a small laugh.

"At least you're still alive."

"I don't know if that's a good thing."

Lukas hesitated. "It is. Trust me."

He shifted and reached under the bed, pulling out something that Aidan prayed wasn't another chamber pot. He was in luck. It was a tray with a covered bowl and a chunk of bread.

At least, he hoped he was in luck. There was no promising the bowl wasn't filled with excrement.

"They brought us dinner," Lukas said. He leaned over to set the tray on Aidan's side. Normally, Aidan would have made some quip about the guy bending over him, but as broken as he was and without Fire's urgings, all thoughts of sex fell flat.

"Delightful." Eating was the last thing on his mind, right after sex and anything remotely pleasurable.

"Don't worry, I already ate mine. It's not poisoned. Could use a bit of salt."

Aidan coughed again. Tried to gracefully hide the phlegm and blood that came up.

"Though," Lukas mused, "it doesn't look like you'll be tasting much of anything."

Aidan grimaced and shook his head. He didn't reach for the spoon or the bread. Not yet. He could barely raise his hand, and he didn't want Lukas to see him shake trying to achieve the most basic of human functions.

"A few days ago I brought down the most powerful Howl in Britain," Aidan said bitterly. "This wasn't exactly the outcome I expected."

Lukas reached over and tore a chunk of bread from Aidan's

tray. Somehow, the guy managed to smell good. Aidan was mostly just impressed he could smell through the blood clogging his nose.

"Karma's a bitch," Lukas muttered.

"You saying I earned this?"

He expected Lukas to backpedal. Instead, the guy chewed Aidan's bread thoughtfully and stared at him. "Didn't you?" he asked quietly.

Aidan opened his mouth to say no, he didn't.

Then he remembered the way Vincent smelled when Aidan burned him alive. The harsh, choking rasp of his screams. Trevor's eyes, right before they went glassy. Memory melted with the countless other deaths he'd been responsible for. The Howls who had been innocent and human, once. The necromancers who definitely had it coming. The bystanders who definitely hadn't. They ticked through his brain, a barrage of marks against his soul. Too many to keep up with. Too many to remember. And yet, he felt every single one as sure as the cuts tracing his flesh.

For the first time in three years, Aidan felt the abrasive, drowning pull of regret.

He wanted to hate Lukas for being a dick. For saying what Aidan was beginning to think.

Maybe Lukas had a point.

Maybe Aidan was right where he deserved to be.

CHAPTER THIRTY-SIX

"YOU HAVE EVERYTHING WRITTEN DOWN, RIGHT?"

Aidan rolled his eyes and held up his phone, showing Dad the screen of his full itinerary. "Who writes shit down anymore, Dad?" he asked. "It's all on here."

"And what happens if you lose your phone?"

"I ask Mom. Or find a computer somewhere since it's all on the cloud. Besides, it's only two weeks." Aidan went back to looking at his phone, thumbing through photos on his feed. Everyone his age had already gone off on a dozen adventures. Now it was his turn to see the world, to get out of this backwoods New England hellhole.

Now was his chance to actually *live*.

The fact that he was doing it with his mother, well…not his first choice, but at least it meant he was getting out of the country. Finally.

He was honestly surprised his parents had even come up with this idea. Take two weeks off of school? In a way, he almost felt bad. The entire reason they were going was to strengthen his relationship with his mom and get her away from the ghosts of this place. If they were willing to let him skip school, their relationship must have been truly failing.

Then again, now that magic had been discovered, the entire field of education was shifting. Very few of Aidan's classmates actually showed up to class anymore. It didn't feel worth it.

Dad grabbed his phone. "This is serious, son."

Son. His dad only used that phrase when he was pissed.

"I'm going to Scotland, *Dad*," Aidan replied. Were they really going to have this conversation again? "They have electricity there. And internet. They don't all just live in castles by firelight."

"I know. I've been there. I just want to make sure you two are safe."

"We'll be fine." Aidan tried to level out his words. He and his mom left for the airport in a few hours. She was out running last-minute errands while Aidan finished packing.

This was the last time he'd see his dad for two weeks. He might as well try to make it a pleasant memory. "Promise. I'll call you the moment I get there."

"Liar," his dad said with a grin. "You'll text first."

"Calling is for old people." Aidan smiled.

"And yet you'll call me when you get to the airport and let me know everything's on time. If nothing else, so I know your phone still works."

Aidan groaned. "Yeah, yeah, sure."

His dad reached out, took his hand. Aidan tried to ignore just how bad Dad's hand shook. "I love you, Aidan."

Aidan smiled and turned his hand up, clenched his dad's hand. "I—"

The door slammed open.

Dad snapped back, shocked, as the Howls poured in. Kravens, putrid and decaying, their stench and gurgling filling the kitchen as they skittered forward on mangled legs, their flesh slopping across the floor.

They reached for his father, yanked him from his seat, their talons digging red into his shoulders, their teeth gnashing. Aidan screamed. He tried to stand, but he couldn't move. He was glued to the chair.

"Aidan! Help me! Please, help!"

His father's voice. And his mother's.

But Aidan couldn't move. And that's when he realized he wasn't stuck there. He was scared. He was too scared to move.

He yelled out again as the Howls dragged his father out of the room. Screamed for his dad. For someone. Anyone. Anyone to help.

He screamed.

Only when the door closed behind them was Aidan able to move. He jumped from his seat. Wrenched the door open.

The yard was empty. In the distance, he heard the bleating of sheep.

"Dad?" he called, his voice trembling. Nothing. Fear clenched his chest. No. No, he had to find him. He couldn't be gone, he couldn't—

"Dad!"

Aidan jerked awake, covered in sweat in the deepest darkness.

"Mate, calm down," Lukas whispered. A hand on his chest, holding him fast to the bed. "It was just a nightmare. Your dad's not here."

Aidan collapsed back on the thin mattress. Stared up at the darkness. Wished against everything else it would consume him, wished the pain that seeped back into consciousness would take him away. The pain, and the everlasting cold.

For what he had done, he didn't deserve anything better.

CHAPTER THIRTY-SEVEN

AIDAN COULDN'T FALL BACK TO SLEEP. HE TRIED after Lukas went back to his own bed. He curled beneath his blanket and shivered, cold and aching, his body a mix of needles and ice cubes and frigid blood. He listened to Lukas snore in the cot beside him.

He considered waking the guy up. Considered trying to make small talk, even though he hated small talk. Something, anything to pull his mind away from his thoughts.

Because he felt like he was going crazy.

As he stared at the ceiling, his memories collected and congealed, the thousands of shadows he'd been burning too brightly to see. But he knew the phrase—the brighter the light, the deeper the shadow.

He'd spent three years ignoring what he'd run from. And now, that past was as thick as tar. It sloughed around his heart, made every pulse ache. He remembered.

Deboarding the plane with his mom, that first glorious taste of Scottish air—the mist and the freshness, the taste of green and stone. Back when this country was an adventure. A chance to mend. To make things better.

Calling his dad. Always calling his dad. When they got past customs. When they made it to their hotel. His dad had wanted a phone call every day. And Aidan had called him. Every day.

Until they went to Skye. He'd planned on calling that evening. Honest. After he and his mom were snug indoors, maybe by the fire in the common room. By the time he tried, the phones were already down.

He never heard his Dad's voice again. Didn't even know if he was alive, or had suffered the same fate as his mom, or had been turned, or...

No. He couldn't go there. Not again. Never again.

He squinted and rolled over, moaning against the pain. Not that this hurt more than the memories shifting around in his head. He didn't know how Water users managed this, the constant despair, the depression sticking to his veins. All he wanted was to open to Fire, to burn the doubt and the regret and the shame.

That was the greatest blessing of his Sphere. In its heat, there was no regret. There was no doubt.

Now, he was wracked by both. The physical pain was just the icing on the damned cake.

It wasn't just the past that haunted him, but the present. Where was Kianna? Had she made it out alive? There was a chance she had slipped free of the Church. Wouldn't be the first time she managed to sneak her way out of a bad situation. And if she had gotten free, there was a chance she had trailed them. A chance she was going to send help.

He just had to hold on until that help came.

If the coming day was anything like the one he just survived, the chances of that were slim.

He almost felt bad that he didn't care about Margaret and Gregory. He *should* care about them. He should be worried for their well-being.

Trouble was, even now, even without Fire making him bold, he didn't care. He just wanted out. Him and Kianna. He wanted out. Apparently, at his core, he was still just a heartless dick.

With every tick of his thoughts was the looming dread that the only thing awaiting him was a cold, meaningless death.

Death at the hands of a zealot in a shadowed room. Lost to history. Nameless. Forgotten.

Exactly as he deserved.

At one point, he even found himself whispering Tomás's name, his body aching for any sort of heat, any sort of hope. But even that was in vain. Tomás never appeared, in dreams or in the flesh. Why had the Howl sent him down here, without warning him of the Church's takeover? It was impossible that he wouldn't have known. Was Tomás truly on his side?

He knew he was an idiot for trusting an incubus. Just as he was an idiot for thinking he had the upper hand against a Kin.

Those thoughts and worse cycled through his head for what felt like days. With no light, he couldn't tell the time.

When the door opened—jolting Aidan back to consciousness with a painful shock—he flinched away, suddenly wishing the night would go on forever.

The guard said nothing. Just set two trays on the ground and stepped out, sending them back into near-darkness. The guard had been kind enough to leave a lit candle on one of the trays.

For a moment, Aidan thought it was stupid for them to leave a weapon like that in a room with two prisoners, especially around a Fire mage. Then he realized he wasn't a Fire mage anymore, and even if he used the candle to set his bed ablaze, all it would accomplish was burning him and Lukas alive. The walls were too thick for it to spread.

At least he had an easy way out, if the torture got bad enough. At least there was one way to go out in a blaze. Even if not of glory.

Lukas didn't move, his breathing still heavy and deep.

"Food," Aidan said. He pushed himself to sitting and winced.

Lukas snorted and rolled over.

"Suit yourself," Aidan muttered.

He wasn't hungry in the slightest, but he ate anyway, trying to restore some strength. It didn't take a genius to know what today would entail: Jeremiah would bring him in for questioning again. The man had made it abundantly clear that Aidan was to be his entire focus until Aidan's sins were gone. There was no hope of getting out of it. No hope of avoiding days or weeks of torture until death or the cavalry arrived.

As he sat, eating tasteless porridge and some lukewarm water that was probably supposed to be tea, he once more wondered how Kianna was. He let himself think the worst— what if she hadn't gotten away? What if she was in the cell beside theirs having the same bland breakfast? What if she'd been killed already?

Something twisted in Aidan's heart. A pang.

This was all his fault.

Kianna never would have gotten into this mess if it wasn't for him. She had wanted to part ways, years ago, once she'd realized the resistance building in Inverness was in shambles. Wanted to leave him at the makeshift Guild and carry on by herself—especially after he'd used the opportunity to get attuned to Fire. He'd followed her out into the world anyway. She threatened to punch him, abandon him in the night, kill him if he didn't get out of her face. But she never had. Somewhere along the line, they had become friends.

Since then, he hadn't left her side.

Now, unless she had managed to get away, she was locked up somewhere in this mess. Getting tortured. Hopefully not tortured. She didn't have a mark to burn off, didn't have any magic to atone for. Though he doubted she would hold her tongue. She was smart, but she hated the Church with the same resolve that she hated magic.

If anything, she was probably only making her sentence worse.

He had to believe she was still alive, though. Giving the Inquisition hell. Making them work. Aidan almost felt proud, knowing she would never snap. Knowing she would sit there, bloodied and smiling and making them sweat for her sins.

The smile slipped.

Or, she could have told them that he had killed his commander. That he truly was a pawn of the Dark Lady. Was that how Jeremiah knew? Had they already gotten to her?

You killed Trevor in cold blood, he thought. And this time, there was no hiss of Fire to convince him otherwise, no assurance that he wasn't a murderer. There was just the darkness and the cold, the knowledge that what he had done was unforgivable. No matter what he told himself, he had killed Trevor solely because he wanted to rule. It wasn't for the good of the country. Wasn't for the good of mankind.

Aidan was a murderer.

He was, at heart, no better than the creatures he'd thought he was seeking to kill.

Aidan tried, vainly, to reach for Fire. To burn the thoughts and emotion away. Every time he clutched at that hollowed space within him, he gasped in pain.

Instead of fending off the thoughts, all he did was inflame them.

Behind the dark of his eyelids, he saw Trevor's face when he realized Aidan was going to kill him. When he knew in his heart that Aidan had betrayed not just the warmth between them, but the very cause they had stood for. And there, too, Aidan saw the other memories: waking up in Trevor's arms, studying the guy's face before slipping quietly away. His lips against Trevor's neck, kissing down to his clavicles while Trevor groaned in pleasure. The nights spent in Trevor's study, discussing tactics or how to manipulate the council.

Trevor had done everything Aidan had ever asked. Had been everything Aidan could have wanted.

Until Trevor had exiled him. Until Aidan let Fire speak for him.

Aidan forced down the thought. Tried to. Tried to find the spark. Fire had been the only thing driving him forward, the only thing telling him that victory would make every sacrifice, every death worth it.

Without Fire, he questioned everything.

If this was what real life felt like, maybe he should just piss Jeremiah off and get this salvation thing over with.

"You look sad," Lukas said. Aidan jerked up.

Lukas lay watching him, his pale eyes reflecting the candlelight, his hair a mop of flame. Something about Lukas's freckles made him look, well, innocent. Even if that was belied by the scars and tattoos that crossed his pale skin, or the knowing, serious look on his face.

Aidan felt like he was being studied. Not in the way that Jeremiah studied him. No. This was somehow more intimate. Lukas didn't look at Aidan like a straight dude would—his expression was soft, open. A question or an offer. Or maybe that was just the lighting.

"I take it you didn't sleep well?" Lukas continued.

"You could say that," Aidan muttered. He slid Lukas's tray over with his foot. Tried not to make eye contact. The boy... even with his thoughts of desolation, Lukas made his blood warm. Made him want to go snuggle in closer. And seeing as they were locked in a cell surrounded by zealots filled with hellfire, that was probably not a good idea. The Church still didn't look too kindly on the queers.

"Nightmares?"

"I mean, I did wake you up screaming."

Lukas nodded and picked up his tray. "Yeah. But I guess I'd hoped you slept a bit better after that. You know, knowing I'm here to protect you and all."

"I don't need protecting," Aidan said on instinct.

"Clearly," Lukas replied, not even looking up at him. "That's why you're locked in a cell and covered in bandages."

"'Tis only a flesh wound."

Lukas snorted. At least he got the reference.

Lukas ate in silence while Aidan wondered what tortures would await him at Jeremiah's hands today. He gingerly touched the bandages wrapped on his arms. The worst of the pain had died down, but the wounds were still tender.

"You wanna talk about it?" Lukas asked.

Once more, Aidan jerked at the noise. Jesus. Without Fire, he was twitchy as an addict. Maybe Kianna was right. Maybe he had gotten too dependent on magic. "Talk about what?" Talking about his feelings was definitely not his strong suit.

"Why you think you're here."

"I'm here because I was captured."

"You know what I mean. Jeremiah doesn't torture everyone who comes in here."

"Says the boy who was tortured."

"For an hour," Lukas said. He took a moment to sip his tea. "You were gone all day. And, judging from the way you look right now, I'm guessing you aren't expecting the worst to be over, even after all that. So. Why are they spending so much energy torturing you?"

"You're awfully nosy for a stranger," Aidan said.

Lukas just shrugged. "Air user. Old habits die hard. Ended up having to attune to Fire as well because my friends said I was acting too cold." He laughed bitterly. "And now look at me."

"Preaching to the choir, my friend."

"The choir isn't answering my question."

Aidan watched shadows curl around his feet, wondering about the shadows lacing through his heart.

"I'd rather not talk about it," he finally said. "I don't know. Honestly. I think Jeremiah just has the hots for me."

Lukas laughed, terribly loud for such a small space. Then he winced and went silent. "Sorry. But yeah, okay. I get it."

"What I *don't* get," Aidan said, "is how the Church managed to hijack all of London. *And* capture the entire army without a single warning being raised. Even with a civilian coup, you'd think someone would manage to escape." Aidan paused. "Do you think we could throw a rebellion of our own?"

"Doubtful. The Church has numbers we never expected. And our Guild wasn't just captured." His eyes narrowed. "They were killed. There are only a few of us left. The ones who weren't mauled by the civilians or killed during the uprising have been massacred."

"But how?" Aidan pressed, almost frantic in his fear. "London was *huge.* Your army was the biggest on the continent." *And mine was second.* "The Church couldn't have converted that many."

"They didn't have to," Lukas said. He glanced at his wrist, to where his own mark was burned and buried beneath scar tissue and bandages.

"What do you mean?"

"I mean, I'm starting to worry that we were wrong all along. That they're protected by God, and the rest of us are damned." Lukas's voice was fragile in the darkness. "It should be impossible. But they're immune to magic."

Aidan didn't think it was possible for his blood to get any colder, but in the light of that revelation, his whole body turned to ice.

Howls were immune to the Sphere they were pulled from. Weapons were immune to magic if consecrated in their user's magic or blood. But humans didn't get to be immune to magic. Humans were *made* of magic. The Spheres weren't some other-worldly force—they were what drove the body, what fueled it. To be immune to magic was to be…well, inhuman.

"How?" It was the only word he could speak.

"I don't know," Lukas said. "They haven't exactly given me the chance to ask."

Aidan's sluggish mind tried to race as panic set in. This changed everything. If the Church was immune to magic, they could take over any Guild with barely a fuss. Sure, Hunters were trained in combat. But magic was what turned the tides of battle. Magic was what ensured you lived to see an-other fight. Magic was what humanity relied on to survive, even as it caused the world's downfall.

The tiny candle between them snuffed out.

A few minutes later, the door opened. Jeremiah and his guards entered.

Aidan didn't even fight when they lifted him up and hauled him away.

CHAPTER THIRTY-EIGHT

"HOW ARE YOU IMMUNE?" AIDAN ASKED.

He tried to keep his voice steady, tried not to wince as Jeremiah slowly unwrapped the bandages from his arms. Slowly, because the dried blood peeled at his skin, ripped open scabs, and sent fresh streams of blood down his flesh. Made him wince and fight back the darkness. Even the unwrapping was another form of torture.

"By the grace of God," Jeremiah said. "In His glorious light, not even shadows may seep."

"That's impossible."

"Nothing is impossible, when you have faith."

Aidan knew he would get no further. Not when ideas of faith were involved. "But why?" he asked through gritted teeth. "Why did you take over the Guild? I thought we had a treaty. I thought we were on the same side!"

"We were never on the same side." Jeremiah paused his unwrapping to stare Aidan down. "You made that abundantly clear when you kicked me and my followers from Glasgow.

Do you have any idea how many we lost in those early days? How many fell to the darkness? No," he continued, resuming his work, "we were never on the same side. You may have destroyed Calum, but you have no love for the living. None who use magic can truly value the world they desecrate. Liberation can only be gained by the erasure of your kind. All who use magic must be brought to the light."

"That's genocide."

Jeremiah grunted. "The Lord works in mysterious ways."

Jeremiah didn't give him a chance to question further. He placed a bare hand on Aidan's arm, right over the brand, and squeezed. Blood trickled between the man's fingers, but he didn't seem to mind.

"Magic will be banished from the land," Jeremiah said through Aidan's scream. "But first, you will find your way to the light. And you will do so by telling me how such darkness entered your heart. The Dark Lady stirs within you. I will know how she got there. I will know how her words became your own."

"I don't know what you're talking about," Aidan managed, his words more gasps than anything.

"I think you do," Jeremiah whispered. He reached into the folds of his cloak, and Aidan flinched back, expecting the worst.

What he hadn't expected was the onyx shard Jeremiah pulled from his pocket. The same shard as he'd seen in the vision. The shard that Tomás and the Dark Lady both wanted him to find.

Aidan tried to keep his expression calm, stony. But he couldn't keep his heart from racing with recognition. He hoped Jeremiah didn't notice the slight increase in surging blood.

Jeremiah held the shard in the glittering firelight. Examining it. And examining Aidan's reaction.

For his part, Aidan tried to look anywhere but the shard. This close, however, and the crystal felt like a whirlpool. It pulled at his senses and snaked through his thoughts, demanding attention. Demanding worship. He could no more pull back from its power than he could from the siren song of Fire.

Aidan's eyes were glued to the crystal, to the serpentine coil of silver wrapped around its length and the sigils sketched into the surface, their sharp shapes inlaid with pewter.

Symbols that seethed with power.

And maybe it was his imagination, maybe it was a trick of the candles, but shadows seemed to ooze around the shard, drifting over Jeremiah's palm like fog, twining to and from the crystal, as though it absorbed and expelled the light. Even the runes seemed to twitch and move, dancing in patterns he could almost understand. In those movements, Aidan heard a whisper. Faint and feminine. The same unearthly hiss as Fire. *Consume, devour, destroy. Burn them. Burn them and be mine.*

For some reason, that voice filled him with hope.

"Yes," Jeremiah said, his words fogged. "It calls to you. You cannot deny its pull."

Aidan blinked. Peeled his gaze away from the shard, which felt like tearing off another layer of skin. "I don't know what you're talking about."

"Your lies are opaque as blood," Jeremiah said. He turned the shard back and forth in the light, but he wasn't looking at it—he didn't stop searching Aidan's eyes. "What does this speak to you? What does *she* speak?"

Aidan shook his head. He refused to look at the shard again. He'd already given too much away with his shitty poker face. "It's a rock. What makes you think it would say anything?"

Jeremiah just smiled, pocketed the shard, and turned toward the table of torture instruments.

Aidan struggled against the bonds. He had to stall. Had to get Jeremiah to talk. To do anything. Anything other than continue the torture Aidan knew awaited him.

"Please—"

That was the only word Aidan could manage through the fear that choked his throat. Fear, and need.

If he could get the shard, he could get out of here. He was so close. So close. But the only thing in his future was pain.

Jeremiah didn't acknowledge Aidan's plea. The man's bloody hand hovered over his tools, their silver dulled with Aidan's caked blood. Jeremiah's fingers waved slightly as he selected, and he actually hummed to himself, something that sounded less hymnal and more '80s rock. Sweat dripped down Aidan's skin despite the chill in the room. Jeremiah enjoyed this. He loved every minute of it. Even this was a part of the torture—the long, drawn out anticipation as Aidan awaited his fate. The knowledge that literally nothing Aidan could do would prevent another session.

"Hmm, yes," Jeremiah mused. Aidan shrunk at the pleasure in his voice before even seeing the instrument. "Yes, I think this will do quite nicely."

Jeremiah picked up an object, and the blood drained from Aidan's limbs.

He struggled against the bonds as Jeremiah stepped over, holding the bloody cheese grater before him like an offering.

"I seem to remember you reacting quite favorably toward this one," Jeremiah said. He knelt down before Aidan.

"No, please," Aidan began, but Jeremiah shook his head.

"Begging will get you nowhere, my child. Only repentance. And you will only repent through answers." He reached out and placed the cold, serrated metal against Aidan's chest. Right above his nipple. Aidan's breath burned his throat, quick as a rabbit.

Jeremiah looked positively delighted at the fear in Aidan's dilated pupils.

"You will scream. But even that is music to our Lord and savior. That is the song of redemption." He smiled. "When the screaming is over, your secrets will flow freely. We will learn why the Dark Lady seeks you, and through our work, we will free you from her clutches.

"So sing for me, my son, and let your sins burst free like blood."

CHAPTER THIRTY-NINE

AIDAN DIDN'T LAST NEARLY AS LONG THE SECOND round.

He came to with a jolt, breaking from blissful unconsciousness to his waking nightmare. His breath was hot and frantic as he waited for the next cut, the next burn, the next scrape. It didn't come. The room was silent. He looked around. No one. His wounds were freshly wrapped, blood seething through cotton in Rorschach-like clots, stains of sins he hadn't known he'd committed. Not that the wrappings did anything to numb the pain that settled on his skin like shards of ice. Every breath shifted the cloth, made wounds sting and burn. Every pulse of blood felt like another day of life lost.

And after Jeremiah's session, Aidan had definitely lost a great deal of both.

Aidan was proud of himself, though—he hadn't broken. He'd spent the entire session with his teeth gritted and blood dripping from his lips and wounds, but he hadn't said a word. Not about himself, or the Guild, or the shard.

Neither of them had gotten any answers, and Aidan knew Jeremiah was far from finished with him. So he sat in the silence and waited for the worst.

Was this another form of torture? Was Jeremiah behind him, waiting to literally stab him in the back? Aidan tried to turn, tried to see, but he couldn't move an inch. The bonds were tight enough that he couldn't feel his extremities.

That's when he realized Jeremiah had left something behind.

There, right on the table in front of him, was the shard. Glinting amid the torture instruments, a fragment of black in a pool of blood.

Aidan tried to check the room. Not that he could move. So he closed his eyes. Went as still as possible, calming his breathing until he could hear every beat of his reluctant heart. He tried to convince himself he could hear that the room was empty, that he wasn't being watched.

Once he was certain, or hoped he could be certain, he struggled. He clenched his teeth and tried to pull his arms from the leather straps. Tried to shift his weight, to topple the chair over. And even—desperately—tried to open to Fire. It felt like grasping for a ghost in the dark—vain and terrible, knowing it was there, haunting him, and forever out of his reach.

Nothing worked. Not that he expected anything else. Hope was a dangerous thing.

He didn't know why he had to get the shard. Only that Tomás wanted it, that the Dark Lady needed it, that it would grant him power and supposedly bring his parents back, and maybe then he could get Fire back, as well. And maybe, when he got the shard, Tomás would appear and pull him out of this hell. Maybe this was all some elaborate, sadistic test, and Aidan just had to prove he could pass. Tears welled in his eyes from his wounds. Pain, and the frustration of being so close. So close to getting the fuck out of here. So close to getting it all back.

He couldn't entertain the other possibilities, even though they gnawed at him. And without Fire to burn away the worries like pests, their voices grew louder as his struggle grew more fruitless.

What if, now that Aidan could no longer use magic, Tomás would have no use for him?

What if the shard would do nothing?

And then, the thought he'd been pushing away since that morning: What if Tomás had played him, sending him into the Inquisition's clutches just to be done with him?

The thought took hold, and he stopped struggling.

He'd thought he was the one playing Tomás. Thought he'd been in control. But here he was, broken and beaten, as far from power as he'd ever been, and Tomás was nowhere to be seen. He had failed. Just as he had failed his mother. Just as he'd failed his friends. Just as he'd failed Trevor, the one man on this island who cared enough to look past Aidan's faults—Trevor had loved him, and Aidan had failed him by giving in to his own primal need to win.

He couldn't help it. Despite himself, he began to cry.

Big, fat tears filled his eyes, blurring the room and the torture instruments and the shard, dripping to mingle with his blood.

He didn't know how long he sobbed. Didn't care. He

couldn't hear anything else over his burning cries, over the constant voices in his head, telling him he had failed.

He had failed, and he had pulled so many others down with him.

He had killed Trevor for power.

He had killed Vincent in cold blood.

He had killed countless others under his command, solely by leading them into the battlefield.

And he had killed his mother by coming here.

"Oh, God," he sobbed, his heart drowning under images of his mother succumbing to the Howls.

"Your God is not here," came a voice.

A finger against his cheek. Wiping his tears away. Before him, silhouetted in the flickering candles...

"But your mother answers."

Aidan gasped another sob. There was no way. It couldn't be—

"Mom?"

And it was her. Kneeling before him. The same brown eyes filled with warmth. The same loving smile. The long black hair, the full cheeks. She glowed in the dim light. Radiant.

Alive.

"It's me, Aidan." She smiled wider. "It's really me."

"Impossible," Aidan said. But her hand was on his knee, and her touch was firm. Warm. Soothing. "You're—"

"Dead?" Her smile twitched, and there was a flicker in her eyes. A darkness. "What is death, when you could control life?"

"No," Aidan grunted. The panic was back, stronger now,

worse than anything Jeremiah could conjure. "No, this isn't real. You aren't real."

The facade slid, her features shifting like shadows from one moment to the next. Dark hair bleaching blonde, clothing melding black and sinuous.

"I am very real," the Dark Lady said. "And you are so, so close to bringing her back. I gave you my word. Now you must deliver on yours."

"I'm not serving you," he said. It was the last fragment of self-respect he had, the last sliver of humanity. "You're evil. You did this...all of this."

The Dark Lady shook her head slowly.

"I never took you for one to believe solely because others tell you to. Look around, my child. You are tortured by those who say they are righteous. I have done nothing but aid you, just as Tomás has lent his hand."

She leaned in closer, and when she spoke, there was true sadness in her voice.

"I am not evil, Aidan. I never created monsters. I created gods. Just as I have created you. It was mankind itself that turned them evil, that painted them as villains and demons. I sought only the secret to life. And these people, this *Church*, gave us only death."

He hated himself for believing her. Hated that when she touched the side of his face, he didn't flinch away. If anything, he wanted to lean in.

"I will give you everything your heart desires. I will set you free."

Aidan knew the answer he was supposed to give. He should push her away. Deny her. See through what had to be lies.

He was a trained Hunter. Sure, in dreams he had been co-erced into believing he would help, believing she could work miracles.

But this wasn't a dream. The Dark Lady was here, in the room with him, even though she was dead, even though this was the heart of the Church. She was here, and she was the reason his mother had died, the reason this hell had broken loose in the first place. He had been trained to kill her. To resist her.

Yet he knew in the pit of his soul that she would deliver on her promise. He knew she was telling the truth. About everything.

"What...what do you need me to do?" he asked.

She smiled and stood, and in that sweeping motion she transformed, the shade of his mother once more.

"I knew I could count on you, baby," she said. His mother's voice. It was his mother's voice. He didn't realize just how much he'd missed hearing it.

Just how much he'd give up to hear it again. A cry bubbled up in the back of his throat. *He could hear her again.*

She stepped over to the table. To the shard.

"These men have stolen so much from me," she murmured. "From us. From our families." She looked at Aidan. "They tore us apart. It was never my desire to create this hell. I wanted only to make Eden. A world where death was not the end, but a transition. One that could be postponed. Or reversed." Her fingers hovered over the shard, so close, yet not touching. "They ended my work. But with your help... I could resume it."

She jerked up. Distantly, he heard footsteps down the hall.

"There is so much to teach you, but we don't have time. We will though, baby. I promise. Just keep fighting. For me. For us."

"The shard——"

"Is just the beginning," she said. "Bring it to Tomás. He needs it. We need it."

Then, before he could ask anything else, the door opened and his mother vanished in shadow.

Three figures stepped before him. Jeremiah. And the two guards from yesterday.

Aidan could barely focus on them. *Had that just happened? Was that my mother's ghost? The Dark Lady?*

"I'm afraid we must change tactics, my son," Jeremiah said. He walked to the table and pocketed the shard as though it were nothing. Just a stone. A rock. When Aidan was beginning to realize it was so much more. "You have proven that physical pain is not enough to break you. And so..." He gestured to the guards. They moved to Aidan's sides, undoing the straps binding him to the chair and then hauling him roughly to his feet.

Their hands on his wounds nearly made him black out again.

"What are you going to do to me?" Aidan gasped through the pain.

"Not to you, my son," Jeremiah said. "Not quite. Just remember...this—all of this—is by your hand."

CHAPTER FORTY

AIDAN TRIED TO KEEP TRACK OF THE HALLWAYS they trudged through, if only to help him try to escape later. Church members in black and violet robes walked with hoods drawn and faces down. Weapons and furniture lined the walls, as if every single room had been emptied, renovated. Aidan could only wonder if each of those rooms had been turned into a torture chamber. Heavy incense pooled against the ceiling, cloyingly sweet.

As if trying to hide the scent of blood that lingered every-where they turned.

Aidan lost track of the turns and stairwells. Not that his brain was functioning properly anyway. He couldn't force himself to believe that the scene with his mother had been an illusion. He'd *felt* her touching his face. He'd heard her voice as clear as day. His mother's voice, and the Dark Lady's. One and the same.

What did that make him?

Then Jeremiah pushed open a door that led outside, and

Aidan's thoughts were burned away by the brightness of the afternoon.

Aidan barely registered what was around him—the rows of sandstone buildings towering up, the ruined street, the stunted trees. He squinted against the light. *Of all times for it to be sunny.* His brain didn't want to congeal on what was actually before him. Because here was gathered what felt like the whole of London—hundreds of people, some in tattered civilian garb, others in the black and purple robes of the Church, pressed together in a large outdoor square. The sight of so many people made his head reel. As did what they gathered around.

At first, Aidan thought they were just telephone poles. But no, the thick poles stuck side by side in the mud were surrounded by kindling. Five charred stakes in all, and the scent of smoke and something sicker mingling in the air. He didn't want to know when they had last been used. He didn't want to know when they would be used again. Though he had a guess, and the very thought made him struggle against the guards that dragged him.

Not that he had much struggle left, and a swift punch in the gut pushed the remaining fight from his lungs.

A makeshift platform had been constructed on the opposite side of the stakes, civilians and priests mingling at its base, and that was where Jeremiah led him. The crowd parted for the priests, but they made no attempts to hide their disgust toward Aidan. They cursed and spit at him, a few braver men slipping through the crowd to punch Aidan in the chest and face. Aidan's entourage did nothing to prevent the beatings, and every thrust sent pain lancing through his body and blood spraying from his mouth.

These were the people whom the Guild had kept safe. Innocents who had lived solely because Hunters like Aidan were willing to die for them.

Oh, how fast they forgot.

Rage flared, brief and fierce—he should burn these people to the ground, kill them for betraying him so quickly. So easily. The Dark Lady's words whispered through his mind: *I never created monsters… Mankind itself painted them as demons.* None of this was the Dark Lady's fault. None of this was made by Howls. This was all mankind's doing.

But the anger faded in a moment, replaced by dread. By the realization that these people who had once composed his countrymen no longer wanted him. He would never get their appreciation for what he'd done. They would never see him as a savior. Instead, abject hatred burned in their eyes.

They had painted him as horribly as the Dark Lady herself.

He couldn't meet their glares. Instead, he watched the blood dripping to his feet and let the Inquisitors drag him up the steps to the platform, where Jeremiah stood with arms raised in reverence.

Aidan wanted to convince himself that if he was going to die, he would do so with dignity. Public execution or no.

He wanted to, but all he could do was look down and hope it was over quickly.

"My children," Jeremiah called out, silencing the crowd immediately. "Today, we have cause for celebration. For today, we bring more lost souls to the light. Today, we rejoice in the purity of our Lord, and His continued battle against the Dark."

He gestured Aidan forward, and the guards pushed Aidan to Jeremiah's side.

"For too long, our world has been overrun with heretics and magic-users, all of them pawns of the Dark Lady. They parade themselves as heroes even as their work drags the world down to darkness. But you have found salvation. The Church has opened its arms to you, and you, my children, have opened your arms to the Light. Today, we bring that work to those who would deny it. Today, the very leaders who tore our world asunder will pay for their actions.

"Bring them forward!"

On cue, a group of black-and-violet-robed Inquisitors stepped out from the shadows, a long chain in their hands. And linked to it by heavy manacles, Aidan's comrades stepped out into the light.

If Aidan had thought the jeers that followed him had been bad, the ones that erupted at his comrades' entrance put them to shame. He felt it—the crack within him as his spirit broke and fell to his feet. Kianna walked at the front of the chain, hands bound behind her, her skin bruised and slicked with blood. One eye swollen shut. She didn't drop her head, though. Even as people screamed and punched and spit at her, she held her head high, gaze forward. Gaze straight at him.

He knew he should have felt proud. Proud that even now, at the end, she was staying strong. Stronger than he was, at least. If anything, the sight of her just made him feel like a failure. Here she was, end of the line, and she was more composed

than he. Because she'd never had magic to be ripped away from her. Because she'd already been through hell and back.

She looked like a woman who couldn't be broken by the world.

If anything, it seemed to make the world try harder.

Jeremiah didn't shut up, but Aidan didn't hear him. His head filled with a high-pitched buzz that drove every thought away. He watched as the Inquisitors chained Kianna to the charred stake. He wondered who had been killed there before. He caught nothing from Jeremiah's tirade, save for words like "salvation" and "repentance" and the usual bullshit. None of it mattered.

He could only watch as Kianna stood calmly at her own funeral pyre, as Margaret and Gregory struggled at her sides. Like her, they were bruised and bloody. Unlike her, they strained and yelled at the Inquisitors who bound them to the stakes. They weren't ready to die.

Seeing Aidan on the platform, rather than at their side, made them pause. Aidan couldn't meet their gazes. The hurt. The confusion. Why wasn't he up there, with them, when he was the reason they'd all fallen into this hell?

It took him far too long to realize that Jeremiah had stopped speaking. The crowd's collective gaze had turned toward him.

Aidan started, broke his stare from his comrades. Looked at Jeremiah. "What?" he asked.

Jeremiah's previous words began leaking into his brain. But no, he couldn't have heard the man right.

"I said, it is your choice," Jeremiah replied. "We must cleanse your soul, Aidan. And the best way of doing so is to

have you aid in the Lord's work. By banishing magic and evil from the land, you will be one step closer to salvation.

"I will give you a choice. Not all need burn to taste salvation. One, perhaps, is strong enough to find their way into the light. I will let you choose. One to live in the hope we can save them. Two to burn and let the Lord judge their souls. Who will it be?" He leaned in closer. "Should you decide *not* to decide, I will ensure that all their deaths are painful and slow. And that you watch every second of it. Either way, they—and you—will be cleansed.

"Choose wisely."

At those words, a guard dragged him off the platform, through the parted crowd.

The faces of the now-silent gathering blurred. Everything blurred. He wanted to run. Wanted to throw up. Wanted more than anything for this not to be real.

Only days ago, he had killed Trevor to secure his place in history. A man he had slept with. Had maybe even cared for. He had killed without question. Without pause or shame. And now, he was being forced to kill, and he wanted nothing more than to hide away.

He stared between Kianna and Margaret and Gregory. He hated himself for so many reasons right then. But the worst was that this wasn't even a choice. He should have at least felt a small desire to save the others—and he did, to a degree— but there was no hesitation when he reached the stakes.

"I'm sorry," he said, looking to Gregory. Then to Margaret. His eyes teared up again, and his words were a choke. "Truly."

He pointed to Kianna.

Wordlessly, two Inquisitors untied her from the stake.

Kianna once more refused to struggle or show any sign of emotion. The others, however, realized what he had done and began to scream.

Aidan tried to block them out. Margaret and Gregory cursed at him. Screamed his name. But he refused to look anywhere but Kianna. Her face was stony, her eyes boring into him with more meaning than he could define. He knew one thing, though—she wasn't grateful.

The guards dragged her to the side. She finally looked away. Looked to the two people he had sentenced to die.

For a moment, he wondered if saving her from burning had only damned them both in a different way.

"Well then, my child," Jeremiah said. Aidan jolted as Jeremiah clapped a hand on his shoulder. "We now move on to the next step of your salvation." Jeremiah reached down and grabbed Aidan's wrist, placing something hot and metallic in his palm. Aidan glanced down, his heart dropping to his feet.

A lighter.

"What?" Aidan looked from the lighter to Jeremiah. There was no way he was saying what Aidan thought he was.

"You have led these men and women to the doorstep of the Dark Lady," Jeremiah said, louder this time. "In following you, they turned to magic, and in turn spoiled the land and their very souls. It is only fitting that you should be the one to help bring them to the Light. Redeem yourself and cleanse their souls. Spark the fire that will bring them to redemption."

Margaret and Gregory had gone silent. They stared at Aidan with wide-eyed horror. Not only had he refused to save them, he was the one who would murder them.

He couldn't move. The lighter burned in his hand and he was frozen. Paralyzed.

This couldn't be real.

Jeremiah's hand squeezed tighter.

"Either you set the fire, or I do. And then I will throw you and your dear friend on the flames."

Kianna still refused to look at him. What was she thinking? Did she hate him for this? For saving her, and forcing her to watch her comrades die?

Since when did he care what she thought? Since when did he care about people under his command losing their lives?

The truth struck him harder than he could imagine.

Without Fire, he was still the weak, pathetic little boy he'd thought he left behind on the shores of Loch Lomond.

He looked down to the lighter, and the painful irony of this struck him. A few days ago, he could have done this with magic. Now he needed a lighter to do the trick, and he couldn't convince himself to strike it.

They were defenseless.

They had relied on him.

And as they watched him deliberate, he knew they were hit by the same realization: even though Aidan was broken in more ways than one, he was going to light the kindling. Because it was the only way to save his ass. He wasn't about to sacrifice himself to save them. In spite of everything, that selfish part of Aidan hadn't changed one bit.

It made him sick.

But it also wouldn't make him change his mind.

"Please, don't do this!" Margaret said, coughing blood. "Please! We trusted you! We believed in you!"

"You can't," Gregory said, and when Aidan looked at the guy, he knew that Gregory was thinking of the night they'd spent together. The hurt of betrayal was thick in his eyes. "Please. Please!"

Aidan didn't move.

"If this is your choice—" Jeremiah began, reaching for the lighter. Aidan jerked away.

"No." Aidan gritted his teeth. Lowered his voice and tried to find resolve—if he was going to make this right, he had to live. He had to get the shard and get out of here. That was the only way to make any of this worth it. The only way to redeem any of his actions. He had to live. He had to fight. And even though he hated himself for it, he knew it wasn't a choice. "I should do it."

He stepped forward and clicked open the lighter. A thin flame poured out. Weak. Pathetic. Just like him. The flame seemed as unassured as he was, as if even the fire doubted Aidan's ability to wield it.

Another step, and the two bound Hunters' pleas turned to screams.

He looked down to the flame in his hands. Knelt before the kindling.

"I'm sorry," he said. Perhaps to himself. Perhaps to his pleading comrades. Perhaps to the memory of his mother and everyone else he had failed along the way.

He held the lighter to the kindling.

It took a while for the straw and twigs to catch. Then they flared, and the screaming of his comrades grew louder, and he didn't move. He kept his hands by the racing flames, let himself try to find some semblance of comfort in the warmth.

Some echo of memory from the heat that seared his knuckles, his tattoos gleaming ominously in the light.

BURN THEM

BURN THEM

BURN THEM

He'd gotten them as a promise to himself. Now he saw
them only as a curse.

He stayed there. Kneeling before the fire. Head bowed. As
his comrades screamed and choked, as the flames and smoke
leaped higher. He stayed there, as if praying for forgiveness,
when in reality he was praying to the flames. To come back
to him. To embrace him. To help him forget, to help him
burn this mortal weakness away.

Fire crackled. Sparks popped. Embers flared against his
skin. Burning him. Making his muscles twitch from pain.
Sweat broke across his skin. His comrades' screams finally
diminished. Choked and sobbing, gasping into silence.

He couldn't move. Couldn't help the tears welling in his
eyes for what he'd done. But more than that—for the absence
of Fire. The burning, starving flames before him seemed
alien, when once they'd felt like family. Every ember that
scarred his skin was a reminder of how broken he was. How
he was no longer himself.

He should have hated himself, for sitting before his burning
comrades and thinking only of himself. He should have, but
that was the one thing that the Inquisition hadn't taken away.

At the end of the day, Aidan would fight for himself. If
only because that was all he had left.

Finally, the guards grabbed him under the armpits and
dragged him back from the flames.

He didn't look up. Just stared at the ground as they pulled him away, as his body immediately shut down with cold.

That was a lie. He looked up and back once. To see his comrades still burning on the pyre. And Kianna staring at them solemnly. Her face unreadable. Like a queen, even with her hands bound behind her back.

For a brief moment, the sight of her gave him hope. She looked in control. Like she could get them out.

Then a guard punched her in the gut, and she dropped to her knees, and Aidan remembered she was still as screwed as he was.

They were still going to suffer and die.

And the suffering, he knew, was only just beginning.

CHAPTER FORTY-ONE

"I'M SORRY."

Those were the first words out of Lukas's mouth when Aidan was thrown back into the cell, the door slammed and locked behind him. Another candle burned in the center of the room, a mockery of the inferno Aidan had just endured.

Aidan didn't answer.

He collapsed on his bed and curled in on himself. Squeezed his eyes shut and tried to block out the sights and scents of his burning comrades. Tried to find some spark of hope against the suffocating darkness, to block out the pain that coursed through his body and the dread of what would continue to happen.

He'd spared Kianna's life and subjected her to more torture. All he'd done was buy the Church more time to hurt them. He would never get out. He would never get Fire back. He would never be avenged. Never remembered.

Everything—every death, every day—had been for nothing.

Despite himself, he began to cry. Again. And the amount he hated himself for it just made him cry harder.

He couldn't stop. Couldn't muffle the ugly sobs. Not even when Lukas sat once more at his side, hand light on his broken body.

To his credit, Lukas didn't tell him it would all be okay. That he'd find a way out of it. Lukas didn't lie, and in some small way, Aidan was grateful for the lack of comfort. It was easier than getting his hopes up. Lukas just sat there, silently, gently touching Aidan's shoulder, while Aidan broke apart.

He hurt. Every inch of him hurt. His body. His heart. His soul.

What hurt most, though, was the small shred of relief he felt inside.

Relief that it hadn't been him on the pyre. Relief that he was still alive. Breathing. Even if only for a little bit longer.

Even though every inch of him screamed in agony, at least he was able to feel that pain.

That relief, that sheer betrayal of his body, hurt worst of all.

Aidan was dragged in for torture a second time that day. Or third, if you counted the pyre. Which he did.

And this time, he wasn't there alone.

Kianna was already bound to a chair when he was brought in. She stared straight ahead, in her tattered pink T-shirt and bloodstained black denim. Same room as before—same dripping candles, same bare walls, same instruments coated with his blood. Beside Kianna was a second table, covered with clean instruments for her own interrogation. The stark silver made him wince.

Aidan halted in the doorway at the sight of her. At the thought of being tortured and questioned side by side. At the thought of the secrets they might spill about each other. His hesitation made a guard punch him in the gut. He was lifted like a sack of potatoes and thrown into the empty chair. Aidan blacked out from the pain, just for a moment, and when he came to he was strapped down and facing her.

Great. Front row seats to each other's misery.

She stared at him with the same hard, unreadable expression she had at the pyre.

She didn't say a word.

Neither did he.

"Ah, here we are," Jeremiah said, closing the door behind him. "Old friends reunited at last. I have often wondered how deep your relationship goes. Today, it seems, I was right in believing it ran deeper than you let on. Perhaps we should find out just how deep your bond goes, and how we might use that to bring you both to salvation."

Aidan didn't answer. He didn't know how *to* answer, didn't know if anything he said would make it worse for her. Or him.

"Are you asking if we fucked?" Kianna asked. Her words were flat, humorless. "Because I sure as hell don't know him biblically."

There was a crack and spray of blood as Jeremiah smacked her across the jaw with a baton.

"I heard you had a tongue." He paced around Kianna, eyeing her up and down. "Perhaps it is time for you to lose it."

"The ladies won't like that," she replied. Still humorless. Still unaffected by fear. "Or the lads." She peered past Jeremiah to look at Aidan. "Am I right? I've heard your tongue is legendary in the Guild. I know the boys like it when you—"

"Silence!" Jeremiah yelled. He hit her again with the baton, this time so loud Aidan was certain her jaw had dislocated.

Her head jerked to the side. But she didn't wince or cry out like Aidan would have done. She just gathered her saliva and spit blood on the floor.

"We are not here to discuss your perversions," Jeremiah said, his voice tight. "We are here to discuss your salvation."

"Good," Kianna said. She righted her head, stared Jeremiah down. "Because I don't think you have time to discuss the first."

Jeremiah thrust the baton into her gut, making her cough. Then he used his baton to stroke her unmarked forearm. Unmarked, save for the welts from her bloodletting.

"Such a unique specimen," he said, as though Kianna wasn't gasping for breath in front of him. "No magic to speak of, yet you willingly surround yourself with the damned."

"Sex with sinners is better," Kianna said dully. "Usually."

"Kianna," Aidan hissed. He didn't want to see her beaten again.

To his surprise, Jeremiah only shook his head.

"How have you survived so long outside the walls?" he asked, his voice low and musing. "Without magic or the Lord's grace, how have you managed to avoid death?"

"Death doesn't want me."

"We shall see."

Jeremiah looked back at Aidan. His smile made Aidan's skin go cold. Colder.

"I see why you picked this one," Jeremiah said. "I don't believe even the fire could have saved her. She will take work to break, this enigma. But that is why I have brought you."

He set down the baton and moved away from Kianna. Stepped closer to Aidan.

"Leave him out of this," Kianna said. And for the first time, Aidan noted a hint of desperation in her voice. Things clicked. She had been trying to incite Jeremiah to pick on her and only her. Because she knew she could take the torture. Aidan didn't know if he felt proud of her or angry that she felt the need to save him like that. He just knew he hated that it was true. "He has nothing to do with this."

"Oh, I think he has *everything* to do with this," Jeremiah said. He picked up a pair of pliers from the table beside Aidan, examining them in the flickering firelight.

"A magic-less Hunter and a speaker for the Dark Lady. What a fortuitous pair to fall into my hands."

"The hell you talking about?" Kianna asked.

"Hasn't he told you?" Jeremiah asked. He set down the pliers. Picked up the awl. Examined it with the same loving intensity. "Or has your dear friend kept that a secret from you, as well?"

Aidan grunted and shifted in his chair. Beyond Jeremiah, Kianna stared daggers at him.

"What is he talking about, Aidan?"

"Oh, this *is* good," Jeremiah said. He looked from the awl to Aidan. "Secrets don't make friends, and it seems you both have many to share. How fortuitous indeed." He looked between the two of them. "We are about to learn so much more about each other, aren't we?"

Jeremiah put down the awl. And picked up a pair of garden shears. They were clean. They were new.

Aidan blanched.

Jeremiah stepped over to his left side. Just out of eyesight.

"Our friend, it seems, has been hearing the words of the greatest evil our world has ever known," Jeremiah said. "And not just hearing them. But acting upon them."

"He's lying," Aidan said.

Kianna's eyes narrowed. She knew when *he* was lying. At least she had the foresight not to call him on his shit.

"The light will reveal all," Jeremiah said. "Now, girl. You will tell me how you have survived so long without magic's touch. Could you perhaps be a different servant to the Dark Lady? A new kind of Howl?"

"Go to hell," Kianna said.

"I don't believe I will." His hand clamped down over Aidan's, grabbed Aidan's pinky. The other brought the shears to the first joint of Aidan's fingertip. "But I cannot say the same for either of you. Your sins run deep. Sins and secrets…"

Aidan struggled. Jerked against his chair.

"No, no please!"

"Speak, girl."

Kianna was silent.

"Please! No!" Aidan screamed.

Kianna stayed silent.

The next sound was the pop of shears slicing through his knuckle.

CHAPTER FORTY-TWO

"YOU FEEL...DIFFERENT."

Tomás's voice curled through Aidan's dream, just as the incubus's legs curled over Aidan's lap. The room bled into focus: leather sofa, blazing hearth fire, white bearskin rug. And the incubus himself, draped across Aidan like a blanket, wearing little more than jeans and a smile. Firelight flickered deliciously over the man's body, over the smooth, tender skin.

Even without Fire in his chest, Aidan sparked at the sight. At the closeness.

At the *heat*.

Despite himself, he reached out and trailed a hand down Tomás's chest, letting his fingers—all five of them—ripple over the man's sternum, his abs. Heat thrilled through him, snaking up his arm and down his spine, igniting pieces of himself he hadn't felt in what seemed like ages. He could touch the incubus for eternity and never feel warm enough. He could press as close as humanly possible, and still feel light-years away from that great internal sun.

Tomás just watched, a small smile on his face and one arm cocked behind his head, the other resting on Aidan's thigh.

"Different how?" Aidan asked. His voice seemed to echo in the emptiness, as though the room were nothing but shadow and furniture and flame.

"You seem—" Tomás began, choosing his words carefully. Aidan knew what came next: *empty, broken, useless.* "—hungry."

Tomás languorously drew himself up to sitting, his hand going to Aidan's chest. Just that touch sent sparks over Aidan's skin, sparks that sizzled and crackled through his rib cage. But rather than filling him with fire like before, they danced around the void in his chest, the heat highlighting the lack he felt within.

That's when it hit him.

Like an ache, a hunger pang, his chest called out in agony, a chord resonating with Tomás's own emptiness. It made him want to draw the Howl closer, to feel the void that stretched between them. He knew the difference, even in the dream: Tomás's Sphere had been depleted, inverted. It devoured heat, rather than creating it. Aidan's was just…hidden. He knew it was there, deep in his chest, knew the energy center still worked, still gave him life, even if he couldn't utilize it to work magic.

That almost made it worse, knowing it was there, just beyond reach. Knowing it was his own limitations holding him back.

Tomás chuckled.

"Still burning, despite it all," he said, still rubbing Aidan's chest in a slow, lazy circle. "What did they do to you?"

In answer, Aidan pulled back the sleeve of his black sweater, revealing flesh untouched by blades and brands—save for the scar seared across his Hunter's mark. Just looking at it made the room tilt, as if even the dream knew how wrong it was.

"These are not the words of any god…" Tomás whispered. He drew his fingers down the length of Aidan's arm, taking his wrist in his hands. Tomás didn't touch the wound. He looked scared of it.

"She's speaking to me," Aidan said. He didn't know where the words came from, or why he spoke them. He just knew that he had to convince Tomás to save him. Had to convince Tomás he was worth saving.

He never thought he would believe it, but the Howl was his only hope of getting out of here.

Tomás jerked his gaze up, something like concern quickly hidden in his eyes.

"Is she?"

Aidan nodded. "I hear her. Through Fire." He didn't tell Tomás he'd seen her. That he'd seen her as his mother. That she promised to bring his loved ones back. He swallowed the thoughts down and prayed Tomás couldn't read them. "I saw the shard. Jeremiah has it."

"Then it should be easy for you to procure." Tomás's touch burned against Aidan's skin, pleasurable as it was painful. His grip was tight. Aidan watched the Howl's eyes. He knew that Tomás wasn't surprised. Knew the Kin had sent him here, into the heart of the Church, without any warning. It had been a trap, and Aidan had hoped that Tomás would show some sign of remorse over it.

He didn't.

"What else does she say?" Tomás asked instead.

"She told me to get the shard for you," Aidan said. "How could she speak to me? I thought she was dead. Killed by the Church right after the Resurrection."

"She is." Tomás's voice was skeptical. "No one has heard her voice in years. Not even me."

Even in the dream, Aidan felt the resentment in Tomás's voice. He sat up straight. "Then why do you need the shard? I thought you needed it for her. How can she need it if she's dead?"

"She rules over life and death," Tomás said, as though reciting something he'd heard long ago. "To die in her embrace is to accept immortality." He shook his head. "The shard contains my brother's power, and the secret of his resurrection. Anyone would covet such a thing." He cocked his head. "Tell me. What did my mistress look like?"

Aidan paused. Admitting this felt too vulnerable. But the ease of the dream intoxicated him. His words fell from his lips like sins. "She looked like my mother."

"She is all of us our mother. What did she say?"

"She could bring my family back. If I served her. If I brought you the shard." Aidan heard the words leave his lips, but he couldn't register the gravity. He was serving the Dark Lady. He was a heretic, just as Jeremiah said. The trouble was, he was beginning to believe that the Dark Lady might not be the villain anymore. "But she's dead," he repeated.

"Death is no barrier when you hold the key. And you, Aidan—you can read the language of the dead gods. You can speak it. In doing so, you could rewrite history. You could reverse even death. As she did. Once." Tomás's hand finally trailed over Aidan's scar. Aidan winced, and images of his torture flashed through his mind.

"If you knew the shard was here," Aidan said, "why didn't you come and get it yourself? Why send me? And why aren't you getting me out?"

"The Church is the one place creatures such as I dare not tread."

"Because of this?" Aidan asked, pointing at his scar. He took his arm back and pulled down his sleeve.

"No," Tomás said, still looking at Aidan's arm. "Not because of that."

Something in Tomás's demeanor shifted. He no longer seemed haughty, on the brink of tipping into madness or sex. He curled his legs into himself and stared at Aidan's forearm, rubbing his own arms, as though the brand had seared itself onto his skin. As though he were a lost little boy.

"I cannot get you out of there, my king," Tomás said. Even his voice seemed smaller. "I am sorry. I have failed you. But I know you will get out. You must. And when you do, we will make them pay. That, I swear."

"Why are you helping me?" Aidan asked. Of all the questions he should have asked, of all the things he should have said, that was probably the last. It was also the one the incubus had yet to truly answer.

"Because she has chosen you as hers," Tomás whispered.

Even in the cold of his brokenness, the statement was an icicle to his heart. It pinned him to the sofa. And as it melted in his disbelief, the cold water of its poison filtered through his veins, a promise inked into his very being.

"What do you mean?" Aidan asked.

"You know what I mean." Tomás didn't move. He didn't tease. All taunting, all seduction, was gone from his voice. He remained curled there, voice muted. As though the Dark Lady was watching. "She speaks to you. She speaks only to you. You are her voice. And through you, she will be reborn into this world."

"I don't understand."

"You will," Tomás said. He unfolded himself as he stood. He looked shorter, somehow, weighted down by the promise falling from his tongue. "But first, you must free yourself from the Church."

"I can't get out of here."

"Then you will die, and the Dark Lady will choose another to serve her." Tomás's stare was unreadable. "You are only special so long as you are useful. Remember this. And until you are freed, you are of no use to us. Bring us the shard, and I swear you will get your retribution. I will help you as I can, but you must still prove your worth."

Aidan swallowed. It was his only chance. It might all be a fever dream, a hallucination. A severe case of blood loss. It was treason a thousand times over, but he was already damned. And when he thought of what awaited him—further torture, the death of Kianna, being another faceless corpse on a pyre—he knew the choice was already made.

He would do anything to get out of here.

Anything to get his powers back.

Anything to make these bastards pay.

He stood and reached out, took Tomás's hand.

"I want your word."

"My word?" Tomás asked. His hand burned in Aidan's, but Aidan delighted in the heat.

"Yes. When I get you the shard, I want my powers back. And then, we will burn the Church off the earth and rule from its ashes."

Tomás smiled. Tightened his grip. "I always had faith in my Mistress," he said. "And now I am certain she chose correctly."

Tomás twitched his hand, pulling Aidan close, their chests touching, Aidan's arm at Tomás's side.

"Follow me," Tomás said. "Serve me. And I will be yours unconditionally. And together, yes. Together we will restore your powers and rule this broken world."

Aidan looked up into the devil's eyes. Saw the Dark Lady staring back.

"Then I am yours," Aidan said. He pressed himself up to tiptoes and pressed his lips to the Howl's.

In Tomás's embrace, Aidan finally felt warm.

Aidan finally felt *right*.

CHAPTER FORTY-THREE

"THE HELL IS THIS?"

Kianna's whispered voice cut through the dark. Aidan woke slowly, consciousness bleeding in like molasses. First the dim light. Then the pain. Then the warmth curled behind him.

He jerked and turned in bed, elbowing the mass that had been wrapped around his back.

Something thudded to the floor with a muffled yelp, and then he saw Lukas struggling to standing in the shadows. Kianna stood by the closed door, illuminated by a candle held in one hand.

"How the hell do you find someone to shag in a torture chamber?" Kianna hissed.

"I— What?" Wait, had Lukas been *spooning* him?

"You were shivering," Lukas said. "I'm sorry. I should have asked. But I thought—"

"Save it," Kianna interrupted. "We're getting out of here."

"What?" Aidan must have lost too much blood. Or been dreaming.

"Get up. We don't have much time. The guard's changing soon."

"How—"

Kianna stalked over and yanked Aidan to standing. He winced at the pain. "Do you *really* want to have this conversation here? I'm saving our asses. Now *move*." She shoved him toward the door and he stumbled, fumbling for the doorknob before realizing he was using the hand missing two fingers. He grabbed it with the other.

"I'm coming with," Lukas said from behind them. "Please."

Kianna snarled. "If I knew you had a cell mate…" she said, glaring at Aidan.

"You can't leave me behind," Lukas whispered. Almost a plea.

Kianna elbowed past Aidan, yanked open the door. "I don't give a shit. I'm leaving. You can follow if you want. But it's every man for himself and I swear to Christ, if you give us away or lag behind, I'll kill you myself."

She pulled open the door and crept through the crack. Aidan didn't hesitate or look back, groggy as he was. His body was on fire with pain and determination, adrenaline coursing through his veins.

He nearly tripped on the body just outside the door. All it took was a glance at the head facing the entirely wrong direction to tell that the guard was dead.

"How did you get out?" Aidan whispered.

"Feminine wiles," Kianna said flatly. Knowing her, that probably meant slamming the door into her guard's face when meals were delivered, or something equally pleasant. He didn't bother to question further.

Lukas followed close behind, their collective footsteps silent in the long hall. For being a prison, the place wasn't heavily guarded. Then again, with the Church in control, there probably didn't seem to be much need for guards down here.

Kianna led them onward, stopped at a flight of stairs. She looked up through the shadows, her candle flickering against the stairwell as she peered up into the darkness. Listening.

"Clear," she whispered. "Come on."

Aidan no longer wondered how she knew things like that. He just assumed it was another superpower.

They crept up the stairs, and with every step Aidan expected to be ambushed. He expected Kianna to get turned around. He sort of recognized where they were, but he would have no chance at finding his way out. She, it seemed, was better at paying attention. In a matter of minutes, Kianna peered through a cracked door, slowly opened it and slipped outside.

Aidan followed into the cool night air, the scent of cinder and flesh heavy in his nostrils. They were in the square, and the charred remains of his comrades still glowed warm and red like a wound in the night before them. He blanched at the sight, but Kianna didn't give them a moment to stare. She darted along the side of the building, keeping to the shadows.

Every step they took, he felt the excitement of escape. And yet…something nagged at him, and he didn't want to admit what it was.

He didn't want to leave here without the shard.

He didn't want to let Tomás down.

No, it wasn't that—he didn't want to give up. If the shard was the only thing standing between him and power, he couldn't just walk away. And yet here he was, running with his tail between his legs, following Kianna through the dark.

It wasn't until they were a few blocks away, far from the sprawling compound that had become his prison, that he stopped.

"I can't."

His words made her turn back. "What do you mean, can't? You about to pass out or something?"

"No." He couldn't find the words. Not without admitting more than he wanted to. "There's something I still have to do."

"You're delusional," she said, and kept walking.

"No." He didn't move, and Lukas stood between the two of them, uncertain.

"What the hell are you talking about, Aidan? We aren't in the clear yet." She gestured out to the warren of tangled streets. "The Guild wall is that way. Still at least two kilometers off. We can't stop until we're past it. And not even then."

Aidan took a step back. "You go. Take him."

"Aidan, I'm not—"

"I said go!" he yelled, far louder than he meant. He lowered his voice. "I have to end this, Kianna. I can't just run away."

"You're wounded, Aidan. You aren't going to end anything."

"Please," he said. "Trust me. I have to go back. You heard what he said."

She ground her teeth. Hands balled into fists. He knew the thoughts warring in her mind: she had just risked her own escape to get him out of there. But she knew he had been lying earlier. Knew he had something up his sleeve. And she knew exactly what he meant—Jeremiah had said that Aidan worked for the Dark Lady, had become her voice. She probably thought he was going in on a kamikaze mission. She was probably right.

"I'm not waiting around," she said.

"I don't want you to," he replied. He nodded to Lukas. "Take him. Get out of here. I'll come find you. Promise."

"You're an idiot," she said.

"I love you, too."

Then he turned and hobbled his way back into the heart of the Church.

Aidan knew time was short. Kianna had killed the guards near their cells, and it wouldn't take long for the guard to change and the alarm to be raised. Worse, he only vaguely remembered his way back to Jeremiah's torture chamber.

But deep within, he felt the whisper.

Every time he thought of the shard, every time he envisioned the image of his mother, he felt the pull forward. He had to trust it, even though it was the last thing on this earth he should put faith in.

He snuck past the smoldering pyres, pausing only briefly to stare at the remains of his comrades, to feel that sick twist of doubt in his gut. Everything he had touched, he had broken.

This was his final chance to make it right.

At least…to make it right for *himself*.

He made his way back through the halls of the old Guild, following his gut and praying he could find his way in. Back to the one place he didn't want to step foot in. He crept through the hallways, following the tug and his own scattered memories, praying to whatever god listening that he wouldn't end up at Jeremiah's bedchamber or something.

Moments later, he found it.

He could smell the blood, just as he could feel the tug in his gut that told him this was the correct door. The tug, and the fear, as though the place were a wound throbbing in the darkness. As though he had left more than a few digits and pints of blood here. As though his soul, his destiny, waited within.

Inside, the torture chamber was exactly as they'd left it.

The tables set out with their bloody instruments. The twin chairs, splattered with gore. His finger nubs, cast on the floor like rune stones. Candles flickering against the blood even now.

But no shard.

Aidan let the door click faintly behind him. Had he been mistaken? Had Jeremiah taken the shard? He stepped deeper in the room, staring at the tables, wondering if perhaps it had been hidden in the blood, or dropped on the ground...

"Looking for something?" Jeremiah asked.

Aidan jerked up as, from the shadows, Jeremiah stepped forward. He was smiling. Aidan looked around, but there was no one else in the room. Just him and this old man. An old man who shouldn't have been a threat to someone trained in combat, but who still made Aidan freeze.

"How long have you been waiting?" Aidan asked. He tried to keep his voice steady, but every time he looked at Jeremiah, he felt the memory of another torture instrument graze across his skin.

"Since I learned you and your friend escaped. Frankly, I'm

amazed it took you so long to get out. I would have thought lessening the guard would have been enough."

Aidan's head spun. "You lowered the guard?"

Jeremiah shrugged, stepping further into the room. Aidan stepped back. Thoughts weren't coalescing as they should. "I wanted to see what you would do. And I wanted to ensure that I had gotten it right. That you truly were in the Dark Lady's fold."

"This was a trap." Aidan's heart fell. A trap to ensure his guilt, a trap to see if he would come back for the stone he swore he had no affinity to. And he'd fallen in headfirst.

"Not a trap," Jeremiah said. "A test. To see if you were truly the one destined for this."

He held out his hand and unfolded his fingers. The shard glinted within.

"I don't understand," Aidan said. "Why—"

"Because, my brother," Jeremiah said. His lips twisted into a smile. "Our Lady works in mysterious ways."

CHAPTER FORTY-FOUR

JEREMIAH'S SMILE DEEPENED AT THE SHOCK ON AIDAN'S face.

"What?" Jeremiah asked. "Did you truly believe she wouldn't have eyes within the Church? There are many within the heart of the Light that follow her ways. *The brighter the light, the deeper the shadow.* We are everywhere, Aidan. As she is everywhere."

"But why?" His thoughts spun. Jeremiah worked for the Dark Lady. Jeremiah was of the Church. How was it possible?

And if Jeremiah were truly working for the Dark Lady… why had he tortured Aidan?

Why had Jeremiah forced him to kill his own comrades?

"Because I do not hear her as clearly as you, Aidan." Jeremiah took another step forward. Aidan pressed back against the door. "Because I needed to be sure that you were the one to whom she spoke." His eyes sparkled in the firelight, fervent. Fearsome. "The shard holds great power, my brother. The power to peel back the barrier between life and death, to rewrite all the wrongs of history. But only to the one who can read her words, who can understand the hidden language. Don't you see? We have been awaiting her return since the Church took her from us. Awaiting the herald of her resurrection. We have been waiting for you, Aidan. The boy who could hear her voice and read her words. The boy who could speak them anew, and complete the work that she herself never finished.

"I had to make sure that you were the one. And you are. You are."

"But my comrades. The Guild..."

"Mean nothing. Their deaths are the first of many offerings made at your altar."

"You *tortured me*. You took my magic," Aidan said. His thoughts were still slow. This couldn't be real. This couldn't be happening.

"I tortured your body to ensure you were fit for her power. And you have succeeded, my brother. What you know as magic is a candle compared to the sun. When you embrace her teachings, the power you know will be beyond measure. A god, Aidan. You will be a god. And the world will tremble at your feet."

He pressed his palm to the top of Aidan's head. As if blessing him.

"When you open to her teachings, the final Sphere will open itself to you. And when Maya is yours to control, the power you've known will pale in comparison."

"Maya?" Aidan breathed. The fifth Sphere. The one that couldn't be attuned to. The one that chose *you*. The one that—so far—had never truly been tapped.

Jeremiah nodded. "The Sphere that has eluded mankind's grasp from the beginning. The power to control the very fabric of Creation."

He took Aidan's hand—the one with all its fingers. Gently. As though he hadn't spent the last forty-eight hours torturing him. As though he cared more deeply for Aidan than anyone ever had. He dropped the shard into Aidan's palm.

"She summons you. And none can deny that call. Embrace it. Open to it. And you will know power beyond your wildest dreams." Jeremiah closed Aidan's fingers around the shard.

A thousand emotions warred within Aidan. A thousand questions. But one thing resonated stronger than ever before.

This was not how it was supposed to go.

Just like with Calum, the moment felt stolen from him.

He hadn't come back to reason with Jeremiah. He had come to steal the shard and kill those who wronged him. To feel like he was on the winning side. To feel power. To feel vengeance. To feel he was taking his place in history.

Not to feel like greatness was handed to him.

His fingers tightened around the shard. It burned under his touch, and now that it was here, in his palm, he felt it whispering to him. He felt the tug in his chest and a sensation he had thought he would never feel again.

Rage.

It burned within him, seeming to emanate from the shard itself. As if it contained more than power. As if it contained every ounce of hatred locked within this accursed place. He shook.

"Fuck you," he whispered. The words ripped from his lips, and he wasn't sure who he was angry at. Jeremiah, for the torture. The Dark Lady, for the lies. Tomás, for the trap. He felt like he'd been led by the nose, through the dark, and he was tired of it. Tired of playing other people's games. Tired of being a pawn.

He looked to the shard in his hand. To the runes that whispered through his mind.

Some, he knew, were for resurrection. He felt them twining through his brain, hissing of the power of the open grave, the overturned casket, the dead spark brought back to life. Just as he'd seen in the vision of Calum. They could be used to pull back a soul from death. And even as he stared at them, at the shifting, jagged edges of the runes, he knew they were imperfect.

Jeremiah had been truthful in that, at least: the language of the Dark Lady, the words of the dead gods, hadn't been completed. He didn't know how he knew, only that they whispered to the deepest corners of his soul. The words were wrong.

The words were wrong, and he knew how to fix them.

He knew the shard was for more than bringing back the dead. The shard was for storing power. He could feel the echo of Calum's flame within it. The shard had ripped out the last of Calum's magic just as it had brought his soul back to life.

Stored it. The magic, not the soul.

And that magic, that *fire*, sat in his palm, begging to be released. It vibrated deep within, a flame at the heart of the void, and he knew the words that kept it locked away. Knew the words that were the key. Words to release the power. To set the world ablaze.

Words he knew that no one—not even the Dark Lady—had ever spoken.

Now, they were his.

"I'm not your brother," Aidan said, glaring at Jeremiah. He didn't know where the anger came from anymore. He had thought all rage had been beaten from him. Perhaps it came from deeper within. Perhaps it came from the stone. He didn't care. All he knew was, he was done being toyed with.

Screw bringing the shard to Tomás. Screw bringing it to the Dark Lady. He was done serving. He was done kneeling.

He was done being anything less than King.

Behind him, the candles flared. "And I sure as hell don't serve the Dark Lady. I serve myself."

Now, it was Aidan's turn to step forward, and Jeremiah's to cower back. Tendrils of fire flickered from his fist, oozing from the stone and his fingertips. Flames coiled around his forearm like serpents, illuminating the raw wound of Jeremiah's brand, the scrapes and bruises and slices from Jeremiah's instruments. Reminders of what this man had done to him. What he'd done to others. What he'd made Aidan do. "You made me kill my comrades. You tortured me. Worse. You tortured my friend. And you made me watch."

"She means nothing," Jeremiah began.

"That's where you're wrong," Aidan cut in. "She means everything."

The candles were torches now, the scent of burning blood thick in his nostrils.

"You must contain yourself," Jeremiah said. "If you attack the Church, you will be forever hunted. You cannot complete her work if you are dead."

"I don't plan on dying." He took another step. "And I'm not here to hide. Didn't you know? I am here to rule. And I will start by bringing you and your bloody Church to its knees."

Aidan didn't speak. He reached through the shard and whispered the words that flickered in the shadows of his mind, words that went beyond language, that were more sensations than sounds. Words of power. Of release.

Of destruction.

The shard grew white-hot, searing his palm, flaring between his fingers, **BURN** highlighting in a promise. Liquid dripped between his knuckles. For a moment, he thought it was blood. Then he realized the shard itself was melting. Power seeped into him. A power so great his limbs shuddered. A power so great that even his starved Sphere filled past the brim.

Power flooded him.

Filled him.

A flame he held tight in his chest. A flame he couldn't hold for long.

He glared at Jeremiah, fire sparking in his eyes.

"What are you doing?" Jeremiah fumbled backward in fear. Smashed into the table of torture instruments. They clattered to the ground, ringing like church bells.

"I'm accepting my destiny," Aidan said. He smiled, and fire curled from the cracks his teeth. "I hope your faith is true, Jeremiah. Your Creator awaits."

The words weren't his. The words were never his.

Fire burned through him. Charred through his veins. Burned through his soul. Calum's fire. Aidan's fire. And a power even deeper, a strength even darker. *Her* power. The fire of hatred that burned so brightly on this godforsaken earth. The rage that coiled deep within the soil for every sin committed, for every treason, for every ache.

And oh, how that fire yearned to be released.

Flames flickered around Aidan. Swirled deep within his chest.

The fire wanted a voice. And now, it had one.

He opened his mouth. Opened his palms. Let the remains of the shard melt silver and black across his bloody palm. Let the Fire consume him.

And when he screamed, he gave all that pain, all that agony, all that hatred the voice it craved.

Fire exploded.

Everything went white. White and red. White and red and screaming.

Jeremiah's screams.

Aidan's screams.

As the world around them burst into flame. As the flames burst from his body. As the skin ripped from his bones. As he flared in the face of humanity's rage. As his voice charred his lungs and burned through the corridors. As the flame burst from the building, stretched across the expanse of London.

As the rage spread. As the rage consumed.

As he burned atop his own funeral pyre.

As he burned the whole world down with him.

CHAPTER FORTY-FIVE

"YES, MY HUNTER," THE DARK LADY SAID. "YOU HAVE done well."

He knelt before her in the void. She shifted. Now his mother. His smiling mother. Crowning him with a coil of flame and shadow. He remembered what he'd done. Reading the runes of the shard. *Speaking* the runes. Words he shouldn't have known.

Words even *she* hadn't known.

Words that broke the world.

Words that built it anew.

He remembered the flame. The explosion.

He remembered burning all of London to the ground.

"I didn't mean to—"

"You did. And you did so perfectly. You have done greater than I could have ever dreamed. My child. My son. I am so, so proud."

He had wanted to spite her. But how could he spite her? His own mother?

She touched the side of his face. Wiped the tears that slid from his eyes. Kissed his forehead, his crown burning with cinders and sin.

"You will continue my work," she promised. "And at the foot of your throne, even the reaper will kneel."

CHAPTER FORTY-SIX

"WHAT HAVE YOU DONE?"

Tomás's words pulled him from the depths of Hell.

No, he was still in Hell. Fire burned around him, everything hot and charred, orange and red and black, and as he stared at the night sky, embers floated into the heavens, charred stars falling in reverse.

Tomás towered over him, demonic in the hellfire.

"The shard," Tomás demanded. "Where is it?"

"Gone," Aidan said. He looked to his hand. His palm was bloody and raw, and when he turned it over, he saw that his knuckles, too, were ripped and bleeding, burned apart from liquid stone. He laughed, a sudden bubble of giddiness at the sight of his bloodied flesh. "I melted it."

"What do you mean, *gone?*" Tomás knelt. Grabbed Aidan's hand, pressed open his palm. Aidan was so numb, he couldn't even feel Tomás's fingers prodding the wound. *"What have you done?"* he roared. "I told you to get the shard. Not burn down all of London."

Aidan tilted his head to the side, scalp rolling against hot ash. Hot ash, but cool beneath his smoking skin. As far as he could see—which wasn't far, through the flame and falling cinders—London had been leveled.

Aidan giggled, heady with power. His brain in flames.

He had done that.

He hadn't just burned down London. He'd burned down the whole world.

Or, if he hadn't, he would.

The thought seared him with elation.

"Maybe I don't need you after all," Aidan said. Giggled again. So much power. All his. All his.

"I should kill you for—" Tomás stopped. Stared out at the horizon with narrowed eyes.

"What?" Aidan asked.

Tomás glared at him. "We aren't finished, Hunter." He squeezed Aidan's hand. "Remember that you are only important so long as you are useful to me. And this makes me doubt your usefulness greatly."

Then, with a flash of magic, he was gone.

Aidan closed his eyes. Waited for Kianna and Lukas to appear. They were out there, surely, running back. To make sure he was okay.

He was okay. He was okay.

And that meant they were okay. He just needed to let them know where he was.

He reached for Fire, but the Sphere still eluded him. It didn't matter, though. Calum's power still rode through his veins. The elation of so much heat, so much magic. He needed to let them know where he was. Send up a flame. A brighter flame.

He must be a brighter flame…

Another magic. A flare of power, of blue light. A power that was not his.

"Where are we?" came a voice. Masculine and strong. American.

What were Americans doing here?

"I don't know," came another man's voice.

Someone coughed, and with another flare of magic a breeze blew around him, chilling him to the bone as the flames swept aside.

Aidan looked over.

Four people. Three guys. One girl. She was very pale. A ghost. Not Kianna. Not Lukas. He didn't care about Lukas. Just Kianna. Where was she?

"There is a survivor," not-Kianna said.

The tall guy raced over, dropped to Aidan's side. Aidan's eyes flickered closed. None of them were important.

Where was she?

"He's lost a lot of blood," the guy at his side said. "And he's horribly burned."

"And naked," came the first guy.

Aidan tried to open his eyes. Saw the other three figures standing above him. A guy with blond hair. The ghost girl. A guy with a crimson scarf around his neck.

And the one at his side. Aidan rolled his head to the kneeling boy. Dark hair. Washed-out skin. Water and whispers swirling around him in waves.

The boy from his dreams.

The boy who would try to destroy him.

Tenn.

"You—"

"Shh," Tenn said. "We're here to help. I'm going to heal you, okay? This may hurt."

Dimly, Aidan felt hands against his arm. Where his Hunter's mark should have been.

He felt nothing else.

Moments stretched.

"Impossible," Tenn whispered.

"What is it?" asked the girl.

"I can't heal him," Tenn said. He looked up. Then back down to Aidan, his eyes creased with pain. "Magic has no effect."

It took a moment, through the cinders of Aidan's mind, for the words to connect. When they did, he thought he must have misheard. Must have.

He couldn't be healed.

Magic couldn't save him.

Something bubbled up inside of him. A sob? Despair?

But no. He felt none of those things.

Surrounded by the flames of his destruction, staring up at the boy he had promised to kill, Aidan began to laugh.

★ ★ ★ ★ ★

ACKNOWLEDGMENTS

No book is created in a void, even though at times it may feel like it. Countless people have helped shape the world of *Runebinder*, and I'll try to hit them all. But *Runebreaker* isn't your average book, so I'm not going to do the average list of thank-you's.

Yes, I want to thank my amazing agent, Laurie McLean of Fuse Literary. And my endless gratitude goes to the team at Harlequin TEEN/Inkyard Press, with special kudos to my editor, T.S. Ferguson, for stepping up to bat, and Mark O'Brien for making this book sing. My thanks as well go to the friends and editors who have supported this series from the very beginning: Patricia, Asja, Michael, David, Bea and Will.

But mostly, I want to thank the people who probably don't even know this book exists.

Aidan has been called "difficult" more times than I can count. Unlikable. Narcissistic. Anger-driven. Over a decade ago, when *Runebinder* first came to light, I poured a great deal of my own emotions onto the page. As I struggled with what it meant to be gay, as I yearned for a world where I didn't have to constantly explain myself, a world where I could be heroic, so was Tenn born of fear, of sadness and of the great desire to be normal. To be important to someone. And to something.

Aidan is more than the opposite end of that spectrum. Aidan is the next step in the narrative.

In that vein, my thanks go to the countless beautiful creatures who allowed themselves to feel and further the burning passion to overcome, to overturn. The revolutionaries who knew that being queer didn't pigeonhole our narrative, who knew that we could be so much more than a foil or fodder. We weren't put here to become normalized, to hide away, to be ashamed or snuffed out.

We were put here to burn.

This book is for the many who have lit the way, both for me personally and for the world at large. For those who—every day—fight to show that we have a place in history, and it is as glorious and beautiful as we are. For those who show that it is okay to be angry, that it is okay to be driven, that it is okay to be fierce and ferocious and yes, most definitely yes: fabulous. We must always temper that flame, lest we become what we fight against, but we must never, ever let our spark wink out due to fear.

Which means, dear reader, that my deepest thanks go to you. Not only for falling in love with this world of magic and monsters, but for carrying the torch inside of you, for being the change and the hope we so desperately need.

You are the light in our current darkness. You are the flame that will burn evil away.

Resist the urge to sink into despair.

Resist. Forever Resist.